TREE OF JESSE

by J.R. Mattison

TREE OF JESSE

by J.R. Mattison

Rothco Press • Los Angeles, California

Published by
Rothco Press
5500 Hollywood Blvd., 3rd Floor
Los Angeles, CA 90028

Cover design by Rob Cohen
Cover image by J.R. Mattison

Portions of this book were previously published as The Tree of Jesse by
Rochester Books, Copyright © 2013 by J.R. Mattison.

Rothco Press is a division of Over Easy Media Inc.

ISBN: 978-1-941519-27-1

Electronic ISBN: 978-1-941519-00-4

Mes•si•ah \mə-sī-ə\: One who saves the people.
An anointed or chosen one. A king.

"*There will be signs in the sun, moon and the stars. On earth nations will be in anguish. At that time they will see the Son of Man coming. When these things take place, stand up and lift up your heads, because your redemption is drawing near.*"

Luke 21:25-28

PROLOGUE

Sea of Zo'ar, Jordan, 1947

The desert sun scorches the West Bank as a Bedouin herder roams near salt reefs that line the stretch of sea, searching for lost goats. He grips a rough handled cane to guide the rocky path, a bead of sweat trickling from his brow. He wipes it away and whistles, calling to the animals as he shakes his head. *I only turned my back for a second.* He thinks, legs weary, mouth dry.

Up ahead he sees a cave embedded into the mammoth stone hills. He makes his way towards the entrance and once near tosses a rock at the opening to attract the attention of whatever may be inside, hoping to find the stragglers from his herd. But instead of bleating goats he hears a distinct sound.

The sound of something shattering.

Intrigued, he enters the cave, eyes darting. He squints, searching the recesses for signs of life. Catching a glimpse of something in the shadows he steps forward. The sound of pottery crushing under his sandal startles him as he enters farther into the cavern and finds several urns still intact and a single broken urn set apart from the others. He moves closer, noticing something frayed and yellowed protruding from its jagged edges. He sets his walking stick on the dirt floor then crouches down and reaches inside, pulling a parchment from the opening. He carefully unrolls the document, its edges weathered with age.

In the dim light, he can just make out markings covering one side. He shuffles toward the entrance of the cave, allowing the sun's rays to catch the symbols.

Aramaic.

He scans the scroll, eyes burning with excitement. Searching the ancient writings he reaches a particular passage; then rereads not believing his eyes. He raises his weather beaten face and gasps.

"Al Moshiach." he says aloud, breathless, the sun blazing behind him.

Chapter 1

Death Valley, California, Present Day

The white lines of the highway shimmer as I sit, head pressed against cold glass. This old bus and I have seen better days. It's two hours till my 33rd birthday and I'm about to play another gig in another desert town in the middle of nowhere.

As I tap my fingers in rhythm with the pounding inside my head we pass desolate miles of Joshua trees until Artie finally pulls to a stop on a gravel driveway. I can barely see his dark skin in the pale moonlight but I notice that he's smiling.

Good old Artie, smiles through all the shit.

A dim neon sign hangs in the front window advertising live music. Somewhere in the distance the wind slams a screen door open and shut. The sound feels like it's trapped inside my head, pushing to get out.

"Jesse. Come on man, let's go." Pete shoves my guitar into my hand. "You fuck this up I'm gonna forget we ever met."

"Take it easy man, everything's okay." I give him a wink and grab my Fender, hands shaking.

I step off the bus and notice a line of kids dressed in black anxious to cross the threshold. This place is like a mirage in a wasteland of dried cracked earth and thirsty foliage. It used to be the Death Valley Drive-In and the rusted old sign still hangs from a single nail, then a guy named Buddy Levine bought the place and made it into the coolest club in the desert. Which isn't really a tall order since it's the only club for a hundred miles. But still, I'd heard good things and it's our first shot at a regular gig. Lucky for me since I need a new toaster and to pay my last three months rent.

Guess I picked a bad time to be on the wagon.

Usually I take some flash so I can give the people a good show. Give them their money's worth. But lately the stuff's been ruining me. I had to make a change. And then we got this gig.

The universe has an interesting sense of humor.

We enter through the back door and I hear a sweet voice sing a sad song, the sound small and frail. I walk backwards trying to catch a glimpse and bump a waitress dressed in dark layers, tattoos lining her arms. One of red wings lays dazzlingly displayed on her exposed stomach.

"Hey, watch it." She shouts. Then her eyes, liquid blue lined in black kohl, shift to the guitar hanging from my shoulder. "Oh, hey, sorry. You playing tonight?" I nod my head as she glances at my shaky hands. "Don't let Buddy catch you with anything. He's Mr. Clean these days and doesn't take kindly to us heathens." She gives me a wicked grin then heads back to the bar lined with customers.

I try to smile but my face feels tight. My whole body feels tight, strange and foreign. I feel enveloped by limbs and sour breath and the flickering lights make me dizzy. I watch Pete push his way to the slick wood bar and hail for the bartender. A minute later he's next to me with a tumbler of Jameson as I stand staring, lost in a cloud of nothing.

"Here you go pal. You're lookin' worse for wear."

I chuckle but the sound gets trapped in my throat.

"I'm tryin' to be a good boy." I reply then take a swig.

"Don't try too hard." He's so close I can smell his last cigarette on his breath. "We need this job. Give the people what they want, man. I'm counting on you." He gives me a hard look and walks away.

I empty the glass and slam it on the bar. The stuff has no effect on me anymore. It might as well be water. The only thing that'll save tonight is the crystal.

I can't let the guys down.

I'll deal with my fucked up life tomorrow.

Chapter 2

Jerusalem, Israel, 4:18 pm

As the sun warms golden fields an old farmer walks towards home, his clothes dusty from the long day. A short distance away a heifer can be heard in pain, the tell-tale sounds of labor.

She lies on her side away from the rest of the herd, body bloated, legs drawn in. The man drops his rake and walks in her direction, once near, he crouches down, "It's about time you had your first, old girl." He says and pats the cow's hind leg. She groans as the head of the calf appears. "Good girl, very close." Suddenly her body buckles and with one strong contraction the calf pushes its way through.

The farmer stands unsteady on his feet. Hand to his mouth in disbelief, his eyes wild. On the ground below is a young female calf, perfect in every way yet profoundly unique in that her entire body is a bright and brilliant red.

"Parah adumah, parah adumah!!" The man shouts. Tears stream down his face, his eyes filled with a strange mixture of fear and utter joy.

Chapter 3

Death Valley, California

The stage sits above an old plank wood floor, roof open to the starless sky. I scan the place for a familiar face. Or more specifically the kind of face that deals. The ones that deal always have a special look.

Feral... animal... base.

I spot him in the corner, back against the wall. Not even pretending to enjoy the music. We lock eyes and he glances over at the men's room sign.

Simon shouts. "Man, this place is packed. This joint's gotta pull in at least ten grand a night." He pushes the hair from his eyes and has a good look around. "Wish I could open a place like this. I'd keep my baby in pearls all year long."

Paul spits out a laugh as we enter the cramped dressing room. "Yeah right. I don't think that's the kinda pearl necklace Karri's accustomed to my friend."

"Don't be a douche, man, that's the mother of the fruit of my loins."

"I'll be back." I say. The words hang in the air like a ring of smoke.

Everybody's waiting for me to screw this up.

Paul raises a brow. "Need me to come with you man?"

"Why, so you can hold it for me?"

"Alright smart ass, hurry up and don't let the wolves get you."

"I could take a wolf. I could take him with my bare hands." I whisper.

I weave through the dim hallway, arms folded, scuffing the worn wood with my boots towards a crimson sign that reads "gentleman."

That assumption always makes me chuckle.

As I push open the door I spot him gazing at his reflection, teeth bared. The enamel is stained and his mouth looks painful. A tattoo of a single tear falls from the corner of his eye.

"Gotta get my ass to la dentista man, but those fuckers scare me. They're like sadists and shit."

I grunt a half reply and pull some money from my pocket. He backs against the sink with arms akimbo.

"Whoa man, show some tact. Come on." He motions to a stall and we both step inside.

It's cramped and dirty and the stench of urine pollutes my lungs. We make the deal and he leaves me there, smoking pipe in hand. The familiar rush pumps through me and I feel invincible-powerful-bold. I splash some cold water on my face and catch my reflection.

A ghost. Not quite human and not yet dead.

Paul bursts through the door and spots me. He looks around and smiles. "What the hell man, you want me to shake it for you or what?"

Chapter 4

Jerusalem, Israel, 10:14 am

A man wearing the traditional robe of a Rabbi is seated on the edge of a velvet bench. Perched directly in front of him is a video camera operated by a teenage boy with a black satin yarmulke settled on his hair. Thick curtains open to bold light streaming in from the outside where there are only Judean mountaintops for miles around. The boy waves a hand in the air, a signal for the old man to begin.

"The day of reckoning is upon us my friends, as it is said in the Torah. An important sign has shown itself less than twenty-four hours ago." The Rabbi's ebony eyes flash with wisdom, the lines marking his dark face deep. "What I am about to tell you is part of an ancient prophecy never before revealed. The time of my death draws near and I am burdened with this great secret that has been held by my family since I was a boy growing up near Lake Tana in the city of Gondar. The prophecy was revealed to me by my father before his death, as it was to him by his father and so on. My family has kept this secret for generations knowing that on a fateful day one of us would have the burden and great honor to reveal it to mankind. That day has come." He gazes down at the prayer beads in his hands and takes a shallow breath.

"The prophecy reveals the true location of the Ark of the Covenant and its contents, which as we all know have been subjects of speculation for centuries. The popular belief is that the Ark holds the Ten Commandments engraved by the hand of God onto slabs of stone, and though there is truth in that notion, there are other contents as well. Things that will astound and amaze even the most vigilant of atheists. Proof, solid proof, that God exists and information we could only dream to possess. I will reveal this unto you so that you as a people can carry out the prophecy and circumvent the End of Days." He places a hand to his slight chest, grimacing in pain.

"The story begins with the great King Solomon and his illicit affair with the Queen of Sheba who was said to hail from Arabia; a true beauty whose charms were known the world over and whom Solomon was powerless to resist. A child was born of their secret passion whose name was Manelik... " The Rabbi suddenly shudders and coughs. The fit comes in waves shaking his fragile body. With a practiced swiftness the young man grabs a nearby oxygen tank and brings it to him.

"Dad, please. Don't push yourself so hard."

"Elijah my dear boy, there isn't much time." He takes a deep breath from the mask. "It seems I have less and less moments in the day where my mind is clear. I must use them wisely. The prophecy must be heard, it is our only hope."

Chapter 5

Death Valley, California

The stage is flushed with a red glow. Everything looks beautiful and alive. The crowd pulses with energy.

Hot-liquid-undeniable.

My voice feels strong but distant as if it's coming from someplace far away. A girl stands below the edge of the stage, her arms waving, head flying back and forth. A blur of dark hair. A lone man smokes endless cigarettes —it looks to me as if he's become ash. A flash of crimson appears weaving through the crowd and catches my eye. Her hair long, the color of blood, she seems strangely familiar. I catch only a glimpse then she's gone. Words flow from me effortlessly. Then I taste the sweat in my mouth and the tremble creeps its way back into my hands.

I signal for a break and Peter shoots me a dark look. I shrug and make my way back to the familiar stall. I feel for the pipe. Gone. I remember it jabbing my skin through the hole in my back pocket.

No time.

Need the flash.

I take the powder and dump it onto my hand, the skin chapped and dry.

"What the hell you doin' in there pal?" The voice booms as he bangs the stall door.

Desperate, I inhale the powder into my nose and mouth. I inhale everything that doesn't flutter to the ground and pull open the stall door.

"Whoa, dude, you look like you just ate a dozen fuckin' powdered donuts." The man chuckles, his pitted face animated and ugly in the fluorescent light.

I wait for the rush that doesn't come and wipe my mouth with a damp paper towel.

No flash, only subtle euphoria.

I'll take it.

As I make my way back to the stage Simon shoots me an impatient look and shakes his head. I barely make it to the mike before I recognize the beginning rifts of "Dirty Fingers" pumping from the P.A. I could sing this one in my sleep. I smile at Matt, his bass owns this song, but when he turns toward me he looks wrong, his face twisted and coming in fragments.

The world whips by in a blur, my mouth feels dry, and the floor looks like it's tilting towards me. The crowd is a thousand serpent heads and my body shakes more violent than before. I hear the screech of a guitar die suddenly then silence fills the room—full.

I feel tired, like I could sleep for days. I'm ripped off stage as I puke my insides out, my stomach and intestines and liver. I'm shoved violently forward and manage to open my eyes as the pavement rushes up to greet me.

Everything goes black.

Chapter 6

Jerusalem, Israel, 12:40 p.m.

Blue veins pump through translucent skin as the Rabbi smoothes his hair with a frail hand. "I apologize for the interruption, a man's stamina is dictated by the temple that provides his soul shelter." He gives a wry smile, "As I was saying, unbeknown to all except the Falashas, a small tribe of indigenous Jews in Ethiopia, the illegitimate son of the Queen and Solomon is a very important figure in modern Christianity and Judaism. For the true story is that the Queen was not an Arab, but a dark skinned woman of Ethiopian decent. And the final resting place of the Ark is purely a consequence of her son's bitterness at being forsaken by King Solomon and being denied his birthright. The Ark was rumored to be held in an Ethiopian city in a temple created to house it near the mouth of the Blue Nile.

It is speculated that Manelik, who was the son of Sheba and Solomon, went to Jerusalem and stole the Ark from Solomon's temple, bringing it to Ethiopia around 940 B.C., just before Solomon's death. As I said before the Ark of the Covenant is said to contain the original stone tablets of Moses with the commandments etched onto them by the finger of God... and so it does contain stones. But it also contains something else. Something that we as a society have been searching to find for many years... the lost pages of the Dead Sea scrolls.

The scrolls were traditionally divided into three groups, Biblical, Apocryphal and Sectarian... and then there are the pages never before revealed... written by none other than Christ himself...

Chapter 7

The light hurts my eyes, everything distorted and strange. My body made of lead. The hum inside me feels electric, like an idle engine, its raw current flowing through my limbs. I feel hot but shiver.

Maybe I'm dead.

I look around. Unfamiliar. Disorientation makes me swim and that's when I see her, the one with the crimson hair. She sits on the floor, her long legs crossed in front of her, in men's underwear and a plain tattered t-shirt. A brown cigarette with an impossibly long ash dangles from her elegant fingers.

She scribbles fast and furious into a small worn notebook, her delicate features animated and her tongue touching her lip in a childlike yet erotic way. She looks up at me, surprised, and just then my eyes feel heavy and my body jerks and shivers until again there is nothing but blackness.

* * *

Journal Entry, April 6th

He's been asleep for 16 hours now. He woke up once for a few seconds, his eyes looked glassy but so beautiful.

The blood on his head is dried and painful looking. I think he hit it pretty hard when they threw him out of the club. I watched it happen but felt frozen. It showed me a side of people I don't like to see or believe exists, a darkness that makes me shiver every time I think about it. One of his band mates literally kicked him when he was down. It made me feel sick. I had this bizarre need to protect him so I had Ralph help me bring him here. Ralph is good to have around. When the natives get restless he makes no bones about showing people to the door or showing them the bottom of his boot. Lucky he was there or else I don't know how I would've got him here.

His fingers are calloused; probably from playing his guitar, and he's got a scar across the top of his eyebrow that looks like it's been there a long time. I want to touch it but I don't. I already feel like some freaky voyeur watching him and listening to him talk in his sleep.

I don't know if I'm doing the right thing, maybe I should call somebody. That bump looks kind of bad. I mean the reality is this guy isn't my responsibility and if he dies in my bed I don't know how I'll explain it.

But there's something about him that makes me hurt inside. His skin is so pale and he seems... broken somehow. And then there are the words.

The words he says in his sleep.

I don't understand them.

Chapter 8

Journal Entry, April 7th[th]

He ate some chicken soup today (Campbell's of course, not homemade) and kept his eyes open for a minute or so. They're the color of amber, like the necklace daddy gave me before he left for good. But the shaking is becoming more violent and he groans and shivers. I don't exactly know how to help him, so I did a spell mamaan taught me with some white candles. It cleanses the aura with a raw egg. At least it's supposed to.

I circled the egg around him then took it to where the four corners meet down the road and watched a car crush it. It felt like it weighed a ton. This guy must have some sort of burden, like he's carrying the weight of the world.

I don't know much about taking care of anybody except for when daddy got sick that one time. mamaan said to leave him be but I just couldn't watch him suffering so I snuck in and laid his head in my lap and told him the Hansel and Gretel story I knew. This guy is shivering like daddy did that night but worse. Somehow I don't think Hansel and Gretel's gonna cut it this time.

I borrowed a couple blankets from Jack next door but they still don't seem to be enough. I heard this is all part of it though. That's what Jack said and he would know. Jack's got some hard miles on him.

I've been writing down the words he says in his sleep. It sounds like some other language, something old, not Latin but something else. Whatever it is, it feels important. I'm writing it down just like it sounds and maybe when he finally wakes up he'll tell me what it all means.

* * *

She's feeding me again. I like how her long fingers break off a piece of bread and dip it into the bland broth. The way she looks at me with her dark green eyes makes me feel naked and vulnerable yet infinitely safe. Like she can truly see me. Her hair is tied back in a satin ribbon the color of the ocean during a storm and her baggy cotton dress covers her elegant body head to toe, the print a muted paisley that makes me think of a tablecloth from the Middle East. She looks beautiful.

Clean and pure.

I'm not sure how long I've slept but it seems like a long time. My body aches in ways and places I couldn't have imagined possible and my head feels like it's trapped in a vice.

It hurts to open my eyes too long; especially when the sun is shining through the big windows this place has lining every wall. I think we're in the woods because all I can see are trees and she doesn't have a single curtain or blind to block out the world.

The bed I've been sleeping on is in the middle of the room and covered in the softest white sheets, a pile of blankets and white Christmas lights strung across the headboard. This place looks like a cross between a fairy's cottage and a hunting lodge with its wood walls and beams.

She has candles everywhere, most of them half burned, and crystals in all shapes and sizes hang from hooks and nails. It suits her, this place. Everywhere I look there's a clue to who she is and what she loves.

Sometimes I see a flash of light and the ache in my head is blinding. The pain leaves me breathless.

Why is she helping me?

The last thing I remember was Peter kicking some dirt in my face and an angel sitting with her hands on me, her hair blowing wild in the desert wind. She yelled at Peter but I can't remember what she said. I want to talk to her, thank her, but my throat hurts too much.

I don't deserve her kindness.

God help me I'm a fuck up.

Chapter 9

Jerusalem, Israel

The Rabbi sips from a small glass teacup, "What if I were to tell you that the stone tablets were in fact two meteorites? In the very same way the black stone embedded into the Ka'ab wall of Mecca is said to have been a meteorite that fell from heaven to Adam. These stones were called betyls, they stem from Smatic origins and the sacred stones are said to possess a divine life. Stones with a soul so to speak. But just as the stones can do good, they also have the ability to do great harm, as anything powerful usually does.

This power explains somewhat the fact that the Ark is said to emanate light. In fact, legend states that when the high priest of Israel would enter the temple of Solomon, he would be guided only by the light of the Ark of the Covenant.

So what do stones, lost scrolls and King Solomon's temple have to do with saving human kind? I am sure many of you have heard of the seven signs. The so-called signs said to be the indication of the Messianic age that popular culture has written about so prolifically. But alas, this is Hollywood's rendition, not what was said in the holy books. There are in fact six signs that Jesus himself revealed, another two told by the apostle John and eleven other signs, which I will reveal to you. I only hope there is enough time."

Chapter 10

Journal Entry, April 8th

I think the worst is over. The shaking has settled and he's eating more. He still hasn't said a word to me. He just looks around the place, studying it—and me with those soulful eyes.

It's a little unnerving.

I'm not sure if he's embarrassed or in shock—maybe when he hit his head on the concrete something broke inside him. Either way, I talk sometimes and he just nods. He looks so sad. I heard him crying last night while I pretended to be asleep on the couch. And I can tell that his head hurts something fierce but he doesn't make a peep about it. It's like he's used to suffering in a weird sort of way. I find myself wondering about him, where he's from, if there's someone out there worrying about him, wondering where he is. Maybe he has amnesia like you always see on those soap operas. It's strange, but I've started to get used to him being here.

I don't want it to end.

I catch myself staring; watching him sleep, and it makes me feel something deep inside that I don't understand. Something I've never felt before.

Four notebooks are full now.

Full of words that I don't know the meanings of, maybe soon he can explain.

* * *

I wake with a jolt. It's raining hard and I can hear her breathing soft nearby. I think it's been three days. I can't stay here. The angel has delivered me and now I have to leave.

I can't fuck up her life too.

It's dark outside. The only light is the glow from a stained glass firefly plugged into the kitchen wall. My legs shake as I stumble to the bathroom and piss like I'm the luckiest man alive. The room is small but there's an old iron bathtub on one side that reminds me of something from a magazine. There are half burned candles on a shelf and some dried sunflowers hang from a nail. I open the medicine cabinet just because I'm curious but the only interesting thing in there is a box of condoms. Extra large.

In the mirror my face looks gaunt and bruised. I've got to get away from her and figure out a way to repay what she's done for me.

Maybe send some money.

I bet she could use it.

The water feels cold as it hits my face and something about it reminds me of the times I'd swim in the swamp near our trailer back home. I think it's the smell —like cool moss. Seems like everything reminds me of back home these days.

I grab my tattered shirt from the bedpost and as I throw it on I notice my Fender in the corner. I pull the strap over my shoulder wondering how she got it here—or how she got me here. She can't weigh more than a buck ten.

"What, were you gonna leave without sayin' goodbye?" Her faint southern accent sounds more pronounced than when I've heard her talking to herself. She stands and comes to me, putting her pretty hand on my forehead. "Well, it looks like you're gonna survive. You seem okay. Wish I could say you looked okay but I think that's gonna take more than a couple days sleep and some canned soup." She smiles up at me. "I'm Mara by the way, and I think I've earned the right to know your name."

My throat aches but I manage to croak, "I'm Jesse."

"Well Jesse, I guess you're welcome to go ahead and leave in the middle of the night but if you don't tell me what in the heck all these words mean I may just lose my mind." She walks towards the couch then tosses a notebook at me, which I grab from the air. "Nice catch, looks like your reflexes were spared."

She gives me another smile and it makes my heart hurt just to look at her.

I can't stay here.

I can't fuck her up.

"Well, don't leave me hangin', what kinda language is that?"

I glance down at the open book. "I have no idea what this says. Why would I?"

Mara laughs. "Are you shittin' me? You've been spoutin' that stuff for three days straight. I wrote it exactly how I heard it. Exactly how you said it."

"There's some sort of mistake. I don't speak another language." She gives me an odd look and walks closer to me. Her scent, a cross between rosewater and cinnamon, makes my mouth water and I suddenly want to cry. To lay in her arms and weep for all the suffering and for the mother I never knew and the life I always wanted. I turn and bolt towards the door.

"Don't go," She whispers. "I don't know why but I think you're supposed to stay with me." She speaks the words simply.

I turn and look into her porcelain face and realize that I will never forget it. "I can't stay here... I would only hurt you."

"I feel like an idiot saying this but something is telling me that I am supposed to protect you. Like you were brought to me. If I believed in God I would say he brought us together... "

Her words make me shudder and though somewhere deep inside me I know what she's saying is true, I can't stay. I burst through the door and run as far as my legs will take me, the strap of my Fender flapping with every step.

Chapter 11

Journal Entry, April 11th

I'm trying to translate the words. I still work nights but wake up early so I can spend my days in the library at the college just down the mountain. It's pretty much a high school with ashtrays but today I found out about a professor that studies ancient languages. Something about the way the words sound makes me think they're really old, from a language no one speaks anymore. I'm hoping this leads to answers because something inside me can't let this go. I see him sleeping, his chest rising and falling, then I wake up —sad to realize it's just a dream. I can't stop thinking about him, sometimes an image of the two of us sitting side by side holding hands flashes through my head and some-times I see myself with a big round belly but he's no where in sight. That vision scares me the most. I do everything I can to stop thinking about him but sometimes it feels like I'm going crazy. What's happening to me?

I'm obsessed with these words and with him.

I see him everywhere.

* * *

I've been watching her for a week. I followed her from her house one day and watched her read books in the library and then she peddled booze at that bar half the night. She seems haunted, like she's looking for something —no —more like something is chasing her. Her delicate hands are always nervously twisting a lock of her hair or playing with her lighter.

Every time I sit and put my pen to paper I can only think of her. And then I turn into a fucking schoolgirl and just end up writing her name over and over on the blank page. I like watching her, I know it's kind of sick but it makes me feel close to her somehow. Like I'm part of her world. I know, I sound like some crazy stalker

I can't help myself.
I'm drawn to her.

Chapter 12

Death Valley, California

A sliver of light pushes through the seam of the closed double doors as Mara walks down a hall lined with trophies, passing photographs of graduates collecting various medals and golden statues. She reaches an inner office where the door is propped open with a heavy brass elephant the size of a coffee mug. "Professor Rajwani?" Mara says as she peeks around the door. Inside the smell of cloves and an aromatic spice linger in the air, a reminder of something unfamiliar and exotic.

"Yes? May I help you?" Rajwani, an olive skinned man wearing a corduroy jacket with faded elbows looks up from his desk, a pair of tortoise shell glasses propped on the end of his long pointy nose. He eyes Mara with a guarded curiosity.

"I heard you know about languages... old ones. I need to know what language this is and I can't find a thing in the library. I'm about ready to pull my hair out."

Rajwani's lips curl into a faint smile. "Well, we can't have you ruining such a lovely head of hair now, can we. Here, let me have a look." He holds out a thin hand, takes the notebook from her, and quickly begins glancing at the cryptic writing. "Phonetic, I see... is this something you heard?"

"Yes, my... um, friend was sleep talking and I started keeping a log of everything."

"Interesting friend. Do many of your friends speak Aramaic?" He looks up at Mara and motions for her to take a seat in one of the leather chairs. The edges are worn and they make the room feel cozy. Complete.

"What's Aramaic?"

"It's an ancient language, used in the book of Ezra and Daniel in the Hebrew bible. This version is the biblical version not the imperial. It's been hotly debated whether it comes from 6th century B.C. from a document called the Targums or 5th century Elephantine Papyri... Either way, I'm amazed that there's someone in modern society who is not only familiar with it but speaks so fluently. Where exactly is your friend from?"

Mara bites her lip nervously, "I don't know, but I want to find out..."

Chapter 13

The sharp clap of wood stuns the members inside the Lodge as their leader, a man with a pure white hooded cloak, slams a gavel onto a pulpit decorated with an ornate five-pointed star, his eyes from beneath the hood alive with fire.

Behind him a tapestry hangs embroidered with the words Ahavat Akhim in a thick golden thread. "We must not jump to conclusions my brethren, when the One arrives surely we will know what needs to be done. Though our leader has passed at an inopportune time with the appearance of the Parah Adumah I will take his body into my own so that he may be reborn. We will be instrumental in bringing the world under the wings of Shakinah as it is prophesied in the *Zohar*. Nothing will stop us."

A young boy carries an oblong cup to the pulpit and bows, handing it to the older man. "Thank you Yaniv," The hooded man says and accepts the golden cup inscribed with a hieroglyphic representing Isis, the Egyptian queen, and puts it to his lips.

He drinks from the cup and glances up at the crowd, his teeth stained with blood. "Pray with me. Bless me and increase my border and your hand is with me that I may not come to harm." The group bows their heads in silent prayer. The hooded man takes a fleshy object from inside the bowl and holds it in both hands, raising it in the air. "Gilgul Ha'ne' Shamot." He chants as the young boy lights seven white candles from the flame of another in a brass holder on the opposite side of the pulpit.

Blood drips down the man's hands staining the pristine robe. He draws the raw flesh to his lips, "Gilgul Ha'ne' Shamot," He chants and looks across the room at his fellow brothers then opens his mouth to take in the human heart.

Chapter 14

The full moon never ceases to amaze me no matter how many times I see it. Lately I feel more connected to it. Like its force is pulling me towards something.

Towards a life that I've lived before.

Deja vu.

I stand awed by its glow as she turns into her long gravel drive way; I'm surprised that old Jeep makes it up the mountain. Never understood why they call this place Lone Pine. There are pine trees everywhere.

As she dips her boot clad foot out the car door I realize that the way she moves has grown familiar to me. That her essence has become tattooed on the recesses of my mind in ways I couldn't have imagined possible. And that I can't imagine a day without seeing her run those long fingers through her hair or watch her light up one of those thin brown cigarettes. And just then I suddenly see myself clearly. I've become the kind of man that watches what he can never have. That lingers too long in alleyways waiting to catch a glimpse.

Someone frightening and grotesque.

I've become less than good for nothing, just like my father always said I would. I've become a monster who stalks in the night.

I have to stop this.

I turn on my heel and race into the woods as fast as my legs will take me, never looking back.

* * *

Journal Entry, April 13th

I saw a man run into the woods tonight. I couldn't make out any of his features, but I felt it was Jesse. Or maybe it's my mind playing tricks on me again. Something is happening to me. Most days I feel like I'm in a fog. Everything seems dreamlike. Almost like I've had this experience before or I've been meant to live it. As if everyday I've lived has been leading me to this moment.

The professor has translated more than half of the notebooks but he's still not saying a word. Every time I see him he looks more sober and confused... It's almost like he doesn't believe me. He keeps asking me who Jesse is but what else can I say? That he's some musician I barely know who crashed on my couch for a few days?

But deep inside I know there's more to this.

It's strange to think about but it feels like there's something or someone guiding us, like he and I were destined to meet. Or maybe I really am just going nuts from living in this place alone with Aapa, I think I'm becoming the crazy cat lady.

I feel detached from the world, day to day life feels frivolous, irrelevant, all I think about are his words.

They haunt me.

I can't go on like this anymore, I have to know what the translations mean...

* * *

Lone Pine, California

"Professor it's Mara. I'm sorry to call so late but I can't sleep. I can't stop thinking about what the words... Professor, are you still there?"

He clears his throat, his voice gruff. "Yes, I am. Allow me a moment to I go into the study so I don't disturb my wife."

Rajwani makes his way down a dimly lit hallway to his study brightened only by faint moonlight. He slides into a worn madras plaid chair with his hand against his head and sighs.

"Miss Mara I fear that you haven't told me the whole truth."

Mara blinks twice, confused. "I don't understand... "

"The words. These notebooks you gave me... they're filled with prophecies. And in perfect Aramaic no less. Words of astounding wisdom and truth. I simply cannot believe your explanation that this mysterious acquaintance of yours said all of this in his sleep. It's implausible. The phrases are so eloquent. Like poetry. It's simply not possible."

"I wasn't lying, what I told you is exactly how it happened. I know it doesn't make any sense but you have to believe me. This man, the one who spoke the words, he's a virtual stranger to me. I don't know anything about him except that he's a musician. I'm telling you the truth, professor, there's no reason for me to lie. Can I please have the translations now? I need to know what they say... "

"I'm not quite through..."

"I'll take whatever you have. I'll see you at your office tomorrow morning." Mara slams down the phone harder than she intended. She stands in the kitchen shaking as she reaches for the bench tucked under the window and slowly sits, lights a cigarette and stares at nothing in particular.

Rajwani glances at his watch and dials another number. "I told the girl. She is coming tomorrow to retrieve the notebooks." He nods his head then gently replaces the receiver in the cradle and takes his second deep sigh of the evening, a profound sense of dread weighing heavy on his body and mind.

Chapter 15

Jerusalem, Israel

Arm draped across the back of the bench, the Rabbi gazes steadily at the camera and rubs prayer beads between his fingers. "Did you know that in one month alone this year there were over two hundred documented earthquakes felt around the world? Quite a marvel I think." He wraps the string of beads around his wrist. "For example lets compare seismic activity of a hundred years ago. Between 1890 and 1900 there was only one earthquake in the world, and yet in modern times there are several hundred quakes during the course of a day. This new level of seismic activity is staggering and yet is this coincidence? I doubt it. Jesus himself said that it would be so in the end of days, that there would be earthquakes all around us." The Rabbi puts the beads to his lips. "But, my friends, do not be afraid of these rumblings of the earth, be afraid of the tremors of your heart, for those will be the true death of us all." The Rabbi puts up his hand. "Please turn it off."

Elijah does what he's told then sits next to his father. "What's wrong, do you need oxygen?"

"No. But I can feel myself leaving." He takes a long and labored breath. "I must rest, my mind is cloudy," He lays his head against the plaster wall, looking out onto a starless sky.

Chapter 16

Abruzzo, Italy

"Thank you, Excellency, for coming, we didn't know who else to turn to." The bishop glances around the tiny room that houses a few battered pieces of furniture, the smell of burnt bread lingers in the air and the fireplace is cold and empty except for old ashes.

"Well, my dear, I was very much intrigued by your message. I haven't performed an exorcism since my early days at the monastery." He studies the woman's worried face. "I'm glad your mother said to phone me, please give her my regards. Now why don't you show me to him, we shouldn't waste any time."

She leads him up a narrow stairway and up another smaller passage until they reach a converted attic. The curtains are drawn and the only illumination comes from a dim night light. A figure lies on a narrow bed, the bedclothes crumpled around it. The stench of sweat and sourness fill the small room so completely that the bishop pulls out a handkerchief and puts it to his face. "Is he asleep?" He asks as he approaches the bed. A young boy suddenly sits upright and rubs the sleep from his eyes.

He looks at the bishop dreamily with a good-natured smile. "Hello, who are you?"

The bishop glances at the woman, confused. "My name is Father Augustus and I am a friend of your mother's. She was worried that you are sick but you look perfectly well to me."

The boy again smiles at the older man, his bright teeth gleaming in the dim light. "No, Mr. Augustus I feel quite good. I'm sorry to have worried you, mama."

The bishop frowns and squints his eyes trying to get a better look at the child. "Here now, let's have some light, open a window so the child can catch a breath." He exclaims and crosses the room toward the curtains.

"No!" A growl is heard from the bed as the child shakes uncontrollably and urinates himself, his body thrashing in the sheets.

Suddenly a wooden dresser slides across the room hurling towards the bishop. He moves swiftly out of its way then grabs a large metal cross from the pocket of his robe and approaches the now laughing child, his large teeth glowing in the darkness.

"Cunning serpent, you shall no more dare to deceive the human race. The most high God commands you." The bishop shouts and opens the curtains letting in piercing sunlight and distant views of the surrounding rural countryside. Skin smoldering the child writhes, screaming in an old and forgotten language. The contents of the room thrash from side to side narrowly missing the bishop who stands unwavering, hands clutching the talisman. "God the Father commands you, God the Son commands you. The sacred sign of the cross commands you, the glorious Mother of God commands you, she who by her humility and by the first moment of the Immaculate Conception crushed your head."

Suddenly the boy's back arches with great force and a gust of wind sweeps through the room. The nearby window shatters and the howling wind escapes through the opening. The child's body, now limp, falls back onto the bed.

"The Blood of the Martyrs and Saints commands you... " The bishop whispers, slowly approaching the now quiet, still child and lays a hand on his flushed forehead.

"mama?" The boy's chin begins to tremble, a flood of tears behind frightened eyes.

"The spirit is gone. He is your child once again," Bishop Augustus says as he watches the woman approach the child with arms outstretched. He turns to look out the shattered window, thoughts flooding his mind as he slowly makes the sign of the cross. *God help the next person who he possesses. The demon is here for something and he will not be stopped so easily.*

Chapter 17

The man with the white cloak stands in the center of a darkened room facing the east, eyes closed, touching the tip of a dagger to the middle of his forehead. "Ateh." He whispers and imagines the light of energy running down the length of his spine. The dagger is brought down quickly in front of his body so that it points down to his feet. "Malkuth," he murmurs in hushed tones then touches the tip of the blade to his left shoulder and utters the word. "Ve-Geburah."

Sweeping his hands in a circular motion he chants, eyes fluttering. "Le-OLAHM-Adonai," his body lurches forward to the ground and he carves triangular shapes onto the thick plank wood floor. "Yhvh," he cries then turns to the north and stands in the center of the etchings, his body shaking. "ADNI," then to the west, "AHIH," and finally facing due south, "AGLA". A glow of light surrounds him that enters from a small circular dome in the ceiling, flooding the entire space. He imagines the Goddess Shekinah, her force powerful.

A young man enters the room. "I'm sorry, sir, I didn't realize you were in the midst of ritual."

The older one pulls back his hood to reveal a cherubic face surrounded by short-cropped black hair and thick eye brows with a generous touch of grey. "No problem, I was just finishing. Have you brought the photographs, Michael?"

"Yes, Mr. Berg... "

The man puts a hand in the air. "Ah—ah, it's Stuart now remember. If you are to accompany me to a meeting of the O.R.G. you must always use that name and your new gentile surname as well." He removes the robe revealing a less than trim body in a short-sleeved polo shirt and khaki's.

"I'm sorry, Mr. Stuart, please forgive me." He hands the older man a bundle a photographs bound neatly with a rubber band.

Stuart unwraps them and grimaces as he flips through the pictures. "That fat bastard really did get his hands on the stones. Or at least one of them." He slides the stack into his pocket and wraps the rubber band around his wrist. "We'll get it and we will win this battle. The secret fire is within us, brother, do not forget. In fact, I look forward to the challenge," He exclaims, jaw set hard, then steps towards the windows and opens the thick black curtains. Daylight fills the room revealing a perfectly shaped pentagram carved deep into the planks.

Chapter 18

The last batch of headaches disappeared when the rain arrived. The drops fall hard on the thirsty soil but only stand in stagnant puddles. Seems like nothing can penetrate this baked, dry earth.

I lay with my head against the wall and light what I keep promising will be my last cigarette. I suppose if I'm gonna enjoy a vice this one sure beats poppin' a black beauty. I haven't written anything for weeks. Ever since the night of my birthday it's like something changed inside me. It's like I see things clearer but this life is just too brutal. The world and everything inside it feels like it could swallow me whole with its hate. I can't read the paper or watch TV.

The terror around me burrows into my pores.

People are in pain everywhere I look, their hearts bleeding. It makes me feel helpless.

My connection to the earth seems different too. I threw some apple seeds on the ground yesterday outside my window and they've sprouted leaves today. I feel certain if I only touch them tomorrow they would be full-grown trees baring fruit. That sounds crazy I know, but in my heart I know it's true. Something is happening to me. It's as if I can feel the earth's vibrations. I swear, I can feel its shifts and the temperature of its core inside my body. Or maybe I'm just losing it. If I told someone about this stuff, not to mention my dreams of talking serpents, I'm sure I'd get thrown into a padded room.

I need to find work.

If I don't pay rent on this place that nice old Ms. Helen is probably not going to stay so nice. In fact, I can't believe she hasn't thrown me out already. Maybe it's cause I help her carry in her groceries when I'm around or that I helped her build that bookcase she wanted in her bedroom. Or maybe it's cause she never got married and having a man live close by makes her feel safe. Either way, she's been better to me than I deserve.

I turn the bolt on my door and notice the old lady peep through her curtain. I wave to her to come outside. My place is built into the side of her garage and she lives in a tiny bungalow on the property. The land is about an acre wide but our places are separated by only twenty feet or so. She walks towards me with her umbrella open, her weathered and tanned face looking grim.

"I know I owe you quite a bit of money and I'm sorry I've let it get away from me like this. But I'm going to find a job today and I'll get you paid back in no time," I say with a guilty shuffle of my feet.

A faint smile forms across her thin lips. "Oh Jesse, don't worry. I know you're good for it."

This wispy haired woman that I barely know is the closest thing I've ever had to a mother. I look into her trusting eyes and my throat gets tight with emotion. "I promise I won't let you down." I hear the words pass my lips and in that moment I know I have to make good on my promise. In fact, from this day on I will make good on all my promises. I'm gonna become a man my mother would have been proud of. As I stand there having an epiphany in the driveway, it occurs to me that Ms. Helen might think I'm out of my mind.

Maybe I should stop fighting it.

Maybe I'm destined for that padded room after all.

Chapter 19

Death Valley, California

Mara glides through the empty school hallway, eerie without students' animated chatter. Suddenly she becomes aware of the click of well-soled shoes somewhere behind her, but as she turns to glance behind the sound abruptly stops.

Too still.

Too quiet.

Reaching Rajwani's office door she finds it propped open several inches with the brass elephant fallen on its side.

"Hello? Professor?" She pushes the door further to find the office empty and void of Rajwani's familiar scent. She stops and turns once again to the open doorway, a chill coming over her, then makes her way towards the desk where the notebooks are stacked. A hand written note on thick parchment paper lays on top, the words difficult to make out, written in haste.

"Be very careful and protect the messages in these books, I believe they are very special. I have an idea about where they come from and will try to find out more. I'm sorry I could not meet you today but I have been called to an emergency. Stay in touch. Sincerely, Raj Rajwani."

She looks around the room again.

Something feels off.

Not right.

She quickly grabs the books and bounds from the office door as she spots a man standing in the hall. He taps his foot lightly and forces a smile, his stare singularly focused on Mara's face.

"Find what you were looking for?" The man asks, his elegant clothing and thick accent betraying him as an outsider.

Mara gasps, startled, then nods. She makes her way to the double doors and bolts outside, eager to escape the darkened corridor and the foreign man with the soulless eyes.

The man walks towards the open doorway, watching Mara slide into the Jeep and pull away. He fingers something in his attaché case then pulls out a worn notebook, opening it to the first page.

"Eli Eli lima sabachthani," He whispers, then closes the notebook and drops it back into his briefcase. "It has only just begun."

Chapter 20

Vatican City, Rome

Bishop Augustus lays awake as the wind howls outside his darkened window, a feeling of dread enveloping his body and tearing at his soul.

Something is happening. Ever since I was a boy I remember that when I have this feeling something wicked was coming. But this time it feels different. Stronger.

He sits up and looks around the darkened bedchamber and flicks on a light. He's still for a moment, then suddenly sure of what he must do; he opens a drawer pulling out an old leather bound journal and flips through the pages frantically. He picks up the telephone receiver and dials, glancing at the open page of the notebook. "I need your help, I fear the Rufus Dreco has reappeared. As he did not succeed in his first attempt, I believe the day is coming for a rematch." The bishop shakes his head frantically. "No, I have not gone mad, it is the truth. He may not appear with seven heads but he has come for something, and I have a terrible feeling I know what it is."

Chapter 21

Jerusalem, Israel

The Rabbi sits looking out the darkened open window lost in thought, the camera still pointed toward him. "A time of tribulation. Religion has fallen out of fashion, my friends. People are persecuted for their beliefs and certainly Christianity has become very unpopular altogether. Jesus spoke of this as one of the signs of the end of days." He continues staring out the window reflecting on his words and sighs. "Our world has grown increasingly cynical and detached and yet there seems to be a hunger amongst many for something greater than themselves. Now more than ever people are searching for a bigger truth." He touches a hand to his brow." It is written in the book of Revelation verse 11:19 that the location of the Ark is in heaven. But there is more in the scripture, clues and double meanings that will unlock its true location so that the Temple can be built again..." Suddenly his expression changes and his mouth falls agape, the spark in his eyes gone and a blank stare in its place.

"Father?" Elijah says but already he knows that his father has left the room, only his shell remains, still breathing, but the mind somewhere far away.

Chapter 22

Special Activities Division, C.I.A.

Harold Cooper crams the last of his personal belongings into the cardboard box on his desk. *More than half a century of service and this is all I have to show for it?* He thinks, chuckling. *Still, it's been a great ride.* He picks up the plaque for honorable service, the gold medal he got from the president himself. He smiles as he packs the items. *A bona fide general, who woulda thought a kid from Alabama who barely finished high school could become a general and director of the CIA?*

Not bad, old boy, not bad at all.

Now all I have to look forward to are my days with Gracey. That old cat will outlive us all. He suddenly thinks of his wife, Yasmine, how she looked just before she died, her skin thin and Jaundiced. Heart suddenly heavy, he runs a weathered hand through his hair as the telephone rings.

Now who could that be? He picks up on the second ring, his thick fingers wrapped around the receiver. "Cooper here. Hey, buddy, how ya doin.'" He listens for a moment until a bead of sweat trickles down his face. "You're kiddin' me, right?" He shakes his head and hangs up the phone. "Well, I'll be Goddamned. It's finally come back to haunt me." He exclaims as he looks through the window at the ground eight stories below.

Chapter 23

Journal Entry, April 20th

It's Aapa's birthday, or at least it's three years ago today that she showed up on my doorstep and we're spending it in front of the potbelly stove. It's been raining all day, so it's oddly cold for this time of year. I'm reading Jesse's words while Aapa relishes her can of tuna, my present to her—that along with my old red pumps for her to scratch up. She's a cheap date.

I've been mesmerized by the words since I got the notebooks from Rajwani. He hasn't returned any of my calls about the missing one; it was the thickest of them all.

I almost can't believe it myself that these are the words that Jesse spoke in his fevered sleep. They seem somehow other-worldly. He speaks of how evil we have become to our fellow man, judging, hating what is different, dictating who is allowed to love, and of how the world can be made right through truth and justice.

The messages are seamless, so open and honest yet some-times almost riddles. I have to see him again, find out who he really is...

* * *

I found a job working with my hands. I've always been good at that sort of thing. I'm helping build a place that's going to be a strip mall soon. Another single story stretch of plaster and tile roofs housing anything from party favors to Mexican food. Looks like the work will be steady and I don't mind waking up early. I've even started packing my own lunch. Peanut butter and banana sandwiches.

I like how the nails glide into the wood when I hit them just right and I've already been able to pay Ms. Helen part of what I owe. Her smile made my day—the way her mouth turned up into the widest grin I've ever seen.

I still think about Mara, but I've stopped following her. Sort of. I only go by the bar once in a while with a hat on and sit and watch her serve drinks. She treats everyone the same, with a special kind of dignity that makes me want to know her even more.

The workday goes by slow. When it starts to get dark I know it's time to go home and the foreman usually gives me a ride.

When he doesn't offer I walk the two miles and think about what I want to do with the rest of my life.

"Jesse, time to go. Want a ride?"

"Sure."

We make our way towards Jimmy's shiny red Chevy and he unlocks the doors with a remote. The truck still smells showroom new even though he says it's two years old. He's the same way about the job site. You could practically eat off the concrete slab.

He chews tobacco and spits into a clear plastic bottle, "You can come by and have some supper with Sally and me, if you like."

"No thanks, I've got plans," I lie. I haven't had plans for months. My evening meal consists of takeout from the Chinese place down the street that doubles as a doughnut shop in the morning.

We drive in silence. I watch the trees whip by in a blur until Jimmy slows and turns into my driveway.

That's when I see her.

She sits inside her Jeep with her head resting against the glass, eyes shut, blood red hair pulled to one side trailing down her shoulder. Jimmy lets out a whistle.

"Didn't know you had *those* kind of plans. Boy, you've been holdin' out on me."

I don't reply and jump out of the car, walking towards her. She abruptly opens her eyes, sensing me and gives me a big smile as she rolls down her window.

"You surprised to see me?" She asks. I hear Jimmy's tires on the gravel, the hum of the engine pulling away.

I feel mute. Like the wind has been knocked out of me but at the same time like I can breathe for the first time in years. "That's an understatement. How'd you find me?"

"Well for a while I thought I was going insane —kept seeing your face everywhere. But then the other night I saw you watching me at the bar and I followed you home. So the cat's out of the bag on you're little stalking fetish." She gives me a wry smile then looks away. "Who gave you a ride?"

"No one. Just being friendly with my foreman" I run a hand through my hair shaking off sawdust. "So, what are you doing here?"

Mara opens the door and steps out of the Jeep in a pair of yellow galoshes. "It's supposed to rain later," She says as I look down. "I'm here to make you a business proposition."

I blink twice but say nothing.

"You think maybe we could go in? We've got an audience." She glances towards the old lady's cottage as I turn and catch Ms. Helen peaking out from behind the drapes.

We step inside and she stands looking around the room. It's just a room with a bed against the wall. That's it. Nothing else.

"I wasn't expecting company," I say as I motion to the unmade bed.

"Well it's not exactly the Taj Mahal but you keep it pretty neat for a bachelor." She stares at me silently for a moment then reveals, "I want to be your manager. Now before you say no hear me out. I translated the words you said while you were sleeping. They're beautiful. Their message is something the world needs. I want you to write them into songs... and I won't take no for an answer."

I sit on the edge of the bed and stare at the floor. "What words? I don't understand." She comes to me and stands at the foot of the bed. She's so close; her scent makes me dizzy with hunger.

"Look, I don't know who you are or where you came from, but you're... special."

I laugh. The sound is deep and guttural and gives away more than I intended. "I'm special? You're right, you have no fucking idea who I am. I'm nobody. I never have been, and if you know what's good for you you'll get as far away from me as you can."

She puts her hand gently to my head and we stay that way for a long time in silence. "Listen, whoever you were before doesn't matter. Maybe something happened when you hit your head, I don't know... but you seem to know things. Things that seem impossible."

She tells me of the Aramaic and the professor. She tells me what the words mean. And as we sit together on the floor with the notebooks fanned out in front of us I realize that my life will never be the same. I find myself agreeing to meet her again and promise to write the songs.

Then I get a fresh and violent headache so she puts me to bed and turns out the light.

And flies away like an angel.

Chapter 24

Special Activities Division, C.I.A.

"Don't understand why a man like General Cooper would want to kill himself," The lieutenant declares shaking his head. "Heck, he was damn near dead anyway."

The young man opposite him tries to hold back a smile. "He must've been pushin' eighty, sir, but he looked fit as a fiddle."

"Fit as a fiddle?" The lieutenant smirks. "Chris, you gotta get out more. F.Y.I. he was eighty-four and never missed a day of work in his life, but the man was bound to kick the bucket soon. I want you to investigate this. Find out what happened. I know you've got your plate full with the weapons case but I want you to do this as a favor to me on the down low. The guy was kinda like my mentor. I need to know what happened." He grabs a black jellybean from a jar and pops it into his mouth. "Something's wrong here. It just doesn't make any sense. It's got me stumped and I don't like being stumped."

"Yes, sir," Chris exclaims as he stands and makes his way towards the door.

"Oh, and Chris, you can check the phone recordings and see if he had any calls that day that might explain this."

The young man looks confused. "We tap the phones here sir?"

The lieutenant rolls his eyes. "Duh. We're the freakin' CIA. Of course we tap the phones." He gives the younger man a sly smile. "And we do a lot of other things I'll tell you all about once you find me some answers..."

Chapter 25

Vatican City, Rome

A man walks down a long corridor, his overcoat flapping against a shiny black briefcase. The dark wood walls are etched deep with a fleur de lis, pointed arches, and crosses. Carpets thick under foot are the color of eggplant and a blood red stained glass at the end of the hallway depicting the Virgin Mary catches the light, filling the hall with deep prisms of color. He stops near the end and knocks twice on an arched double doorway. It's opened by the Bishop Augustus in a dark clergy robe with several ornate rosaries hanging from his neck.

"Have you brought it?"

"Yes, Your Excellency," He replies and removes a notebook from the attaché case. "It is as you thought. He has returned."

Chapter 26

Jerusalem, Israel

"As it is said in Matthew 24:14, 'And this gospel of the kingdom shall be preached in the whole world, and then the end shall come.' We only have to go as far as the Internet or television these days to see humankind passing their religious beliefs as fact and gospel. Missionaries travel all over the world spreading the word. Television evangelists speak of wisdom and profound truths as they collect endless sums of money from their devoted followers. I believe Jesus thought his teachings would be a positive thing for mankind and yet we have figured out a way to make it dishonest and hurtful, connected to ego and power." The rabbi's body rattles with a wet cough, his lungs congested. He puts up a hand. A signal to stop the recording. Elijah comes to his father and sits next to him as the Rabbi takes a long breath from the oxygen mask.

"Dad, why have we become so evil?" Elijah asks, his expression brimming with innocence. His father frowns and turns his face once again towards the window.

"I believe, my son that our society has become one where deceit and trickery are applauded. A world where fame is revered more than love or kindness." The Rabbi turns to face his young son. "Are you afraid, Elijah?"

The young boy looks up at his father, chin trembling. "Yes, I am, dad. I'm not ready to die."

The Rabbi puts an arm around the boy's shoulders and pulls him close. "My beautiful boy, you must have faith. We do not know what the future holds but rest assured that whatever it is, God has a plan for us. He will not abandon us in our hour of need. He will come for us and then we will have the chance to choose."

The boy buries his face deeper in his father's robes, his cheeks stained with tears. "What if we make the wrong choice, dad?"

Chapter 27

Journal Entry, April 23rd

He's been trying to write but something's blocking him. I hear him humming melodies but then he stops just as quickly as he started. Sometimes he cries and sometimes the pain in his head is too strong and he just curls up in bed, rocking.

It scares me.

I keep asking him to go to the doctor but he won't. He comes to my house and sits in front of the fire for hours after work. He lights it even when it's warm outside. Mostly I think he likes staring into the flames.

There's a key for him on the porch under the old metal milk can for the nights when I'm at the bar and I made a charm to protect him from the demons that are trying to shake him. It's an old Balloch thing my mamaan showed me when I was small, a bit of white magic. I put the amulet into a leather pouch and he wears it on a thin cord around his neck. Sometimes I fix him a fried egg but mostly he doesn't eat unless it's peanut butter and banana sandwiches with the crusts cut off. Usually, I fall asleep and by the time I wake up in the morning he's gone. Not a trace of him to be found.

I called Rajwani again to see about the lost notebook. No one answers, just the same recording that his voicemail is full. It's like he just disappeared.

The timing a coincidence?

Something tells me no.

I wonder if the notebooks have something to do with him vanishing...

Chapter 28

Jerusalem, Israel

Elijah turns on the camera and stands next to it, eagerly watching his father with adoration. The old man smoothes his hair, a nervous habit. "Are you ready, dad?" The young man asks.

The Rabbi smirks and lays the oxygen mask by his side. "As ready as I will be." He turns to the camera. "I believe if any of you look around our beautiful planet you will find acts of God. Things that are inexplicable and yet so purely undeniable that we simply must believe.

The stone heads of Easter Island, the great pyramids and so many other phenomenon that cannot be explained away by modern science. The only explanation is something otherworldly. I am not saying this in an effort to coax any of you to become zealots or suddenly fall to your knees. The reason I speak of such things is because you must believe that there is something beyond yourselves for the remainder of the story and for the world to be saved. Maybe not God in the traditional sense but just the belief in a higher power is of the utmost importance to save our planet from its fate." He pushes the hair from his forehead now wet with perspiration. "Quite a daunting statement I know, but there isn't much time. You will watch this after the End of Days has already begun and only your faith can stop it.

The signs are among us. The increase in knowledge is another sign. All around us things are changing at the speed of light. New technology is being developed that regularly leaves us in awe. Imagine that only one hundred years ago a crude version of the automobile was being invented? Can you imagine a world without iPhones or laptops or any of the other gadgets that we've become so reliant upon? The Bible says there will be a great increase in technology in the last days. Daniel 12:4 says, 'but thou; O Daniel, shut up the words, and seal the book, for even until the time of the end: many shall run to and fro; and knowledge will be increased.' This is certainly true of the age in which we are living. Currently the accumulated knowledge of the world doubles every 18-22 months. What would our ancestors have thought of this? The mere idea of it boggles the mind and yet it has come to pass and so we have come one step closer to the End of Days."

A phone rings on the nearby desk. "Shit," the young man mumbles then looks guiltily at his father who let's out a chuckle.

"Elijah, my boy, you still manage to surprise me on occasion." The Rabbi stands and slowly walks to the desk, answering on the fourth ring."

"Hello?"

"Rabbi Ashkenazi, I'm sorry to interrupt sir but I thought you should know... he has arrived sir."

"Who? Who has arrived?" The old man cries, confused.

"The One."

Chapter 29

To see her laying there, her skin so porcelain, one could never tell that she hails from gypsies. She says she's from an old tribe and was touched with magic, a power to feel and see a truth that for most people is only an idea. She told me about it one day while making me a cup of coffee. And the way she said it, it seemed like the most normal thing in the word. Sometimes it's hard for me to keep from touching her. The way her skin looks when the light catches her a certain way.

She sparkles.

Mara tells me to write what I feel. But there is sadness inside me that I still can't explain in the music. Sadness for what our world is becoming. I see images around me of people that are deified and for the life of me I can't figure out what they have done to deserve their seat on the public throne. I can't watch TV at all anymore. I try but it revolts me. Every day it seems like we become less tolerant and more hateful.

Soulless.

We blame what we do not understand and attack each other in the name of God. I can't think of anything less Godly. People go to their churches in their small towns then come home and spew vile hate against their neighbor or the man of color walking on the street. So many lost, I wish there were some way for me to reach them. But these days ignorance seems to be winning by a landslide.

Everyone playing judge, jury, and executioner.

Each one worse than the next.

But there are those touched by the light. Like Mara. The ones that make me believe that change is possible.

I think of my father from time to time and wonder what's become of him. He's probably drunk himself dead in that trailer by now. I pull out the photograph of my mother and wonder if she's laughing in heaven, if her hair is still black and shiny like in the picture. It was taken before she was married and the back of the photo says, Miriam Navi 1968. It's the only one I have of her and I've kept in clean in a plastic baggie ever since I took it from dad's liquor cabinet. I think of going to see him a lot lately. And if he's still alive maybe I can help him.

Reach him somehow.

I don't know. Sometimes I think there's something really wrong with me because all I can think about is making things right for everyone else. But I can't escape this feeling that I have to settle things with my father and then maybe I will find my way.

Maybe then I can find the truth in my music.

* * *

Journal Entry, April 28th

He left to see his dad today. I divined, so I knew he was going to go, the old magic comes in handy sometimes.

I took him to the bus station and he bought a ticket to a small town I'd never heard of. The people at the station looked dirty and sad. They had a beaten hollowness that made me feel like their lives must not be worth living. Jesse couldn't stop looking at them. He wrung his hands and his eyes filled with tears as he watched a woman who looked sick inside slap her little boy across the face. It was as if every person had a wordless story for him.

He absorbed them all.

By the time he got on the bus he looked so tired. As if he had sucked in every bad thought and feeling in that rundown station. I gave him the P&B sandwich I'd packed and a bottle of baby aspirins —he likes to chew them when a headache comes on. I like looking out for him. We're connected in ways I can't explain. Sometimes I want to feel his touch so bad it hurts but I keep my distance. It seems like that door is closed. Locked even.

I just hope after this trip he can finally write his truth in the songs... and maybe open up to me...

Chapter 30

Flames burn in patches that rise and fall on dry soil, the air thick and the terrain rough. A man laughs wickedly, his eyes glow red as his hands tighten around the bishop's throat. "Please," Augustus cries, his breath coming in short gasps.

"You dare to think you could defy me?" The demon taunts. "I will get what I came for, make no mistake, the chosen one will not succeed." He presses down until the bishop jerks and shakes. The demon howls in delight as the flames rise, enveloping both of them.

Bishop Augustus bolts awake, startled from the nightmare, sweat glistening his brow.

Dear God, please help me, I must do something to stop this evil.

Chapter 31

A group of trailers form a circle on the open plain, huddled together like a self-contained city. In the center sits a rickety picnic table and a charcoal grill that's seen better days. Nearby a silver Air Stream is draped with a blue plastic tarp, protecting its rust pitted roof from the elements. Inside a man sits in a ragged plaid chair, an oxygen tank at his side and a lit cigarette in hand. He stares out the window at nothing. Hearing a knock at the door he abruptly turns on the TV set and cranks the volume loud. He looks around at the mess on the kitchen counters and scratches his unshaven face. Another knock. He sighs.

"I'm comin.' "

Jesse waits on the other side of the doorway with a pastry box in hand. His hair is combed and he's freshly shaven but his clothes look like a cross between rock & roll and homeless. The front door opens swiftly.

"What can I do you for?" The man asks, no spark of recognition on his face.

"It's me, dad."

The two stand for a long beat, their eyes locked until Jesse breaks the ice. "I brought you an apple pie. You used to like them."

"Well, come on inside, boy. No need to stand here starin' at each other like a coupla fools. The neighbors are gonna start talkin.' "

They enter the dimly lit main room and Jesse glances at the familiar maroon shag carpet, more worn and unraveled than he remembered. The furniture hasn't changed in the two decades since he's been away either, he notes.

His last foster mother brought him to visit a couple times, but dad slapped him in front of the sweet lady for spilling corn chips on the floor and that was the end of that.

The smell hasn't changed much either except now the undeniable stench of sickness floats atop the stale cigarettes and beer. The sour smell of death that makes Jesse's heart ache.

"What brings you to these parts? You need money? Cause I don't got none in case that ain't obvious as a son of a gun."

"No, I don't need any money. I've got a job."

"Well how grand. Good for you boy, hope that works out for ya. Now why exactly is it that you're here?" He scratches behind his ears and looks out the small window. His face is ashen and his cough wet and rattled. He reaches for the oxygen tank and takes a few breaths.

"I wanted to see you... and I wanted to talk to you about my mother."

"Now, Goddamnit, boy, how many times have I told you not to bring her up to me. That was a long time ago and I made my peace with it. Even though she never would've died if it wasn't on account of you. But it makes me tired thinkin' about that." He sighs. There is only silence as Jesse opens the pastry box. "What you want to know about that for anyway?"

Jesse washes a small plate from the pile in the sink and dries it facing away from his father. "I want to know what she was like and if she was happy before she died. I want to know what she wanted out of life. I want to know the kind of soda she liked to drink. I want to know anything you're willing to tell me."

The old man takes another hit of oxygen. "I meant what I said when I gave you away. You're no good. Bad luck. Plain and simple. But I guess if you bring that bribe of yours over here I'll tell you what you wanna know. Though I can't imagine what good it'll do you now... "

Chapter 32

Jerusalem, Israel

A man in his late twenties sits near El Kas fountain with the Rabbi, his face set in a deep frown. He stares at the golden dome of the Temple Mount. "Dad, I thought we had more time."

"So did I, my son, but it appears that we must find him soon. I am sorry to put this burden on you but there is no one else. I knew when you were born you were the 'chosen' one. In fact, your mother knew even before you were born. But she only revealed this to me years later."

"If I were the *chosen*," David replies, a wry expression on his dark, handsome face, "you'd think I'd be able to get an article published."

The Rabbi chuckles. "Don't judge your talents based on the whims of our fickle society, son."

"If I had written reality TV, I'm sure I'd be a huge success by now," David mumbles with a pained laugh as he studies his father's face, searching.

"You are wondering when I will shift and stop being the man you know," The Rabbi asks, "when my mind will give out again?"

"Dad... "

"It's all right, David, I know it cannot be easy. But I feel strong today. The mind is clear."

"That's great, dad," David says with a forced smile. "So where do I start looking? He could be anywhere... "

"Search in the books, there will be clues. And others that you will find in unlikely places. Where there are clues you will uncover them, my boy. I have faith in you."

David glances at the old and weathered man but is heartened by the gleam in his eye, bright as ever. "I won't let you down, father." He speaks suddenly, wanting to keep that sparkle alive.

"And it's most important that you not tell a single soul. If word of this got to the public there would be upheaval. This is your search. You are alone in your crusade for now, and there are others who do not want you to find him. Of that, I'm sure. There will be two who will join you but the time is not right for that yet. You will know when the time comes. Trust your instincts. But for now just be careful of the others. Keep your faculties about you. The trees have eyes."

Chapter 33

Special Activities Division, C.I.A.

Chris stands in the office doorway. "Is this a bad time, lieutenant?"

Eisenberg looks up from his paperwork, his crafty eyes alive with humor. "You may enter, my boy. Tell me you've got something for me, would you."

He settles into the chair opposite the lieutenant, a concerned look on his face. "Well I don't know quite what I have but I know it's something. Maybe you can make sense of it."

Eisenberg's face betrays a hint of impatience. "Well go ahead, spit it out."

"I checked the calls for the day he died. And well, you were right sir. He received a strange call at 1400 hours and the jump from the window happened about five minutes later."

"Did you listen to the call?"

"I did sir. The caller didn't identify himself but it was a man, his voice sounded older and definitely foreign. And from the way he addressed the general, sir, they seemed to be friends. He said, I quote, 'You won't believe it, Coop, after all this time someone's found out about the missing scrolls.' The general said he didn't believe him but the man said it was definite, that he had seen the proof himself. They exchanged a couple more unimportant words and that was it."

Eisenberg swivels in his chair and faces the window along the back of his office, gazing out at the rows of pine trees densely packed. "What would make a decorated general commit suicide based on a call like that? And what damned scrolls? It sounds like an Indiana Jones movie." He turns to face Christian. "I don't want you to talk to anyone about this, okay? I just want you to dig deeper. Get in the muck and swim around. The general worked for the CIA a very long time, look into his past, see what you can dig up."

Chapter 34

Journal Entry, April 30th

He showed up on my doorstep today, the rain had soaked him. The way the drops clung to his lashes made him look so young. Innocent.

He said he was ready to write the songs and asked to see the notebooks again. I made us some hot cocoa and he sat next to me on the floor in front of the fire with his words spread all around us as he searched the pages. His face glowed in the light of the flames and he looked beautiful sitting there with child-like excitement.

He looked less messed up somehow.

Like he had a secret.

***

Lone Pine, California

"So what's the big secret? What happened? You look different."

Jesse shrugs and gives Mara a lopsided smile. "I danced with the devil in the pale moonlight."

She laughs, a loud belly laugh that shakes her whole body. "Are you seriously quoting the Joker right now? Who knew, the man has a freakin' sense of humor."

She stretches and lays on her side, her body curved carelessly. Seductively. She studies him and their eyes lock, neither one can look away. Mara leans in to touch his face but he quickly pulls back and stands, cramming his hands in his jeans pockets. The spell broken.

"My father's alive. Barely. There's still no love lost but I guess I can't blame the man, I did kill his wife."

* * *

She stares unsure of what to say until I tell her my Mom died the night I was born and that dad blamed me for it. I tell her what he said; that she smiled at everyone she met and how she used to wash his shirts for him by hand that first year they were married, back when he had a good job selling insurance door to door.

The words spill from my lips—about how she always had a glass of champagne on her birthday and it made her tipsy. She wore a white cotton gown the night I was born and by morning the bottom half was soaked with blood. She laid there pale and beautiful, eyes closed as if she was still sleeping. She called me her bucket of sunshine when she was pregnant with me and talked and whispered sweet nothings to me inside her womb. She once told my dad that she had heard that plants grew better if you talked to them so why not people. She was pure as an angel and her smile could melt the coldest heart.

I went to her grave.

I left her sunflowers.

He said they were her favorite.

By the time I'm finished, Mara is crying. She comes to me and holds me tight, but I don't feel sad, I feel strong. I know I can write the songs now and I know that this is the way it was meant to be. Then the pain in my head comes like a bolt of lightning.

"Are you okay?"

"Yeah... I remembered when I was sitting with my dad that I used to have these exact headaches when I was a kid. Funny thing is they stopped one day when he cold cocked me. I never got the pain after that... until the night I met you."

She stares at me.

Knows I'm holding something back.

"After he hit me, I never got the feelings either. When I was small I used to be able to feel peoples' pain, look in their eyes and know if they were telling the truth. The nicest thing my dad ever said to me was that I got that gift from my mother. But after that day, it was gone. And I know it sounds cliché but now that it's back, I don't know if it's a gift or a curse. Something inside me is telling me I'm supposed to use it to help people. Help them find their way." I shake my head as I say the last words not quite believing that it's me saying them.

I sound like some pretentious asshole.

"I know it's true, Jesse," She says simply, "I've known it since the day we met."

Chapter 35

Dallas, Texas

A man walks towards a dusty field dotted with churning oil wells. He wears rugged old boots and a pristine white Stetson hat, which rests on his head, contrasting weathered skin. He flicks the remainder of his unfiltered cigarette onto the dirt road as he approaches a white Bentley idling, windows tinted dark. The glass rolls down revealing Rogerson, an older heavy-set man comfortable in the rear passenger seat.

"What's the good word, Roy?" The older man puffs a cigar, his hand lined with several gold nugget rings.

"Word ain't so good, boss. Somebody knows about the scrolls."

"What? That can't be..." He stubs out his cigar and addresses the driver. "Jibril, give us some privacy." The partition rises in acknowledgment.

"A member of the O.R.G. was alerted to some translations done by a professor at some rinky dink college in California. When they compared some of the words it was an exact match."

The fat man slams his fist on the seat in front of him. "Damn it! I want to know everything about this professor and where he got the information. I want to know what he eats, when he sleeps and how often he shits! You got that?"

"Yes sir. There's also a little lady involved." Roy kicks the dirt with the tip of his boot. "Don't know how she's connected yet."

"I want her followed too. And schedule an emergency meeting with all the members." Rogerson plucks a fresh cigar from his pocket. "And get me a copy of that writing. I want to see it with my own eyes."

Chapter 36

Jerusalem, Israel

The Rabbi touches the smooth beads between his fingers as he speaks, "The apostle Paul was infinitely wise. He predicted much of the plague that has desecrated our society for the last several years. The scripture passages Timothy 3:1 through 7 state, 'but realize this, that in the last days difficult times will come. For men will be lovers of self, lovers of money, boastful, arrogant, ungrateful, unholy, unloving, unforgiving, malicious gossips, without self control, brutal haters of good, treacherous, reckless, conceited, lovers of pleasure rather than lovers of God, holding to a form of godliness even though they have denied its power, always learning yet never able to come to the knowledge of the truth.'" The Rabbi raises a brow and turns towards the camera. "Sound familiar?"

Chapter 37

I went back to work today and everybody wanted to know where I'd been. Jimmy made a crack about me and Mara running off to Vegas but I told him it wasn't like that between us. I'd like it to be different but I don't wanna take any chances with her. I could fall off the wagon again.

I wouldn't wanna take her down with me.

I like the work here. It keeps me busy and makes me feel like I've done something real. Solid. And I finished three songs last night. The words flowed from my fingers as if by magic. It was like something was talking through me.

Something divine.

Mara's got some fancy dinner planned tonight to tell me something important, so we're going to a nice place with real tablecloths. She says it's a surprise.

* * *

Death Valley, California

"Are you gonna tell me now or what? I can't stand surprises," Jesse says with a faint grin. The couple sits close together at a small table adorned with a single rose and a lit tapered candle. Mara's curtain of blood red hair falls heavy around her shoulders. She wears a simple black dress that flows down to her ankles and a pair of sterling silver teardrop earrings. Jesse has on a black shirt with a slim black tie and black jeans. His mussed hair falls past his collar and the dark golden pieces shimmer in the flicker of the flame. Restaurant patrons stare at the two in their Sunday best, capturing the light with every movement.

"Who can't stand surprises?" She replies with a taunting smile. "Everybody loves a surprise. Don't be weird."

He fumbles with an unlit cigarette in his hand wishing he could fire it up. "A little too late for that."

"I'll tell you after they bring the champagne. You can drink champagne right? I ordered it ahead of time." Mara is suddenly unsure. "Maybe I'm making too big a deal out of this... "

"I can have a little."

"One glass it is then. I guess I'll have to drink the rest all by my lonesome."

The waiter arrives and sets an ice bucket next to their table. He pops the cork and pours them each a glass. "Celebrating an anniversary?"

The two glance at each other. Mara replies, "Not exactly."

Once the waiter has left she raises the champagne flute. "A toast to the future... and to new beginnings."

Jesse raises his glass. "Okay... ?"

"I got Buddy to agree to let you play the club again. I told him you were clean now and that sealed the deal." She pauses and gives him a wry smile. "Now we've just gotta find you a band."

Chapter 38

Mecca, Saudi Arabia

Early morning light streams through an arched window making the fine dust that floats in the air of the voluminous space shimmer. A dark skinned man finishes buttoning his Nehru collared suit, the white linen crisp and impeccable. His dark eyes flash with danger and curious humor as a young woman enters the room.

"Mr. Abdullah, I am sorry to intrude sir, but I've received an urgent message." She hands him a fax with a date and location marked with only the words: "He has returned."

The man's hand trembles for a brief moment. He reads the words then slowly creases the paper into folds, slipping it into his jacket pocket. "Please ask Omar to fuel the jet. I will be leaving as soon as it is ready."

Chapter 39

We've got two band members already and it's barely past noon. Mara put together an audition at the club. It's strange seeing this place in the daylight. Wrong somehow. You can see all the nasty stains and scrapes that are normally hidden in the dark of night.

So far we've found one bass player that looks promising. Jude —he looks like he's always ready for a fight. And James who's a killer on the keyboards.

"Next, please," Mara calls out. She looks beautiful today in a dark green wool suit she said she's had since the high school debate team. Said she toyed with the idea of being a lawyer for people who didn't have the money to get a good defense but with all the moving around she never got to plant any roots and ended up letting that dream go.

She's good at being in charge.

It comes easy to her.

A young guy comes to the edge of the stage, his hair and clothes disheveled. "Hi, my name is Andy, and when I'm not playing the drums, which is hardly ever, I'm fishing." He sits on a stool in front of the drum set, lifts his hands into the air, holding the sticks high then plays like lighting. Mara glances at me and smiles. She's magic.

Things are looking up for me since this angel arrived.

I hope I don't fuck it up...

Chapter 40

Jerusalem, Israel

The Rabbi paces the small room, cane in hand. "It is said in the book of Daniel that all who seek to calculate the date of the end of days shall perish... so if you continue to listen you are taking a risk. But I ask you fellow citizens of our lonely, crumbling planet, is there any other way for our world to survive?" He takes an uncomfortable breath. "Now before I continue I want you to know that I have this information because I am a direct descendant of the Fashalas, the so-called Black Jews of Ethiopia. The information is true and I have first hand knowledge of all things of which I speak. I have recently received some astounding news so I know for a fact that the time of doubt has past, we must move briskly." The Rabbi motions for his son to stop the camera and sits on the edge of the cot at the far end of the room.

"Please give me the telephone." He states holding out an unsteady hand. The Rabbi dials and abruptly questions the man on the other end of the line. "David, is there any news? Have you found any clues to his location?"

"I'm sorry, father, I've found nothing... "

"We need answers, my son. Track him. Hunt him. Follow the prophecy, thus he will be found. It is our family's legacy."

"I will, dad. I won't let you down." David hangs up the receiver and runs a hand through his dark hair. Deep in thought he begins absentmindedly rubbing the bump on his prominent nose then stands suddenly and goes to a safe on the wall where he retrieves an old map on yellowed parchment. He sits at his desk and takes in a sharp breath.

Wherever he is I must find him before they do.

Chapter 41

Journal Entry, May 5th

The days are flying by. Jesse practices with the band after work everyday and stays up half the night writing lyrics. But we still can't decide on a name. A waitress at Buddy's said we should call the band The Haunted because of the look in Jesse's eyes. It's not half bad. It's not half good either but I guess it'll do for now until the right name comes along. It'll be just like that too. I know it. The name will just drop in our laps and feel right like all good things do.

The guys seem to be bonding pretty well. They all look up to Jesse, except for Jude who's still a little standoffish and maybe even a little jealous. I think he fancies himself a lead singer.

My landlord wasn't too happy but I finally got him to agree to stay with me since he's here all the time anyway. We live like husband and wife yet he never touches me. The tension between us is raw, but he goes outside and keeps himself busy chopping wood when the hunger comes over him. We have enough wood to last three years now but he still keeps chopping.

My feelings for him grow stronger every day.

He's quickly becoming everything to me.

* * *

I've become so strong in the last month. My body seems to have been reborn. An energy surges through me that feels electric... kinetic. And even though the headaches still come, they aren't as blinding. Or maybe I'm just getting used to them. My band is becoming like family and Mara is in the center of it all.

Her strength holds everything together.

I wrote a new song today, just in my head while I built a staircase. It's as if everything is on autopilot, but in a good way. We have practice tonight in Andy's garage, how cliché right? And our first gig is this weekend.

I'm so happy to be alive.

I pray this new life is never taken from me.

Chapter 42

Vatican City, Rome

The bishop enters the empty cathedral, not a soul to be found. He sprinkles his face with holy water then wipes it with a shaky hand. Making his way to the confessional, he looks from side to side. Confirming that he is in fact completely alone he enters the ornately carved booth and closes the thick velvet curtain.

"Bless me, father, for I have sinned. It's been one month since my last confession."

"Yes, my child, continue."

"I have seen the devil, he came to me in a dream. I fear he is trying to steal my soul."

"You have nothing to fear if your heart is with God."

Frustrated, the bishop wipes his damp face with a handkerchief. "You don't understand. I think he is here on earth to do blasphemous deeds, to keep God's children from the truth. I must find him and stop him."

"And why do you think this?"

"I have received some information that leads me to believe that we are near the End of Days." There is silence from beyond the small screen. "Father, please, I'm not mad. This is all true."

"Where did you get such information?" The voice asks.

"I'm sorry, I cannot tell."

"I see. Well, I cannot comment on the accuracy, I can only say that I pray you are safe in your crusade. Do ten hail Mary's and may the Lord be with you," He says then abruptly slams the screen divider between them.

Augustus sits for a moment, his face twisted in grief. He pulls at his thick hair, closing his eyes he whispers to himself, "Maybe I am going mad." He opens the curtain and exits the confessional shaking his head and muttering. As he turns and looks back he sees that the confessor has opened the curtain and is watching him, a strange and dark look in his eyes.

Chapter 43

Special Activities Unit, C.I.A.

Eisenberg and young Christian walk down a long corridor, their shoes tapping the freshly polished floor.

"So you're telling me that he was stationed in Jordan practically right out of high school?"

"Yes, sir. And apparently he became good friends with a younger boy there; a prodigy of sorts that studied ancient languages. The two were inseparable until he got back from the Middle East. Didn't he bring his wife back from there?"

"Yes, Yasmine. It's a good thing she passed before him; I don't think she could've handled this. She was a fragile lady."

"I'm just wondering if the best friend from Jordan could be the same man he talked to the night he died. The accent sounded more East Indian though."

"That's a good question Chris. One you're going to find the answer to, I presume."

Chapter 44

Death Valley, California

"What's going on, Thom?" Jesse asks when the lead guitarist misses cords for the third time.

He shrugs. 'Nothing, just had a late night. Let's keep going. I'm fine."

The band resumes playing but Jesse puts his hand in the air to stop them. "Come on, brother, level with me." He circles Thom, strength behind his gentle voice. "You're in pain," He says and takes Thom's arm.

The younger man winces as he pulls back the sleeve of his shirt revealing a bruised and swollen limb. "I didn't want to let you guys down with the first show tonight but I shut the car door on my hand."

Jude slams his fist on the table. "Son of a bitch, what are we supposed to do without a guitar player, I need this gig man."

James plays a couple cords on the keyboard to lighten the mood. "Show a brother some love, the man is injured."

Jesse moves closer to the guitarist. Taking Thom's hand, he holds it with eyes closed as the rest of the band glance at each other with confused grins. "What the hell, man?" Jude laughs uncomfortably.

"Be quiet. Thom, close your eyes."

"Whatever you say boss." The two stand close together and Jesse mumbles words under his breath. After a few moments, Thom's body shudders, a surge of energy burning through him. Jesse continues to chant. The others look on in silence until he suddenly releases Thom's hand and steps back, unsteady. The guitar player stands dazed for a moment until he wiggles his fingers. He gives Jesse a confused look.

"No way."

Jude snickers. "Doodoodoodoo... and now, we've entered, the Twilight Zone. Come on, man. Really? It's better?"

Thom turns and the two lock eyes. "Like it never happened."

Chapter 45

Bangkok, Thailand

As dense summer rain whips the palm trees, steam rises from the sidewalks creating a thick blanket of humidity. In the distance the sound of a propeller can be heard as an older Taiwanese woman in traditional garb is escorted onto the private jet by a young pilot in uniform.

"Madame Kung, if there is anything else you require please do not hesitate to ask." He says, clearly awestruck by the sheer majesty of her presence. She returns the communication with a simple nod of her head and nothing more, then straps her seatbelt.

She looks out the small window then lifts a set of plain wooden prayer beads, kissing them gently.

Chapter 46

Paris, France

A brisk chill enters the darkened room as a young man soaked from the early summer downpour enters holding a note. "I'm sorry to bother you, Monsieur Montbard, but the lines are down and you've received an urgent message."

A sophisticated man in his forties turns from the picture window where he has been looking out over the storm, pipe in hand. "Thank you, Jean-Michel. Leave it on my desk and take an umbrella with you, there are several in the hall."

Montbard waits until the young man has left then sits at his desk, his face ashen. He reaches for the note, visibly shaken. He opens it and stares, awestruck.

And so it begins.

He leans back in his chair looking onto the raging storm.

Chapter 47

Sweetwater, Texas

Inside a converted cattle barn on a ranch in the deep-south sits a group of fourteen men and Madame Kung. The atmosphere is abuzz with excitement. Mr. Stuart sits in the corner staring at the back of Monsieur Montbard's head, lost in thought. Montbard turns, sensing the attention, and the two lock eyes for a brief moment until a strong voice interrupts.

"What makes you so sure about this Mr. Rogerson?" Sheik Abdullah asks the fat man. "I will need to see solid proof before I put all of my resources at risk. I know you think this man is reciting his version of the scrolls but I need to be sure."

Rogerson's mouth sets in a hard line. "Need I remind you who's in charge here? Since I took over this Organization I've run it like a tight ship." His face is flushed with anger. "Unlike the guy before me. Now I may not come from nobility or whatever like ya'all but I know how to get shit done. My track record should speak for itself. So when I say we've got a Goddamned situation on our hands I mean it. Now listen up." He motions to Roy who holds a notebook in his hands. "Roy, please do the honors. After you hear this, Mr. Abdullah, you will want to risk every precious barrel of oil your family owns."

"The day is near. My heart swells when I see the suffering ripe in the air like a deadly stench. The only way to save ourselves is to change this web we are weaving, to accept one another with whatever god we believe. The time for change is here my people, follow me into the light and we will all be saved from the evil that awaits us. It must start in every heart, in every soul. Mine is the way, the truth and the life... "

The audience sits shell-shocked, the tension in the room palpable until Rogerson breaks the silence. "I assume you understand now, ladies and gentleman, why there isn't a moment to spare..."

Chapter 48

Death Valley, California

The crowd watches enraptured by the music and a young girl smiles through tears, her face a delicate mix of reverence and wonder. Jesse glows under the lights, his voice like a flame that breathes warmth and life into the darkened space, illuminating every corner. Jude plays the last note of the set and the crowd erupts in cheers and applause.

"That's quite a talent you've discovered, Mara." Buddy admires her beauty, vivid in the stage lights. "I always knew you were more than just a pretty face."

"Is that supposed to be a compliment?" She gives him a wry smile and turns back to the stage. "He's really something, isn't he?"

"He's a star. No doubt about it. I think your waitressing days are over sunshine. How about a regular gig for your golden boy?"

Mara raises a brow. "Okay, but whatever you're offering I want double," She shouts as the jukebox kicks on.

"I knew you'd be tough," He studies her, "You ever think about that kiss at last years Christmas party?"

"Don't start, Buddy, that was a lifetime ago."

Buddy glances at Jesse, who approaches the table. He inches closer, stopped and congratulated every step of the way. "I suppose you've got your hands full now, but I'll give you a warning, never mix business and love. Business and sex is one thing but love will kill even the best arrangement." He gives Mara a mischievous grin and slides out of the booth.

"Always the romantic," Mara shakes her head.

Jesse settles himself next to her, the seat still warm. "This is unreal. Surreal. I never expected this kind of response."

"You underestimate yourself." Mara gives him a warm smile and without warning Jesse kisses her. It's a quick kiss, more friends than lovers, but both faces reveal a longing for more.

A longing that races their hearts.

Mara breaks the trance after an uncomfortable silence, "Buddy offered a regular gig. Not bad for your first time up to bat. I think this calls for a round of drinks. A sparkling water, rock star?"

Chapter 49

Bethany, Israel

An overhead fan circles and the tattered pages of a thin paperback flap, their sound marring the exquisite silence of deep night. David stares at the open page, distracted. *What is within these pages, father, and why must everything be a riddle? This Kebra Negast is full of them, like some sort of maze. Was Sheba converted to Judaism as it says or did she leave Solomon's home a heathen as is written in the Bible? And what does all this have to do with finding the one?*

David slaps the book onto the desk in a fit of temper then runs long fingers through his dark hair. He slowly scans the room searching the rows of floor-to-ceiling books for a clue.

A sign.

Anything.

How can the fate of mankind rest on my shoulders? Isn't there someone better qualified? He chuckles and shakes his head in disbelief. *Leave it to father to have a failed scholar be his only hope for saving the planet.*

Chapter 50

Paris, France

Monsieur Montbard sits in a small café sipping espresso. He takes the thin lemon rind from his saucer, gently tracing the rim of the tiny cup with long elegant fingers as he watches nearby patrons laugh and talk with animated gestures. A deep sadness washes over him while he studies the faces. A man from the O.R.G. enters the café. Recognizing Montbard, he veers to the small table set only with a half eaten croissant and the lone espresso.

"Montbard, what a delight to see you here!" The portly man shouts with a heavily affected Scottish accent and a practiced smile. Monsieur Montbard glances up abruptly, his thoughts shattered by the intrusion.

"Oh, what an unexpected surprise, Mr. Stuart. Please join me won't you. You must pardon me, my head is in the clouds until I have finished my morning café."

Stuart laughs, head thrown back, forced and overly jovial. *What an odd man.* Montbard thinks and runs the lemon rind along the rim of his cup once more.

Stuart pulls up an empty chair and glances at the small gold pin with the double-headed eagle on the lapel of the Frenchman's overcoat. Once he's settled he motions to the waiter with a snap of his fingers. Montbard winces. The waiter cocks a finely arched brow in annoyance and approaches the table.

"I'll have a Cappuccino, heavy on the cream and a tart. Make that two tarts in case my companion here would care to partake." He winks at Montbard who watches the exchange with distaste.

"No, thank you, I cannot take sugar in the morning."

"Well more for me then." Stuart snorts as the waiter ambles away leaving the two men in silence. Montbard takes a sip from his cup, briefly studying his companion's profile.

"Where are you staying?"

Mr. Stuart glances at Montbard coolly. "The Relais. But it's no Grand Lodge." He states, focused on Montbard's unwavering expression. "Have you ever stayed there when visiting England?"

Montbard shrugs. "I don't believe so. I'm not familiar with that particular hotel."

Stuart looks away. "A shame. It's quite a special place."

Montbard pushes the empty cup and saucer away. "You live in Jamaica most of the year if I remember correctly."

"Yes. The Scotland winters are murder on the old bones you know."

The two men watch a nearby table of American tourists slather mounds of butter on fresh croissants and laugh too loud.

"I cannot begin to imagine how these people would behave if they knew what was happening..." Montbard mumbles under his breath.

"Yes, I agree. But I try not to give it too much focus and remind myself that it's all under control. Rogerson will take care of everything. He is quite a change from the old leadership but efficient and... well, I certainly wouldn't want to go toe to toe with him. I believe he is well prepared for the situation."

Montbard's expression is hard, unreadable. "Yes, I have no doubt that Rogerson is ready for battle. No doubt at all..."

Chapter 51

Journal Entry, May 14th

Jesse's got a die hard following at the club after only three shows. The place was packed and the parking lot full. He has a hold on the audience like nothing I've ever seen. There's even a journalist who said he'd heard about Jesse and wants to write a review. A couple of the waitresses keep asking if he and I are an item but I don't know what to say so I just smile and shrug. Whatever this thing is between us, it makes me feel more alive and whole than I've ever felt.

I will protect it with everything that I am...

Chapter 52

Castel Gandolfo, Italy

A shaft of light illuminates the bishop's face while he eats his morning bread and cheese, glancing out the window at lake Albano and its ancient woods. *A good night's sleep does wonders,* he thinks as he sits in the familiar comfort of the long time summer home to the papal community, his sanctuary since he was a boy. Memories of swimming in the cool water or lying under the tall cork oaks dreaming of the future flood his weary mind. A future that turned out to be a far cry from what that dream filled child could have imagined. But becoming a man of the cloth was the least he could do. After all, the pope saved him from a terrible fate at the orphanage and Augustus would be forever in his debt.

And now the pope needed him even if he didn't realize it yet, and he must not fail him, he contemplates taking another bite of the thick loaf. *He must find a way. Perhaps he should travel to America himself, as the man from the Swiss guard he had hired seems to be making no additional progress on the matter. He must make sure that the Messianic Age is not circumvented.* A thrill runs through him at the thought of the One here on earth. *But he is so vulnerable in human form; I must find a way to protect him from the Rufus Drego.* The door opens abruptly and a young man enters interrupting the bishop's thoughts.

"Your excellency, the pope is requesting your presence in his drawing room." The bishop turns to him, a blank expression on his face. "Sir? Shall I tell him you are on your way?"

The bishop shakes away his distracted thoughts and sets aside the last bit of breakfast. "Yes, yes of course. I will be there momentarily."

The man shuts the door behind him leaving the older man deep in thought. *I must find my way out of Rome, he thinks. Even if I have to disappear, I will find the demon and protect the One. I must go with the full knowledge that I may sacrifice myself in the process, but there may be no other way. God has chosen me for this task.*

He puts the rosary around his neck and traces the sign of the cross on his chest. *May God be with me*, he thinks and opens the heavy wooden doors.

Chapter 53

I feel a power when I'm on stage that's almost unearthly. I hope the people are hearing me. Really listening.

Another terrorist bombing was on the news right before the gig and I couldn't help but weep. My whole body shook. Mara held me and dried my tears. She's so strong.

She promised some guy from a newspaper that I would talk to him tonight after the show but right now my head hurts so bad I could sleep for a year.

* * *

Jesse sits with his face resting on open palms as a middle-aged journalist enters the room. "I was told it was okay to just come in?"

Jesse looks up slowly. "It's fine."

"That was quite a show, man, I'm at a loss for words. Really. The effect you had on that crowd—I've never seen anything quite like it. I mean, yeah, I've heard about the legends, the King, The Beatles and all but man, I've never witnessed it in person before. I've gotta shake your hand." He holds out a thin tanned arm and Jesse returns the gesture. "Can I ask you a couple of questions?"

"Fire away," Jesse replies with the calm and ease of a man who's done this a million times before.

"What inspires you, Jesse? Your lyrics are quite... profound."

Jesse takes a drag of his cigarette and blows a ring of smoke. "My inspiration is you. It's every person on this planet. I can't believe what we are doing to each other. It's as if there are a million different wars and those wars are waged every day, brother against brother, citizen against citizen. People sit in ornate buildings and fear the devil but I tell you I see the devil in every single face I see. There is no man behind the curtain, no secret enemy pulling the strings. We are not puppets; we are the rulers of our own destiny. But we are destined to crash and burn in a fiery glory, each and every one of us, if we don't wake up." Jesse lights another cigarette and takes a long drag but the journalist does not speak or move a muscle, rapt in Jesse's passion. "Terrorists, each and every one of us, from the suffering we cause our neighbor to the abuse we unleash on the person we claim to love... I feel like our planet's dying many small deaths every day and we don't have much longer on this earth that we have so horribly taken for granted. The future looks grim unless we change our ways." He takes another drag off his cigarette as the journalist leans forward.

"Is this some sort of doomsday apocalyptic type of thing man?" He asks with a nervous laugh. Jesse just stares in reply and takes another drag off his cigarette, the smoke lingering ominously in the air.

Chapter 54

Jerusalem, Israel

The Rabbi holds a delicate white cloth to his lips, a raspy cough rattling his lungs. "The tensions in the Middle East are high as we all know from the media. But what is not a well-known fact is that this tension was foretold as the fifth sign.

"Zechariah 12:2, 'Behold I will make Jerusalem a cup of trembling unto all the people round about, when they shall be in siege both against Jerusalem and against Judah. And in that day shall I make Jerusalem a burdensome stone for all people: all that burden themselves with it shall be cut in pieces, though all of the people of the earth be gathered against it.'

"This obviously speaks to the continued struggle over Jerusalem. The Palestinians want it as their capital but the Israelis will not give up their holy land. Since its creation, Israel has never been at rest. The constant wars and conflict will continue until the Messiah comes. We can only hope we don't all destroy each other with the push of a button before we can be saved..."

Chapter 55

Bethany, Israel

David sits with a map, a copy of the Old Testament and a Hebrew to English dictionary open on the desktop. He studies the pages speaking aloud. "Galilee means circle in English. A district that is circular... " He studies the old map then pulls up Google Earth on the lap top computer near him and punches in the opposite coordinates. It lands on Cheshire, England. No circle district there. He types in another sequence of the same four numbers and another then slams his fist in frustration. "I'm losing it, dad, I don't know where to look!" David's wife enters the room with a cup of tea and some chickpea cookies.

Sophie reveals a sardonic smile. "Have something to eat, you're talking to yourself much more than usual." She sets the tray on the desk. "What are you looking for, my love, what could be so important to keep you up half the night?"

"I'm sorry, I can't tell you, Sophie, but just know that it's for papa. He needs this from me." David sighs running a hand through his hair. His wife moves behind him and strokes the back of his neck.

"Whatever it is you'll find it, David. If you need me I'm right outside that door."

David nods wordlessly, already lost in the books, searching for a clue to the whereabouts of the man who has returned after such a long absence. He punches in the last version of the coordinates. This time, he's taken to France, right in the center of the Chartes Cathedral. David's eyes flicker with recognition. *The Chartes has been said to contain complex messages about the past, the meaning of the prophecies embedded into the stained glass. Could this be? Could this Gothic church built in 1134 hold the secret to His location?*

Chapter 56

The man known by the name Mr. Stuart sits on the floor
of the lodge, his feet bare, the sunset burning in his weary eyes.
Michael enters the large room, it's vaulted dome ceiling reverberating the clack of his shoes on the stone floor. "Sir, it's time to
break the fast for today."

Stuart glances at the open window and speaks without a hint
of accent, "Not quite yet, my friend. The sun is still showing
her lovely face." He smiles. "Did you break your fast already,
Michael?"

The younger man hangs his head. "I was about to sir."

Stuart pats the floor next to him. "Here, sit with me for a few
minutes. Have they taught you in your studies the story behind
Tisha B'av and why we fast?"

Michael shakes his head. "Not all of it, sir. But I was told as a
boy that it would be expected of me when I became a man."

"So you did what you were told like any good boy would
right?" Stuart shakes his head. "A person should never blindly
follow a faith Michael, no matter how many people tell you it's
the right way. Question and educate yourself so you can truly
know why you are doing what it is you are doing. Understand?"

Michael shakes his head. "So what is it about?" He asks as the
sun finally dips behind the hills, leaving the room dim with the
fading light.

Stuart points outside, "We can eat now. Isn't that what you
wanted?"

"Yes, but I want this more." Michael replies with a smile, his
face suddenly animated.

"As you wish," Stuart says with a dramatic bow of his head.
"The Tisha is really a mourning period for us. It was a very sad
day when the First Temple was burned, the Holy Temple. In

fact it is the saddest day of our calendar. That temple was built by our ancestors, Michael, yours and mine under the guidance of King Solomon. The temple stood for over 400 years until its destruction in 587 B.C." Stuart rests his back against the wall and looks out onto the darkening night. "It housed the Ark of the Covenant for many of those years until the Ark was stolen from us. Preparations have long been made to rebuild the temple. The stones have been cut. The robes have been sewn. But until the Ark is found we cannot rebuild the temple and prepare for his return." Stuart turns to face his companion, his voice charged with passion. "You see Michael, this day of fasting is part of our destiny. Part of the prophecy we were put on this earth to fulfill. Only by following the prophecy to the letter can we resurrect the temple and be ready for the arrival of Al Messhiah. We must stop at nothing to reach our goal."

Chapter 57

Sweet Water, Texas

The scent of lemon and sandalwood linger in the den lined with hunting trophies where Rogerson sits staring into a large ornate wooden box. The interior is lined with sapphire blue velvet and the contents have him mesmerized until a sudden sharp rap at the door startles him.

"Come in," He shouts and closes the box abruptly.

The chauffeur and houseman, Jibril, enters with a snifter of Brandy and sets the warm glass garnished with anise seeds in front of him. "Nice night." He states as thunder rolls outside.

"What do you mean 'nice'? That storm is near blowin' the house down."

Jibril makes his way towards the window and in a somewhat grand gesture, unusual for the soft-spoken man, places his arms on either side of it, looking out. "I've always loved a good storm. The world feels cleaner afterwards. As if it's been purged." He stands for a beat, his back to Rogerson. "I know I haven't been here long but I believe I have become an asset to you, wouldn't you agree sir?"

The fat man is intrigued, "I believe so, yes. What are you playin' at, Jibril, you want a raise or something?" Rogerson asks, perusing the younger man's long and lean frame. "You got it if that's what you're carryin' on about."

Jibril takes a sharp breath. "It wasn't about a raise, sir, but now that you mention it I don't mind if I do."

Rogerson grins and takes a swig from the etched glass that catches the light from the lamp above him. "Well played, Jibril. So what's on your mind then if it isn't money? With most men there's only two things, money or women. Thank the good Lord

I was blessed with not much of a taste for the fairer sex. Lucky thing for me."

"Yes, lucky." Jibril turns away from the storm and locks eyes with his employer. "Whatever is going on, I can help."

There is a long beat of silence as Rogerson considers the man in front of him. He reaches for his cigar box, takes a fat Cohiba and taps it lightly on the leather matting. "Now what makes you think somethin's goin' on, boy?"

Jibril looks to the ground and speaks softly. "Nothing. Nothing at all. I just wanted you to know that I am at your disposal sir. Anything you need done... and I do mean anything, I am but your servant."

He abruptly exits leaving Rogerson open mouthed. "Now what in the Sam Hill was that all about?" He mumbles to himself lighting the cigar. He reclines in the leather chair and reopens the ornate box. Inside sits a large black stone about one foot wide etched with intricate writing. *We're gonna have to keep you safe now aren't we?* He thinks as he touches the primitive letters. *You're my ace in the hole.*

Outside the room, Jibril crouches peering through the keyhole of the hand carved door. He stands abruptly, brushes off his dark jacket and quietly makes his way down the polished stone hall.

Chapter 58

Rome, Italy

The Romana Termini bustles with passengers rushing to board their trains, its vaulted atrium abuzz with the typical sights, sounds and smells of a crowd. Augustus glides to the magazine rack studying it momentarily. He pulls his fedora down further and darts his eyes searching for a familiar face. Distracted, he grabs an issue of Time Magazine with a crimson colored calf on the cover, checks his watch and approaches the young clerk.

"Will this be all for you, sir?"

"Yes. Actually no. I'll take a bar of Lindt. Dark please." He pulls several Euros from his coat pocket as he catches a glimpse of himself on the mirrored wall. He shakes his head in disapproval, still not accustomed to the plain clothes. *I cannot believe I'm doing this*, he thinks.

"So do you believe the world as we know it is coming to an end?" The young man asks with a grin.

The bishop suddenly jolts backwards. "What?" He looks around frantically. "Who are you? Who gave you that information?"

Confused, the clerk smiles and holds up the magazine. "It's right here sir, the Red Heifer. I thought that's why you were buying it. It's a pretty cool story actually."

The bishop rests his hand on the counter, embarrassed and weary. "Yes, yes, of course," He replies unconvincingly. "Please hurry, I must catch my train," He says as he shoves the bills towards the clerk and grabs the items.

I'm getting paranoid, he thinks and makes his way towards the far end of the terminal. Boarding the train he gives one last look over his shoulder and breathes a sigh of relief. He enters the train car and quickly opens the magazine, a dark crease across his forehead.

Chapter 59

Special Activities Unit, C.I.A.

"So as I said, he was stationed in the Middle East practically out of high school." Christian watches as Eisenberg takes another bite from his fish fillet sandwich, tartar sauce squeezing out the sides.

"Okay, I remember, but what does that have to do with his untimely death?" Eisenberg asks, mouth full, wiping his face with a napkin.

"I'm just getting to that, sir. Apparently there was a rumor that someone who worked in the CIA at that time put together a deal for the illegal sale of artifacts. Antiquities that were said to belong to the Jordanian government."

The lieutenant glances up mid bite then puts down the sandwich. "Okay, now you've got my attention."

"Turns out when General Cooper returned home to Atlanta after 2 years abroad he bought his parents a brand new Buick and a big house in the nicest part of town. I wonder where a 22 year old kid gets that kind of money?" Chris sits back in his seat; a smile plastered across his all American face.

"Interesting," Eisenberg says as he taps the end of his nose with an index finger. "Nice detective work, son. I suppose that could be the secret he was trying to keep. But it sounds pretty crazy to go throwing yourself off a building for some antiques." He swivels his chair from side to side. "Do me a favor, don't mention this to anyone. Obviously. I want you to do some more digging, see if you can't find some information on what it was he sold and why it would make a decorated general want to eat the pavement."

Chapter 60

Death Valley, California

"He called you 'the Prophet.'" Mara says and tosses a folded newspaper that lands onto the old scrubbed pine kitchen table. Jesse, startled, looks up from his mug of black coffee, cigarette in hand.

She smiles. "Not too shabby for your first time in print."

He glances at the paper, "I'll take your word for it," then takes another sip of the hot coffee, "I just made it, you want a cup?"

"Sure. But remember... "

Jesse cuts her off. "Lots of cream and lots of sugar, I know." The two share a smile, lost in each other's gaze for a pregnant beat. Mara's expression is wounded as he turns away.

"Do you ever wonder what it would be like between us?" She whispers.

Jesse stops pouring, his back still turned.

He turns without meeting her eyes and reaches for her hand, intertwining his gentle fingers with hers. And for that brief moment the small gesture of intimacy quenches Mara's deep thirst. Her body shudders with the force of their connection. Electric. Jesse feels it too. Much too strong and deliberately releases her hand and stands. He grabs his jacket, pulling it on as he heads out the door.

"I'm going outside to... "

"Chop some wood, I know."

Chapter 61

Paris, France

David slides into the driver's seat of a rented Peugeot outside the terminal at Charles de Gaulle. He opens a guide map of northern France, spreading it across the steering wheel. *So if I cross the Siene, I should be able to get to the Chartres in just a few hours, but more than likely the cathedral will have already closed for the day. I'll go first thing tomorrow morning and stop for some French pastries along the way. Though this is certainly no pleasure trip, who knows when I'll return to France again.*

He starts the engine and winds his way through the heavy Paris traffic, his mind consumed with thoughts of his father and the family legacy. If there is anything he can do to assure that his children live in a better world than this, he will do it. He ponders the stained glass pictures and what clues they might hold. The prospect exciting, yet terrifying.

What if they hold nothing? What if I return to father empty handed...

He pushes the thought from his mind, determined to reveal the secret and to discover the location of the only person that can save the planet from catastrophic doom.

Chapter 62

Sweet Water, Texas

A photograph of Mara exiting a grocery store drops onto Rogerson's desk. "Well, well, who's this little lady?"

Roy settles into a nearby chair and crosses his legs. "That's our ticket to the golden boy."

Rogerson squints his eyes with interest. "Real pretty red hair on her. I want her followed, but at a distance. See who she interacts with, what her job is, that sort of thing. We can't make any assumptions. He could be anyone."

"I got it, boss." Roy stands and makes his way towards the open doorway as he glances at the ornate silk wallpaper and the rich fabrics lining the windows. "You know, you sure have some fancy taste for a boy from Broken Arrow. I thought us Okie's would always feel most comfortable in a place like when we were kids."

Rogerson frowns and rubs a hand across his mouth. "Now what in tarnation makes you think I'd want anything that reminds me of that Godforsaken ass backwards little hick town? In case you haven't noticed, I'm somebody now, Roy. So I don't want you to go bringing up any of that crap from when we were kids. Cousin or not I'll fire your ass so fast it'll make your head spin."

Roy pulls the toothpick from his mouth then turns to face his cousin, a smirk on his weather beaten face. "Oh, I see how it is now. Don't worry, boss, I'll do just as I'm told." Jibril, having witnessed the entire exchange, ducks behind an antique armoire in the hall as Roy turns to leave.

The butler watches as Roy slowly limps his way to the double doors and exits, slamming the door with a force that reverberates across the slick stone floors.

Chapter 63

San Lorenzo, Italy

Bishop Augustus sits deep in thought as the sleeper car jerks and hums beneath him. The faint glow of the light above falls on the open magazine, the article entitled "The End of Days". He thinks of how he has spent so many years behind the confines of the Vatican walls living a life of chosen ignorance. *How could I have not heard of the red calf being born,* he thinks. Surely the pope must know. Why would he not share the information? How many other occurrences and experiences do I not know of or hear about? The life of a man of the cloth is lonely and isolated.

He suddenly thinks of Amelia, her sweet smile, the dimple high on her cheek. He had barely turned thirteen and she was the only thing in his world that helped him survive the orphanage. At times they would sit together nursing each other's wounds under the old olive tree, its gnarled limbs shading them from the sharp sting of the Italian afternoon sun. He recalls the bitter time when the headmistress had beaten Amelia so badly that she could not lay on her back for weeks. He shifts in his seat and sighs, remembering the vow they made to meet again and marry someday. *I wonder where she is now, he thinks. Married with beautiful children, I'm sure. Maybe a daughter who has her smile and sharp wit. She could always disarm me with the things she would say.* A perfect tear forms in his eye when he remembers the day she left. It was her twelfth birthday and he waited for her under the olive tree with the present he had made but she never came. Dusk arrived and he went back to look for her in the dining hall only to hear that she had been adopted by a family that very morning, the best birthday present of all. She left him a note under his pillow telling him to find her when he got out and that was the last he ever heard of her. *Dear sweet Amelia, where are you now?* He thinks as he lays his head on the pillow and stares at the metal ceiling, the overhead racks above casting shadows on his pensive face.

Tomorrow I will set foot for the first time outside of Roman soil. *I look forward to this strange new experience,* he thinks, his eyes growing *heavy, I only hope it is fruitful. Though God help me I fear for my life...*

Chapter 64

Journal Entry, May 18th

The outdoor venue was standing room only. Somehow word has gotten out. There were probably a thousand people, all there to see Jesse. It was unbelievable. The band played like they had been together for years.

Everything was flawless.

There was a black limo that pulled up near the stage and sat there for over an hour. It made me nervous and excited at the same time. I'm not sure what to think of it all.

Watching Jesse onstage is like a revelation. The way he moves, the way he closes his eyes like he's unaware of his audience... the audience that began chanting the word "Prophet," as their plea for an encore. I'm thinking we've found a new name for the band.

It's surreal how quickly he's catching on.

Like wildfire.

Chapter 65

Michael and Stuart walk along the outside of the lodge through the tall pines that engulf the perimeter, keeping prying eyes away. A ritual carries on inside, the chants drifting out of the open windows as the two speak in hushed tones. "I received some information about the location of the Ark, we need to leave immediately. Are you sure you're ready for this?"

Michael's face lights up. "Yes, yes I am."

"Do not speak of this to anyone, not even your teacher. Pack a single bag, one you can carry easily, and I will meet you just past the gardens at one o'clock. Bring a camera and a small flashlight and make sure your shoes are made for walking." He says with a wink.

"Where are we going, sir?" Michael asks, his voice shaky with anticipation.

Stuart smiles enigmatically. "You will find out soon enough, my boy. It will be a journey beyond your wildest dreams."

Chapter 66

City of Angels

Professor Rajwani walks briskly through a crowded market in Chinatown, wearing a fedora pulled low to shield his eyes from view and clutching a small leather attaché to his chest. He has the look of a hunted man.

He approaches a phone booth and climbs inside then reads the numbers scribbled on his palm and dials.

"Hello?" Mara answers her cell on the second ring to the sound of static on the other end of the line. "Hello?" About to hang up, she stops when a familiar voice breaks the silence.

"Miss Mara, it's me, the professor," He says, his eyes darting, searching the crowd through the glass booth.

Mara smiles. "Oh wow, I just about gave up on you. So you got my message; you have the other notebook?"

"Mara listen, I don't have much time ... I made a mistake, a very grave mistake. I mentioned your notebooks to someone. A person I had done business with long ago. I now have reason to believe that this person is linked to an underground society. One that may be looking to do you and your friend harm..."

Mara steadies herself against the kitchen table. "What? What are you talking about?" She rubs her temple, trying to make sense of Rajwani's cryptic revelation.

"I cannot explain all the details just now, but I will contact you again and we can talk further. I just want you to be careful ... and whatever you do protect that friend of yours. As unbelievable as it may sound he is the ... " The line is suddenly dead.

Mara stands shouting into phone, "He is the what? Hello? Hello?!" Frustrated she throws the phone to the ground, "Who is he?" She whispers to herself, silence her only reply.

Chapter 67

Jerusalem, Israel

His oxygen mask on the seat nearby, the Rabbi continues, face drawn and pale. His eyes are glazed, the sparkle that once shined, gone. "Forgive me, I believe I have forgotten where I was."

"The tribulation, father."

"Ah, yes, thank you, my son. The fourth sign is predicted in the Bible in a time that nuclear weapons had not yet been conceived of. It speaks of this time as tribulation hour. Nuclear weapons are one of the biggest threats our world faces, and this threat is a grave premonition that the end of our time is near." A coughing fit suddenly rattles the old man's body. He limply reaches for the oxygen mask as Elijah turns off the camera and comes to his aid.

"Some water." He says in a raspy voice.

The young son pours a glass from the copper pitcher nearby and puts it to the Rabbi's lips. "I am not a child, Elijah, I can do it myself." He snaps, then shakily takes the glass and drinks the contents in one gulp. He wipes the excess from his mouth with the back of his hand and says softly. "Please, call David. He must hurry. Time is running out ... "

Chapter 68

*I can't believe the whirlwind this has been since the angel took me under
her wing. Since then my life has seemed like some sort of dream ... all the
venues, the clubs. Maybe now my message will have a chance to reach people.*

Inspire change.

*Mara doesn't let me go anywhere alone anymore. The pain I see around
me is too much and it makes the headaches come on without warning.*

She's so protective.

Like a mother.

*Like how my own would have been I think. I wrote a song for her today,
it poured itself from my soul and onto the blank page. As if I had written it
long a long time ago and it was being recited back to me.*

Strange and wonderful these gifts and curses.

* * *

Journal Entry, April 21rst

Someone is definitely following me. They're slick but I can
feel it. Mamaan always said Balloch women could feel a change in
the current around them if someone meant to harm us. Whoever
this is most definitely does not have good intentions.

Rajwani seems to have dropped off the face of the earth. I
wonder if he knows the identity of my stalker. I have a feeling he
might.

The mountain gets warmer everyday. I swim in the pond near
the cabin sometimes at night when I can't sleep.

The nights when my body aches for him.

Chapter 69

Chartres, France

David climbs the steps of Chartres Cathedral studying the carved stone statues on either side of the arched doorway. A thrill runs up his spine. "Something is here, I can feel it. If only I can get to father before it's too late."

He glances at his watch. Nine a.m. The Cathedral doors swing open in that instant and David bolts up the remaining steps. An old nun in a habit stands in the doorway smiling at him, her teeth dark and rotting with age. David returns the smile and dashes towards the door.

"What on earth are you in such a hurry to see here young man? Whatever it is it's been here a long time and it's not going anywhere." She says in broken English.

David looks at her haggard face and gives her an even broader grin. "I'm here to unlock a secret centuries old."

The old woman laughs heartily. "Well, good luck, my boy, and may the Lord be with you."

As David moves past her, he mumbles under his breath, "He's with us more than you know." His cell phone rings, the chime reverberating on the Gothic stone walls. He searches inside his messenger bag but the ringing stops before he can get to it. Too eager to reach the area of the cathedral he came to see, he decides to check for a message later. He makes his way down a long dim corridor bathed in red light until he reaches the first of many stained glass windows.

One of the one hundred and seventy images I have traveled across the globe to see, he thinks with excitement and a sense of awe. Legend says that the stained glass tells a story, clues to the Messiah. According to the guidebook he picked up at the entrance this one is number sixty-four, and its called Noah. Somehow in the next three days he must search every window in the twenty one thousand foot cross-shaped building for hidden messages.

A clue that will lead him to the One.

The fact that his arrangement of the coordinates from the old map brought him here to the fabled location of the Gnostic Gospel of Thomas, the scripture said to have been written by Christ himself, lets him know that the clues indeed lay within these walls. He just needs the wisdom and intelligence to decode them.

A tall order.

He studies window number sixty-four, quickly recognizing a pattern. The story begins from the bottom left and weaves in an S like pattern through out the window. Small stained glass sections tell the story in art all the way up to the forty-second piece depicting the angels after God made a covenant with Noah and his wife.

Realizing the piece as a dead end, David moves swiftly to the next, Lubin's window. He suspects this beautiful cut glass will not contain the clue he needs but he must see each one with his own eyes to unlock their meaning. He can't afford to miss a single message. A small voice inside his head mocks his arrogance. What makes him think he would be able to find and correctly interpret clues that thousands of prominent and published scholars before him had apparently missed?

I must believe.

It's my only hope.

He pushes doubt aside and gazes upward. This window is far more intricate than the previous one and he studies it for several minutes before a pattern emerges. The glass shows the story of St. Lubin, the son of a farmer who worked the fields until he was able to convince a monastery to take him in. He eventually became Bishop of Chartres and was known for performing great miracles until his death in 558 A.D.

Beautiful but not of importance, he thinks and moves on to the next image as he glances at his watch, the ticking hand a taunting reminder that time is running out...

Chapter 70

Special Activities Unit, C.I.A.

Photographs of weathered and delicate parchment cover Lieutenant Eisenberg's desk. "Okay, son, you've got me stumped. I have no idea what these are."

Christian puts his hands behind his head and stretches his legs. He flashes Eisenberg a winning smile. "Don't you even want to guess?"

"You're really enjoying this, aren't you?" Eisenberg asks, his face alive with humor.

"Immensely. This reminds me of that game I used to play when I was a kid. Clue. You know the one. 'Was it the professor in the library with the candle stick?' It was my favorite." Recognizing impatience in the lieutenants face, Chris straightens in his seat and clears his throat. "Sir."

"So glad we could take that trip down memory lane. Now why don't you tell me what these pictures of rotting paper are all about."

"They're the Dead Sea scrolls," Christian reveals with a smirk. Eisenberg sits silent in his chair, not moving a muscle. "You know what those are don't you, sir?"

Eisenberg retrieves his signature scowl. "Of course I know what they are, Goddamnit. I'm a Jew for Christ's sake!"

Chris shifts uncomfortably in his seat. "Right. Sorry, sir. I didn't know."

"With a name like Eisenberg, are you kidding? I might as well have Jew tattooed on my forehead. Anyway, what in the heck do the Dead Sea scrolls have to do with our dearly departed buddy, Cooper? This is getting rich."

"Well, sir," Christian leans forward in his chair, "it turns out the artifact that general Cooper sold back in the forties was a missing part of this collection."

Silence hangs like a dense veil as Eisenberg studies Christian's face. The boyish good looks, the cleft chin and pale blue eyes sparkling with excitement. "You wouldn't be pulling my leg now would you?"

"No, sir. This information was confirmed by several sources in the Jordanian government. Apparently the only antiquity found in 1947 was part of the Dead Sea scrolls. They found the other pages from 47 all the way to 1956. Fascinating no?"

Eisenberg sits back in his chair and lets out a breath. "Beyond fascinating. The question is, who did he sell it to and why did they want it?"

Chapter 71

Elephantine Island, Egypt

A dark man leads Michael and Stuart toward the ruins of an ancient temple. Stone and mortar lay crumbling as evidence of the forgotten place. "It is said that the Jews who built this in 650 B.C. had brought the Ark down the Nile to keep it safe. This being a most suitable place they built a temple almost identical to Solomon's to house the Ark of the Covenant." He points towards an opening. "There it is said that the Holy of Holies was held for many years."

"Take us inside." Stuart says, his voice commanding.

"I'm sorry, sir. That is not possible, it is very dangerous."

Stuart pulls a crisp bill from his pocket and neatly folds it into the hand of the guide. "You seem like an adventurous fellow, Mr. Mubarak. Let's have a look shall we?" He climbs the low dirt mound towards the interior of the ruins calling behind him, "Tell me about the Papyri they found. What did they say?"

Mubarak shrugs. "Many things. Some very mundane. Legal documents, divorce papers, manumission of slaves," He pants, trying to keep up, "All written in the Aramaic. There is no doubt that a community of Jews lived here. Most likely they converted the people who became known as the Falashas. The Black Jews." As they duck under a crumbling arched doorway the bright light of the desert sun disappears. "I have no flashlight Sir."

Stuart stands, eyes closed head tipped back. "It's alright. No need to go further. I just want to feel the presence in here."

Mubarak gives Michael a strange look and shrugs. "Okay. I will just wait outside." He exits leaving the two men in darkness.

"What is it, Mr. Stuart?"

Stuart's eyes open and land on Michael. "It was here. I can feel it. The prophecy is real and if we follow the path of those men down the Nile we will find the Ark and fulfill our destiny. It's there for the taking ... "

Chapter 72

New York, New York

La Guardia airport bustles with energy. The bishop, weary from the hours spent in the cramped airline seat, rounds a corner heading for the men's room. A man, breath foul and teeth stained with tobacco, bumps his shoulder as he enters.

"Hey, man, why don't you look where you're going?" The man shouts, pushing the bishop with rough hands.

Augustus is clearly shaken. "I'm so sorry, sir, I didn't look where I was going."

"Yeah, clearly. Jesus H." The man mumbles and walks away.

Augustus shakes his head. *Friendly people, these Americans,* he thinks as enters a stall and pulls off his trench coat. He notices that it feels unusually light and frantically searches the pockets for his billfold. *How could I be so naïve,* he thinks to himself; *of course that awful man meant to steal my wallet, it was all a charade.* The bishop exits the stall, his face weary. *Now what will I do? In a foreign country with no money.* He shakes his head and stares at his reflection in the graffiti etched mirror. *Augustus, what in the devil have you gotten yourself into?*

Chapter 73

Death Valley, California

Mara enters the dressing room as Jesse sits shirtless at the long vanity, the circular lights making his pupils dance and shine. "You have a visitor..." She says, barely able to contain her excitement. He looks up with mild curiosity, cigarette dangling from his lips as she continues, "Some big record producer saw the outdoor show, he wants to talk about a deal."

"What kinda deal, like another regular spot?" He asks applying charcoal liner to his eyes.

She tries to hold back her excitement. "Not exactly... He wants to talk record deal."

Jesse drops the pencil and gives her a tentative look. "You wouldn't kid about a thing like this now would you, Mar?"

Mara smiles wide and rests a hand on his shoulder. "You deserve it, it's your time."

He stares at his reflection in the mirror. "Well, I'll be damned."

She stands and heads for the door, "I'll go get him... and you might want to put a shirt on or something... or not. Whatever." She says, still smiling.

Jesse glances at his reflection and sighs with relief, a sense of joy washing over him. He grabs a worn flannel shirt off the nearby stool and pulls it on, leaving the buttons undone. He lights another cigarette from the butt of the one still burning as a thin man in his early fifties walks through the door. His eyes are wild and his teeth huge and bright white. He wears a t-shirt displaying a faded image of Billy Squire barefoot and a pair of distressed designer jeans held up by a snakeskin belt. He holds out a thin hand adorned with several large silver rings.

"Hello, my man. A pleasure to meet a legend in the making."
He flashes his unnaturally pearly whites.

Jesse holds out his hand to shake as Mara enters balancing
three cups of coffee on a tray. The older man gives her a smile.
"Hey, you're pretty good at that."

"I used to be a pro before I became his manager." She replies
with a good-natured grin. "Cream and sugar, Mr. Abaddon?"

"It's Mandy, and no thanks, black is fine." He considers
Jesse then sips the hot drink. "The quiet brooding type aye? The
press will love it ... and so will the ladies. You know all these little
girls grew up reading Bronte and whatnot. They just love their
Heathcliffs. You've struck gold Miss Mara." He flashes another
smile. "Now lets get down to business shall we?"

Chapter 74

Chartres, France

David paces the room at the Château Desclimont, the only hotel for miles with a vacancy and certainly more than he can afford. Unable to sleep, his long strides carry him from the stone fireplace then back to the velvet-draped bed where he slumps, his arms limp at his sides. The oversized four-poster makes him think of Sophie. *She would have loved the city and the hotel, much more grand than the one where they spent their honeymoon. I hope someday to bring her here,* he thinks. When my work sells. Then the fear in the pit of his stomach at the probability of his impending failure takes hold.

Why am I not more like father? Why can't I believe that everything will work out? Maybe it's because I seem to fail at everything I do. He shakes his head. *Sophie would call that a defeatist attitude. And she would be right. I must keep the faith for Sophie, for father, for Sarah... and for the world.* He walks to the gold leafed mirror above the fireplace and stares at his reflection. A shudder runs through his body. *One more day to find the clue. Is it even possible?*

Chapter 75

Death Valley, California

As traffic whips by, Jesse and the foreman shake hands in front of the structure soon to be the Desert Breeze Plaza. The large man pats Jesse on the back in a paternal gesture, brimming with good will. "Knew you were cut out for more than this from the day I met you. Good for you, we'll be listenin for you on the radio."

Jesse kicks the dirt beneath his boot. "It still doesn't seem real."

Jimmy gives him a solid look. "It'll sink in. Sally's so proud she's practically your biggest fan already," He chuckles, "Now don't you forget about us little people once you become a big ole rock star, all right? We'll still expect you for supper every now and again."

Jesse laughs. "I'm counting on it. Thanks for giving me a chance."

"One of the best workers I've ever had. Sad to see you go." The two men look up at the half finished building, hands in their pockets.

"I know it's not rock and roll or anything fancy but something about building a thing with your own two hands is about as fulfilling as I can imagine life to be," Jimmy reflects, studying the thick beams and joists holding the massive structure together, "It feels right for me and I feel lucky to have this work. The Lord's been good to me—my wife, my kids. I hope he blesses you in the same way, Jesse. You deserve it."

Jesse's voice is barely above a whisper. "When I was a little boy I always wanted to build things. I used to go out into the field behind our trailer park and find old pieces of wood that people had dumped there. After a few months I had a fort big enough for me and one other person. I didn't really have any friends but there was a girl in school I liked. She was the only one allowed in my hiding place and then one day she didn't show up. I found out at school that she had a new boyfriend. So third grade was my first run in with heartbreak and the first time I realized I was good with my hands."

"Now heck, Jesse, that's the most words strung together you've said since I met you." Jimmy chuckles. The older man gives the younger one another pat on the back. After a few silent moments, Jesse walks toward the Jeep, his new life awaiting him.

Chapter 76

Jerusalem, Israel

The old man sits propped against the wall on a small rolling cot, all pretense gone, his struggle is apparent with every uncomfortable breath. "A one world government is another sign. In the book of Daniel they called it the reviving of the Roman Empire, this my friends I believe will happen when the One is revealed to us. He will be King to us all and will rule with a gentle hand. A one-world order is not as crazy as it sounds. It only takes one. A person so charismatic and so pure that society simply cannot deny his power. I believe this will happen in a short time, one day we will wake up and the One will be in our living rooms, on the radio and inside our heads... "

Chapter 77

City of Angels

Mara unwraps her thick shawl as they are shown into the dimly lit studio attached to Abaddon's gated estate. The record producer opens his arms dramatically revealing instruments and computers that line the walls, and a smaller room enclosed with glass where a microphone is positioned in front of a tall black stool. "This, my friends, is where the magic happens." He laughs and claps his hands. "This is Tiger," he says as he motions to a middle aged man with long permed hair who sits at an instrument panel, "He works his own brand of magic. And this is Billy, he'll get you anything you need during your stay at Casa Mandy, like your own personal concierge if you will. You're gonna be here a while. Weeks, months maybe, so get comfortable."

Jesse walks around the room, holding his Fender like a security blanket, while the rest of the band arrives. "Come one, come all. Let the games begin." Mandy rubs his hands together greedily. "Let's rock and roll ladies."

Chapter 78

Chartres, France

Monsieur Montbard makes his way up the steps towards the open doorway of the massive ornate building. He glances up thinking that the cathedral always manages to leave him awe-struck at first sight. He carries a thin attaché, its worn British tan leather a compliment to his linen summer suit. A pair of espa-drilles adorn his feet and with his dark overgrown hair and five o'clock shadow, he looks like a Spaniard on holiday rather than a descendant of French nobility.

He makes his way through the long corridor appreciating the voluminous space. Prisms of stained glass create a glow all around him. He reaches a particular image and stops. "Glorious." He mumbles to himself as he looks up at the stained glass rendition of Christ on the cross.

"I couldn't agree more." David walks into the chamber and stands beside Montbard to marvel at the masterpiece.

Montbard doesn't so much as glance at the stranger but stands, eyes transfixed on the window called Redemption. "A pity that modern man cannot create such beauty. What we consider art these days is monstrous. Something created in an afternoon or a fit of temper. I like to come to this place when I need to be reminded of what true beauty is."

"You're lucky to live near such a stunning revelation. I've traveled halfway around the world to see this place," David replies thoughtfully. "Where I live there is nothing quite so ornate as this Gothic architecture, though my home it has its own rugged beauty."

"America is but a young country," Montbard replies.

David looks surprised for a moment then replies. "My accent, yes. It gives me away."

"I also detect a hint of something else though … something I can't quite place."

"My father is from Ethiopia and I was born in Israel, where I live now. But I was educated in America and my brother and I grew up with the language."

Montbard's brow creases and he turns to study his new acquaintance. "That's quite a regal place, Ethiopia. May I be so bold as to inquire what brought you here? Tourists are typically not burdened with so many notebooks."

David takes in the man beside him and a feeling comes over him. A strange connection. Surprising even himself he states plainly, "I'm searching for clues."

"What sort of clues may I ask?" He replies, more intrigued than he shows.

David is unsure why feels a compulsion to share his secret with the stranger but continues, "I believe that an apocalypse is near and I came here to look for the signs that legend claims lay hidden in the glass."

Montbard laughs out loud. If one knew him they would see that it was forced, an effort to distract, that he was clearly taken off guard. "That's quite an admission my friend, not one you may be wanting to make to just anyone. They may think that you've gone quite mad," He lowers his voice conspiratorially, "But I could not agree more. So what will you do when you unlock the clues?"

David chuckles. "Why save the world of course."

"Ah, of course," Montbard studies David for a moment then whispers, "It is here, the clue you seek, but it will be revealed only to the purest of heart."

David smiles assuming he's being toyed with. "And how sir, might you know this?"

He glances up at the sunlit image, "Ah, well. One of my ancestors built this place. It's full of more secrets than even I care to know."

Chapter 79

Jerusalem, Israel

"Ezekiel 36:24, 'For I will take you among the heathen, and gather you out of all countries, and will bring you to your own land.'"

The Rabbi runs a thin almost skeletal hand over his dark robe, smoothing it absentmindedly. "Thus the Jews will be brought back to their homeland —the second sign of the apocalypse. According to many experts the day of reckoning will come on the final day of the Aztec calendar, the end of the 13 baktuns. It is not quite as simple as the end of a calendar, my friends. The End of Days is divinely up to us and how we accept Him when He shows Himself. Whether you believe or not there must be some place inside you that fears what I'm saying could be true. I am counting on your fear if not your faith..."

Chapter 80

Sweet Water, Texas

Photos lay spread across the carved mahogany desk in Rogerson's home office where sunlight filters in through the sheer curtains illuminating the rugs, tapestries and desktop in its hazy glow. The grandfather clock chimes five times, filling the hall with its metallic sound that bounces along the gleaming marble floors and through the open doorway. Roy sits sipping a can of Mountain Dew and bites off a piece of beef jerky. His manner is relaxed and easy as he watches his cousin peruse the photographs.

"She's always with that guy. I think he's her boyfriend or she's a groupie or something. He must be a musician, 'cause he's usually got that guitar with him." He takes a swig of the drink. "She's a looker, that's for sure. She seems darned nice too, Rog. I hope we don't have to do her no harm."

Rogerson glares at him in disgust, "Roy, would you keep your trap shut! You're supposed to be following her not fallin in love with her. Now this guy of hers looks like some sort of bum, don't he?" He turns his attention back to the picture in hand with a scowl.

Roy tips the can to his lips before replying, "You know, he's one of those rock and roll types. Remember back when we were kids and we had our band? Those were the days," He smiles lost in the memory, "Boy, were you a rotten singer. I suppose we coulda had a shot at the big time if it weren't for your singin.'" He chuckles to himself.

Rogerson throws him an impatient look. "That talent show was rigged I'm tellin' you. We shoulda won. Anyway you'd think a man his age woulda out grown those kinda pipe dreams by now."

He returns to studying the photographs picking them up one by one, hoping to glean something—a sign.

After a few moments he drops the pictures carelessly onto the desk. "He's nobody." Rogerson pushes the stack away and sits back in his chair, hands folded across his wide girth. "Just keep on her, you're bound to find something. Now, how about we round up some lunch. All this talk has worked me up an appetite. I'm thinkin' of a rare steak, some good ole fashioned beans, and biscuits drizzled with honey and a whole mess of butter. Hot damn, my mouth's waterin' just thinkin' about it." He gives Roy a conspiratorial wink.

Roy smiles and crushes the empty can, tossing it into the marble wastebasket. "Just when I thought you'd gone all city slicker on me Cuz."

Chapter 81

New York, New York

The night sky hangs ominous over the city street, the darkness enveloping Bishop Augustus making the ache in his belly even more distressing. He comes to an old stone building where a sign hangs above that reads, Sacred Heart. Weary and afraid of continuing down the unlit side street, he settles onto the old limestone steps, exhausted and unsure of how to continue. *How am I going to find him with empty pockets? God is truly challenging me,* he thinks and rubs his weary face. *I must carry on and not be discouraged by these setbacks. Sometimes challenge is the Lord's way of testing one's commitment. But, Lord,* he thinks to himself and glances at a bright star above, *I could use a little help.* Suddenly a young nun comes bounding down the street, arms filled with brown bags of baguettes. She approaches the bishop and cocks her head to the side.

"Can I help you, sir?" She asks in a sweet voice.

Augustus looks at her, suddenly awake from his daze. "I'm sorry, I am blocking your way."

"It's not a problem." She smiles sweetly. "Where are you from?" The bishop looks confused. "The accent. I can tell you're not from around these parts."

"Oh, yes. I am from Rome."

"Rome? Wooowee! You're a long way from home!" She smiles wider revealing two deep dimples. "I'm not from around here neither. I'm from Chilton County, Alabama. Lived there my whole life till I was twelve." She plops down on the curb next to him. "I came here after my parents died. And then I just decided to stay. Be a bride of Jesus, you know?" She says with a laugh. "So you visitin' friends or somethin.'"

Augustus shakes his head. "No, no. I have no one here."

"Not a single soul in this big ol' city?" She asks and he shakes his head in reply. "Well, you better come on inside then. We're having beef stew tonight and I just bought the most delicious bread this side of the Mason Dixon line."

Augustus smiles and looks to the sky, the star shining even brighter now. "I would be delighted," He replies and as he takes the last step he turns to see a figure in the distance, its head in the shape of seven serpents...

Chapter 82

Cairo, Egypt

"I will give you two thousand pounds. No more," Stuart waves a stack of foreign currency in the air. The dark skinned man across from him glances at the bills, shakes his head and shouts something in Egyptian to the young boy next to him.

"My father says it is a long journey. One he cannot make for less than two thousand five hundred."

Stuart smiles and shakes his head. "No deal." He grabs Michael by the shoulder and pulls him away.

Michael wrings his hands, "I thought he was the only charter down the Nile? How will we get there now?"

"Don't worry. He'll take us. Let's go to the café across the street and have a Turkish coffee. It'll put hair on your chest," He says with a laugh. The two make their way towards a small outdoor table and set down their bags as the dry desert breeze blows easy, coating everything in a fine dust.

"How can you be so calm, sir? What if he does not agree to take us for the price."

"He will Michael, have faith." Stuart signals for two coffees to the beautiful young waitress. The sway of her hips almost profane as she walks towards the samovar to fill the small glass cups with the rich amber liquid.

"Wow," Michael mumbles as he watches her move.

"Yes, Egyptian women are known for their beauty, the greatest example being Cleopatra of course. Legend says she and King Solomon both soaked in the Dead Sea in the area where the scrolls were found. Many attributed her beauty to the magical salt found in this pool of water with no outgoing channels, and so a major import industry was founded on the Dead Sea salts. A tidbit of trivia for you, Michael, something they won't teach you in your studies," Stuart says with a wink.

The waitress sets down their coffees and Michael stares at her, mouth agape. She glances at him with her large almond shaped eyes and smiles coquettishly then glides away. "Close your mouth, son, you're drooling," Stuart says as the young boy from across the street approaches them, hands crammed in his Levi's back pockets.

"My dad says he will take you for two thousand," He states plainly, his chin set hard.

Stuart takes his glass and raises it in the air looking at the boy's father across the street. "Tell him I will take the ride and that I will pay him two thousand two hundred."

The boy smiles brightly. "Okay! Thank you, sir!" He shouts and runs across the street to tell his father the news, narrowly missing a dented rickshaw.

Michael looks at Stuart with a perplexed expression and sips his Turkish coffee, "Why did you do that?"

"Because it was the fair price. One must never take advantage, Michael. Even if a person will allow it," He says and drinks the remainder his coffee in one swift motion, "Now let's go, we have a long trip ahead of us."

Chapter 83

Lone Pine, California

A full moon glows giving the night a haunted and magical quality as the desert wind comes in gusts shaking the delicate leaves of the Mesquite trees. The two sit outside on the porch swing looking up at the sky. Mara cools herself with an old-fashioned paper fan decorated with pictures of birds in vibrant colors and Jesse mops his face and neck with a cool damp cloth. A coyote howls in the distance and crickets chirp in time with the steady creak of the swing. Mara points up at the stars to a constellation in the shape of a unicorn. "See that one? That's Monoceros. It was my favorite for a long time. Most people say it just looks like a horse but I can see its horn. And that one right there is Orion, the Hunter."

Jesse tilts his head back further. "Where did you learn this stuff?"

"My mamaan taught me. She said that you can always keep track of the people you love by looking at the stars." She glances at him, suddenly shy, "The stars tell you the future and the present. I can read them a little."

Jesse points to a cluster of stars. "So what does that one mean? Is it the future?"

She looks up. "That one is Sagitta. The arrow. It means that true love is nearby."

Jesse clears his throat and grabs for a fresh cigarette. Mara smiles, changing the subject. "It's totally a werewolf night, isn't it?" On cue, the wind howls shaking the swing.

Jesse gives her a sidelong glance. "Really? Werewolves? Oh right, I forget you've got gypsy blood. You believe in ghosts and goblins and creatures of the night." He says with a taunting grin, feeling a levity that's foreign to him.

Mara squints her eyes suspiciously. "Are you mocking me, mister? Because I get the distinct feeling that you are."

Jesse frowns. "I would never mock you, Mar, I wouldn't even think of it."

She elbows him. "I was kidding, don't get all serious on me."

He smiles. "Well, in that case, I actually was mocking."

"I knew it. I suppose I should expose all of my weaknesses now. I also have my original Star Wars action figures in a box under the bed and if you weren't around I'd be sleeping with a night light."

Jesse gives her a look of astonishment. "Star Wars? You're kidding."

"I would never kid about Star Wars. That's sacrilege."

"Okay, well I bet you can't recite all the lines from the *Return of the Jedi*."

"Bet I can," She replies defiantly, "Don't tell me you're a Die Hard fan?"

"The die hardiest."

"Interesting. I knew there was a reason I liked you."

Jesse pulls a Marlboro from the crinkled pack. He lights up and takes a slow drag. "I like you too, Mara. I like you a lot."

The heat between them lingers in the air with those simple words making Mara's heart beat. Hard. She takes his free hand that lays next to her on the swing. Hands intertwined they sit rocking on the porch swing as if they've been doing it their whole lives until a sudden gust of wind whirls around them, its howls distinctly animal. The two glance at each other and a foreboding shudder runs up Mara's spine.

Chapter 84

C.I.A Headquarters

The cafeteria's fluorescent lights cast a sickly green hue on Chris and Eisenberg's faces as they speak in hushed tones. "I am completely at a loss for words," Eisenberg states plainly then takes a bite of his tuna fish sandwich.

"I know, sir. I don't know how it's been kept a secret so long. I mean, can you imagine, scrolls written by Jesus himself?" Christian replies, his ruddy face flushed with excitement.

"So you think this is the scroll that Cooper sold to this group. This O.R.G.?"

"Yes, sir, apparently the group is made up of powerful men, and most recently, women that control major industry. Several of the members are old Yale graduates and also belong to the Skulls and Bones."

"You're shitting me! I heard about that group but I always thought it was more of a joke really, like a fraternity."

"It's a fraternity, alright, but it's not as innocent as you may think. The intel I've gathered says they participate in dark rituals and some pretty shady dealings."

"This is interesting stuff, Chris, I think it's time we clued the director in on it. This O.R.G. sounds like something we should be keeping a keen eye on, wouldn't you say?"

Chapter 85

Chartres, France

David stands in the center of the great cathedral clutching his guidebook, now crumpled and worse for wear. The dim light of the overcast morning barely penetrates the colored glass in front of him and he looks as if he hasn't slept for the three days since he landed. *All of this for nothing? It can't be. I only have a few hours left. How will I face father if I don't find the answers we need?* His breath comes in quick waves. *The Frenchman said the clues were here. Do I not have a pure heart, God? Am I not seeking the answers with the noblest of intentions?*

He stops, weary, resting his hand on a stone pillar, looking up at the gilded dome. *Please, I am but your servant. Please help me find the way. Give me something that I may not disappoint my father. Please give me a clue so I may help save my brothers and sisters.*

In that moment the sun breaks through the clouds, its radiance blasting through a window on the far end of the cathedral. He walks toward the light, his eyes fixed on the image at the top, a depiction of Christ surrounded by doves wrapped in a green cloth. As he reaches the window David scans the guide map in search of the name of this particular stained glass.

"The Tree of Jesse," He mumbles aloud to himself. Then reads the rest of the description, his thoughts swimming. "The Tree of Jesse is a depiction in art of the ancestors of Christ, shown in a tree which rises from Jesse of Bethlehem, the father of King David. The original use of the family tree as a schematic of the representation of a genealogy. It originates in the biblical book of Isaiah, which describes metaphorically the descent of the Messiah. The passage in Isaiah 11:1, 'There shall come forth a shoot from the stump of Jesse, and a branch shall grow out of its roots."

David slowly rolls the guidebook tight. He bows his head for a brief moment then looks at the image once again, the intricate image of Christ searing itself into his memory forever. "Thank you," He whispers, then turns on his heel and walks briskly toward the open doorway now brimming with brilliant light.

Chapter 86

City of Angels

The bishop hobbles through the Los Angeles streets, his clothing dusty and his face unshaven. He holds his derby hat out to passers by for coins and the occasional dollar bill. Despite his frugality he'd used up the money the young Nun had given him on his bus ticket to the west coast. *At least it got me this far,* he thinks. *That sweet girl, I hope she gets out and ventures into the world. I'm sorry to wish for her leave you, Lord, but someone so full of life is not meant to be a bride of the church.* He shakes away the thought knowing he's projecting. If only he could turn back the clock, but what's done is done and he must focus on the matter at hand. The duty to the pope and his fellow man infinitely more important than his sudden yearning for years lost.

I know he is here. I can feel him, he thinks as he makes his way through the busy street during lunch hour, searching the faces of the office workers, as they taste their few moments of freedom. *I will know him when I see him,* he thinks, realizing his chances are smaller than finding the metaphorical needle in a haystack. He scans the faces that speed by, bodies carelessly brushing past his hat and pushing him further and further into the crowd. A young child points in his direction. "Mommy, why is that man so dirty?" The child questions her mother, her expression filled with innocent wonder. The mother, embarrassed, pulls a single dollar bill from her purse and puts it inside the bishop's hat.

"I'm sorry, sir," She mumbles, uncomfortable, and pushes her way through the crowd. The child's eyes stay on the old man, her face sad. Augustus stares at his reflection in a shop window and a sudden rush of emotion overwhelms him. He seems to have aged decades since his days at the papal palace in Castel

Gandalfo, mere weeks ago. *What am I doing? He thinks. How stupid I was to assume I could find and track Satan himself, what kind of folly is this? I must write to the pope and explain my dire situation, I'm not sure I will make it another day alone in this rat-infested city.* The demon's voice begins to taunt him suddenly. Hisses and growls flood his brain, he drops his hat, clutching his head and praying for silence.

Chapter 87

Chartres, France

David stuffs clothes into his faded leather suitcase and pauses to glance at his watch. *Of all the days for me to oversleep.* He curses under his breath with a good-natured grin. *But at least I'm not going home empty handed.*

He grabs the map and his papers off the nightstand, littered with chocolate wrappers from the Château's turn down service. It struck him as decadent on arrival but now, a mere three days later; he wonders how he will do without it. *Maybe Sophie will do this for me at home. Leave a chocolate mint on my pillow at night and untuck my side of the bed. Wishful thinking.* He chuckles to himself. The profound relief he feels at having found a clue just as his father had told him he would, for not returning a failure, is almost euphoric. *In fact he should call the old man, check in, and tell him the good news. No time,* he thinks, *he would have to save the call for later.* He grabs his cell phone and swears again, realizing he forgot to plug it into the charger last night in his exhaustion. *There'll be a pay phone at the airport. No need to panic.* He tucks the cell phone into his backpack and zips it. He grabs the telephone receiver on the nightstand. "Yes, this is Mr. Ashkenzari in room 708, I would like the express check out. Yes, thank you... merci." He laughs to himself. *As they say, when in France...*

He closes the door behind him and glides to the elevator feeling better than he has in months. He sniffs the air and looks around the deserted hallway. *The French, will they never learn that smoking is bad for us? That's one thing I won't miss. Though I would put up with it for their chocolate and fresh croissants everyday.* The doors to the elevator open and he steps inside as Montbard steps out from behind the wall, his cigarette glowing.

Chapter 88

Journal Entry, April 24th

It feels like we've barely left the studio. Jesse works like a mad man. Even during breaks he hums and writes new songs. He seems almost possessed... but in a good way if that makes sense. His voice is so fluid... like mercury, liquid and filling every crevice of the soul. I feel like I'm witnessing something mythical. Something I don't understand yet.

I think Abaddon feels it too. He's practically counting the money already. He took us all to a party the other night and we saw Keith Richards, which was really exciting and surreal. He didn't seem to know I existed but he sat with Jesse all night. They must've smoked four packs of cigarettes between the two of them. I've never seen Jesse so chatty. They were talking about human nature and how the world is ready for change. I just ended up playing gin rummy with somebody's mother who was in town visiting. She drank vodka out of a plastic tumbler all night and still beat me almost every hand. It was two in the morning when Abaddon finally took us home. He brought a girl young enough to be his daughter with him. He called her dessert.

I feel like he's hiding something but I can't put my finger on what it could be. Maybe I'm just being paranoid because of what Rajwani said. I hope the professor's okay and that he'll call again, but as the days tick by it seems less and less likely. I reread the journal translations last night just to see if I could find some sort of clue. A clue to whoever it is that's following us —my gut tells me there's still someone lurking.

Chapter 89

City of Angels

French doors open to a panoramic view of Coldwater Canyon as a gentle breeze blows over the infinity pool and into the cabana at Abaddon's estate, fluttering crumpled napkins around the room. The guys relax on beanbag chairs and a half eaten pizza sits on the stone floor along with several empty pizza boxes and beer bottles. James has his arms propped behind his head staring out at the breathtaking view. "Seriously, man, this is the life. I thank the Lord in Heaven everyday that I met you Jesse, my brother." Jesse sits on the ground, back against the wall.

Thom chimes in, "Seriously, man, I was washing dishes at a roach motel before I got this gig. Who woulda thunk."

Andy grabs another slice. "And now we're the Prophets, ready to invade living rooms and car stereos all over AmeriCalifornia, I think my mom will finally have to eat crow. Hope it tastes good," He says and takes a bite of pepperoni.

"We'll all get our fifteen minutes," Jude props his legs on a rattan ottoman, "Maybe more if we're smart. Feel like I've been waitin' on that fifteen all my life man, and nobody's gonna keep me from it."

"Wow. You sound like one fame hungry mother." Thom laughs.

"Damn straight. Fame is power. It makes people want to know you and kiss your ass," He lights up a joint, "Fame is the thing that every prom queen in the Midwest dreams about at night and wakes up with her panties wet from the urge for it."

"Very poetic. I'll drink to that," Andy says raising a fresh bottle of beer, "To fame. May we all have our taste."

Jude looks out the window and takes another drag, his face tense. "We'll all get a taste. Right, Jess?"

Chapter 90

C.I.A. Headquarters

Christian and Lt. Eisenberg make their way down a narrow hallway bathed in fluorescent light. Each is impeccably dressed in suit and tie and Chris carries a shiny new briefcase at his side. They pass through an open doorway and into a sterile room, not a single picture on the walls. A receptionist sits behind a large metal desk.

"Hello lieutenant," Glancing up from the keyboard she gives him a dry smile, "He's been expecting you." She stands, heads to a door and opens it. "Sir they're here."

"Send them in," Replies the gruff voice of Henry Johansen, Deputy Director of the CIA. His slick bald head shines in the bright sunlight that floods the inner office through the wall-to-wall picture window, a brilliant view of dense forest behind him. "Have a seat, gentlemen." He states in his typical abrasive tone.

"Good morning sir." Chris says, giddy as a schoolboy. "Pleasure to finally meet you."

"Yes, well. What can I do for you?" He asks, eyes darting from one to the other. Eisenberg motions to Christian.

"It's your story to tell, son. Go for it."

Christian opens up his briefcase and begins to take out photographs and several files.

"We don't need a show and tell here, just let me know what you got. I'll look at that stuff later if I think it's necessary."

Chris regains his composure and closes the case. "Yes, sir. Sorry, sir." He then proceeds to tell the deputy director about General Cooper and his suicide and what led them to the scrolls and ultimately the organization that purchased them.

Johansen sits back in his oxford leather chair, hands resting on the wooden arms. "So let me get this straight. You think that there's an elite group out there that's controlling our country, or better yet, the world, and trying to keep the Messiah from coming?"

"Yes, sir," Christian replies, head held high, "I know it sounds far fetched but that's what I uncovered during my investigation and I'm very close to finding the identity of the man who heads this organization.

"Well, now gentlemen, as much as I would love to stay to continue this little chat and peruse the facts in that shiny new briefcase of yours, I've got a true military emergency to tend to. I was told this was urgent so I made time for you this morning but..."

"This is urgent!" Chris interrupts. The room goes silent. "Sir. It is urgent, sir," He states his passion unwavering.

"Yes, well, I can see that you're worked up about it, so why don't we do this. Let's discuss it tomorrow night over drinks when I get back from Washington. I belong to a great club that actually let's you smoke cigars inside. Imagine that." He laughs. "A good cigar and a nice cognac. There's nothing more American." He scribbles an address on a piece of paper. "Be there at seven and ask for Henry's private room, they'll take you right in," His smile is strained, "Good day, gentlemen," He says and the two men exit the office. Johansen immediately picks up the phone and dials. Impatient, he drums his fingers on the desktop. "It's Johansen, we've got trouble..."

Chapter 91

Jerusalem, Israel

The old man looks withered and ashen, his face sunken, bones too large for his feeble frame. His body rattles with a series of coughs. He takes a shallow breath from the oxygen tank then begins again. "The Messiah with come visibly, with power and great glory, with a great sound of a trumpet, accompanied by billions of shiny, holy angels, Thessalonians 4:16.

"This day will be the birth of a brave new world. And as I said we will have only one King that will rule, and he will be benevolent. He will speak truths and show us of our suffering so that we may be reborn. This is the only way we can save our selves and circumvent the End of Days. Most all of the signs have shown themselves in the last decade. I only pray that you all will open your hearts in time for the One... He is here."

Another coughing fit overwhelms the old man, the worst yet. Elijah turns off the camera, his voice anxious. "Are we finished, dad? The Rabbi shakes his head in reply and motions for him. "No, there is still much to tell."

The boy comes to his side, tears flowing freely now. "Is it time dad?"

"No, Elijah, I only want to give you this." He takes a primi-tive silver cross from his pocket; the unskilled etchings that line its edges look as if they were done by a child. "Keep this, and when your brother has found the One, he must give it to him for protection. It will keep him safe against the power of the stones. Now please leave me, I must rest for a short time."

Elijah shakes his head. "No, father, I'll stay. I'll just sit quietly while you sleep."

The Rabbi smiles at his son, thinking how he wished he had been a younger man when this surprise was brought to him and Sarah. Remembering the day so clearly when she handed him the pregnancy test looking sheepish and childlike even at the ripe age of thirty-nine. His dear beloved Sarah, taken from him four long years ago now, who would have thought that he would outlive her being fifteen years her elder. It would not be long now till they would meet again in the kingdom of heaven.

"No, my boy, you must eat and have some rest. You have made me very proud." He takes Elijah's hand who is now kneeling next to him, glossy tears marking his flushed face. They look into each other's eyes for a moment until Elijah kisses his father's hand.

"I'll be back soon, dad."

The Rabbi nods and watches his son walk through the heavy wooden door, closing it gently behind him. He takes an old leather bound journal from under the seat of the bench. *There is so much still left untold, he thinks. So much for David to unearth on his own, hopefully the journal will help him, please God help him find them and the Ark before it's too late.*

He writes frantically revealing thousand year old clues about the location of the Ark, facts hidden in the recesses of his mind, until a cloak of silence envelopes the room and the temperature drops suddenly. The old man shudders, his breath icy and thin. Still holding the diary he folds his hands on his chest, still damp with Elijah's tears, and lays back on the cot looking up at the ceiling. He thinks of his life in Gondar and of the figurines he used to carve from rosewood to help his mother and father put food on the table. The tacky trinkets sold to travelers became a calling card for their tribe and it had made him ashamed.

His thoughts wander to his mother's delicate face, her thin lips curved in a slight smile while she watched him with his small knife, whittling wood at all hours, the smell of her faint perfume lingering wherever she went. His mind shifts to his two sons, the boys who came to him too late in life for him to be a proper father. David, head strong and passionate, a brilliant writer and scholar still yearning for success. The one who can see truth in every religion and holy book. And Elijah, the sweet child who loves like a mother with a gentleness that seems unfitting a boy of eighteen.

After a few dense moments filled with circling thoughts his mind goes to his beloved, and his heart aches for her. Thoughts of his Sarah flood his brain coming in flashes and quick images, the day she gave birth, the first time they met, the way she wrapped her scarf around her pretty hair. The pain in his throat stings; tears and gasps come in waves. *I am coming, Sarah. I am coming to you, my love.* His eyes close and after few moments the shallow breaths are no more. Only stillness remains. A profound peace fills the silent room as the journal slips from his fingers and falls below the bench, out of sight, taking its secrets with it...

Chapter 92

Addis Ababba, Ethiopia

The Nile River rages as Michael and Stuart sit on the deck staring out towards the shore. "We should be there in less than an hour," He shouts over the sound of rushing water.

"It's fantastic." Michael watches the Ethiopian city approach through a pair of old binoculars. "How long will we stay?"

"This is our final stop on the Nile, from here it's all on foot or by taxi. We'll stay as long as it takes."

The young boy approaches them stumbling now and again with the movement of the boat. He sits at Stuart's feet. "It's been a pleasure riding with you, sir. I have learned many new things," He says with his engaging gap toothed grin.

"And you, Ebo, are quite the tour guide, I've learned much myself." Stuart tousles the boy's hair. "What does your name mean? All the names in Egyptian mean something, no?"

Ebo laughs. "Yes, that's true, sir. Mine means born on a Tuesday."

"I see, so you are a Tuesday baby."

"No, sir. I was born on a Saturday, my mother just liked the name." Stuart replies with a hearty laugh as he and the boy slap hands playfully. "I hope you find what you are looking for, sir," The boy states in earnest.

Stuart looks out over the horizon to the looming city of Addis Ababa. "I will find it, Ebo, I will not stop until I do."

Chapter 93

A notepad sits open and blank in front of David in his cramped airline seat. The passenger to his left snores lightly as the woman on his right gazes out the window at the distant sunrise. The sky is awash with a purple and orange glow that gives the outside world an alien quality, the textures of the bold colored clouds haunting and vivid.

I wish I had something more concrete to take to father but I know he will have some idea to how the Tree of Jesse is connected to the location of the One. I just wish I had not been so late for my flight; I shouldn't have taken the metro. It would've been good to call before I left but I suppose seeing his face when I tell him the news will be worth the wait. But at least I was able to charge my phone for a few minutes in the lobby...

"It's quite something isn't it?" The middle-aged woman mumbles, interrupting David's thoughts.

He stares at her vapidly for a moment unable to formulate a thought then replies, "I'm sorry, I don't follow."

She nods her head towards the window. "The sky. The universe. It's amazing. It's moments like this that make me believe in God."

David chuckles. "Only moments like this?"

The woman gives him a wry smile. "Unfortunately, yes. In the world we live in we disconnect from all this, I mean who has time for it these days, right? We only get a few fleeting moments to truly see beauty and it's only when it's forced on us and we can't distract ourselves." She smiles and shakes her head. "I know, arm chair philosopher, right?" David returns her smile. "But lately I've been thinking about these things. I don't know why but they suddenly seem important to me."

He looks into her eyes now brimming with tears. "I understand more than you know," He states simply.

Their fleeting connection is interrupted by the middle-aged stewardess who taps the man next to David on his shoulder, "Sorry to wake you, but we're preparing to descend, if you could fasten your seatbelt, please."

David glances at his own lap where the belt is firmly secured and shudders, remembering the flight from Ethiopia when he was only four. The way the plane jolted during turbulence and how his father had held his mother's hand while they prayed silently. His sweet fragile faced mother with her charming gap toothed grin that made her shy among strangers. How he wished she were still alive so that she could have seen his first born, the sweet baby with her grandmother's name. He suddenly longs for his family with a surprising ache and rests his head against the seat back, holding the arms of the chair tight.

The mercifully uneventful landing complete, David turns on his cellphone and notices several messages. He grabs his rolling bag from the overhead compartment and follows the other passengers to the ramp.

Once out on the ramp he dials his father's room at the temple. It rings and rings. No answer. He gives up and tries his brother's cell phone.

"Hello?" Elijah's voice cracks as he answers on the second ring. A feeling of doom over whelms David and his stomach clutches into a ball of grief.

"Elijah, is he gone?" He asks tentatively. "Did he tell you anything?"

Chapter 94

City of Angels

Leaning against a dumpster in an alleyway stained with splattered mud, the bishop unrolls the tattered Time magazine and pulls from it a blank piece of paper. *I must write to him before it's too late,* he thinks and searches for a pen inside the layers of his clothing. He sits on the ground with his back against the dumpster and writes with a shaky hand:

Your Holiness,

I am writing to tell you about a great miracle disguised as misfortune that has come into my life. I recently performed an exorcism at the home of one of the villagers. When it was over, the thoughts of the demon that had possessed the child consumed me. It came to me in fitful dreams and dominated my daytime thoughts. I knew the Papal community would think me mad so I made the decision to venture out on my own and seek the demon myself. In doing so I have been lead by a great force to the City of Angels. It is nothing like I expected. It is loathful and venomous and there is a palpable desperation in the air. I spend my days wandering the streets looking for the devil himself. I know that he is here and as God leads me I know I will find the truth. But the true miracle is that I believe we are upon the second coming. In fact, I feel as though He is very close, almost near me. Yes, this may sound bizarre but as you know I'm not one to give in to flights of fancy. There is something brewing, Your Holiness. As the old saying goes 'something wicked this way comes' and I will need more than just myself to battle it. Please send reinforcements soon. I have made a map on the back of the page showing my location. I anxiously await your assistance.

Your brother and humble servant, Augustus

Chapter 95

Dallas, Texas

Roy takes a gulp of Mountain Dew then sets the can back on the nightstand of the rundown motel room. "Well golly gee Kathmandu darlin that was about the best romp in the hay I've had in, well, maybe ever," He says as the weathered woman that lays on the opposite side of the bed lights up a cigarette.

"Listen here, Roy, sweet talk isn't gonna get you out of payin.' This is prime U.S.D.A. meat here," She replies with a hoarse laugh.

"Wouldn't think of doin' any such thing. You're worth every penny." He pulls two crisp one hundred dollars bills from his wallet on the nightstand, "Pleasure doin' business with you, ma'am." He smiles and grabs his crumpled jeans off the shag carpet.

"Thank you, doll." She stuffs the bills into her cigarette case. "Now, that doesn't mean you need to rush off now. I like you, Roy, you're sweet as can be. Let's get to know each other a little better," She says patting his side of the bed as he buckles his belt.

"Don't mind if I do for a short spell, but I'll have to get to work soon." He settles back onto the bed.

"What kinda work is it that you do, Roy?" she asks, curling up beside him.

He smiles up at the ceiling, his bare chest rising and falling. "Well, I guess you could say I'm a private investigator of sorts."

"Oh, how exciting. What are you investigating handsome?"

Roy turns his face towards hers. "To be quite honest with you, Charlene, I don't quite know all the particulars except that someone who's related to someone who wrote some old papers has come to town and I'm supposed to find him. He's supposed to be plenty important and so are those papers my cousin has locked up in his safe. That's all I know."

Charlene stares at the ceiling and takes a long drag of the cigarette. "I wonder what they're worth..."

Chapter 96

Paris, France

Montbard walks along the Point Royale Bridge, hands inside the pockets of his long trench coat. The Seine rushes by beneath him and the dark sky crackles as lightning strikes a few hundred yards away. The promise of rain lingers in the dark clouds above him, ripe and ready to open. He stops and looks across the water, his hands resting on the old stone of the bridge, reminded of the river near St. Benoit Du Sault where he used to swim in the summers while growing up on his family's country estate, surrounded by lush gardens and servants. Most of his childhood memories were of the servants themselves since his interactions with his parents were brief and unfulfilling. *Maybe that's why I became so passionate and single minded about this cause, he thinks, maybe that's why I made the crusade my mistress and never even considered taking a wife.*

He shrugs absentmindedly and turns his attention back to the road where a man walks towards him; bolero hat pulled low, his face revealing nothing. He passes Montbard and the two men nod in salutation then walk beside each other for several steps until he breaks the silence. "It seems there is a girl. A woman I should say. I believe she's more important than anyone realizes. She may be of the blood but that is only a guess at this point. I need more time and... "

Montbard smirks in reply. "And more money, correct? I had a feeling that is what this meeting was about." Montbard plucks a long cigarette from his breast pocket and attaches a filter onto it. "Do you mind?"

The man nods. "Of course not, please."

Montbard lights the cigarette with an ornate mother of pearl lighter, bearing a red symmetrical cross, and takes a long drag. He stops and turns looking over the bridge and into the water below. "I don't take kindly to being swindled, Monsieur Moreau. I paid your advance and now you come to me with nothing more than guess work and talk of more money."

Moreau glances nervously from side to side. "Sir, I don't mean any disrespect and I sincerely hope to have more of your business in the future. But I've spent all of the funds on my investigation. I swear I've been frugal but there's much travel involved. I know I'm very close to an answer and proof of His whereabouts, I just need more time."

"And more money, yes, I understand. Do not look so concerned, monsieur; I'm not feeling particularly vengeful today. You shall have your funding but do not call me again until you have something of substance. To disobey my orders would be a grave error." He throws his half smoked cigarette into the river. "You may go, the money will be wired to your account. And please, Monsieur Moreau, remember my warning."

Chapter 97

Langley, Virginia

A haze of smoke circles the dimly lit bar as Christian and Eisenberg are escorted to a back doorway. "Here you are gentlemen, enjoy." The maitre d' exits leaving the men standing side by side in the dimly lit room. Inside the deputy director sits in a deep club chair, fresh cigar in hand.

"Hello boys." He clips the end of the Cohiba. "One of my vices," He says with a smile. "Those Cubans are good for something."

"This is quite a place." Eisenberg pulls off his sport coat. "Had no idea it was here and I've lived in this city longer than I care to admit."

"Oh it's the kind of place that gets passed down through the generations. A bit elitist if you ask me but I don't get involved in club politics. As long as they keep the Hennessey flowing I'm happy to be included." He takes a slow pull from the snifter and motions to the deep mahogany chairs, the leather tufts softened with age. "Have a seat. Drink?" The two shake their heads in reply.

"No thank you, sir."

"So where did we leave off last we met?" Johansen asks after lighting his cigar.

"Christian here was briefing you on his findings, which I must say are quite extraordinary. It started somewhat by accident with me asking Chris to investigate General Cooper's death on his off time as a favor, but what he found was beyond what we could have ever expected. Way beyond a pet project. So we decided it was time to get you involved," Eisenberg replies. "The evidence is good. Backed up and substantiated. This is a real issue that needs to be dealt with, sir."

Johansen sits back in his chair and puffs the Cohiba. "Tell me more about this so-called group. The ones plotting against mankind, as you say."

Christian looks to the lieutenant then begins, "Firstly, sir, I want to apologize for my over zealous behavior last we met. I have just been very excited about these findings and wanted to share them. That being said, I believe you are making a grave error by waiting a day or even an hour to address this situation. These people are powerful and they're pulling strings we didn't even know existed."

"Like?" Henry asks, the flames of the fireplace reflecting in his eyes.

"Like did you know that the funding for the Soldiers of God, also known as the Jullalah, comes primarily from an elite group of powerful men and women? People who have a vested interest in continued terrorism and separation of countries based on religious zealotism."

Henry shakes his head; "The Iranians have been ranting that same sentiment for a long time."

"It's no sentiment, sir. War is big business and the men and women who stand to gain the most from it are funding terrorist efforts all around the globe. In 2008 this group even received financial support from our own government when President Bush pushed through 400 million dollars for funding the efforts of groups like the Jullulah."

"I believe that rumor was started by Seymour Hersh who's since been discredited. You expect me to believe our former president was helping fund terrorism?"

"A Pulitzer prize winning journalist discredited? I'm sorry sir, that's simply not true. It seems that whenever someone disagrees with U.S. policy on war they suddenly get 'discredited'. In an interview with Mr. Hirsh, United Nations weapons inspector Scott Ritter said and I quote, 'The United States needed to find a vehicle to continue to contain Saddam Hussein because the CIA said all we have to do is wait six months and Saddam is going to collapse on his own volition. That vehicle is sanctions. They needed a justification; the justification was disarmament. They drafted a Chapter 7 resolution of the United Nations Security Council calling for the disarmament of Iraq and saying in Paragraph 14 that if Iraq complies, sanctions will be lifted. Within months of this resolution being passed—and the United States having drafted and voted in favor of this resolution—within months, the president, George Herbert Walker Bush, and his secretary of state, James Baker, are saying publicly, not privately, publicly, that even if Iraq complies with its obligation to disarm, economic sanctions will be maintained until which time Saddam Hussein is removed from power.

"That is proof positive that disarmament was only useful insofar as it contained through the maintenance of sanctions and facilitated regime change. It was never about disarmament, it was never about getting rid of weapons of mass destruction. It started with George Herbert Walker Bush, and it was a policy continued through eight years of the Clinton presidency, and then brought us to again through the disastrous course of action under the second Bush Administration. This clearly shows evidence that the efforts of groups to continue warfare runs deep within the American government.' End quote, sir."

"Ritter is a child molester. You can't take the word of a person like him." Johansen scoffs.

"My point exactly. Seems awfully convenient, sir, considering that supposed fact was uncovered by a sting operation in 2001 only *after* Ritter became verbal in his criticism of U.S. policy, especially U.S. policy pertaining to the Middle East, where he cited publicly that Iraq had no weapons of mass destruction."

"Your boy's done his homework." Henry glances at Eisenberg and chews the end of his cigar. "Impressive stuff. I'd like to review it. Can you leave your files or are they your only copy?"

"They are originals, sir, no copies." Chris replies.

"Surely you must have them on your computer?"

"No, sir, it's all up here," He says tapping a finger to his head.

"That's good, son, good work," Henry smiles and slides a silenced Glock from his jacket. He pulls the trigger once hitting Christian in the center of his forehead and for a second time piercing Eisenberg's heart.

Two clean and precise hits.

Chapter 98

Bethany, Israel

Black curls frame young Sarah's angelic face as she plays with a wooden spoon, banging it on the leg of David's desk. He stares absently, lost in thought, his back propped against the whitewashed wall.

What is it that I haven't thought of, father? Why did you have to leave me, I need you more than ever. He runs his hands through his hair. *I can't do this alone. And what am I supposed to do with that cross and how in the world will I find the descendant of King David now with you gone? So many questions I may never get the answers to dad. How could you leave us and not leave anything behind to show the way?*

A single tear runs down his cheek and his little girl looks at him perplexed, "Daddy?" She frowns and holds out her arms.

"Yes, angel, It's okay. I'm all right." He puts his arms around her and gently rocks back and forth.

The door to the office opens and his wife enters, her beautiful face drawn and tired. "I'm back. Everything is arranged for the Shiva. Elijah will stay here and my mother will take Sarah so that she won't be confused."

David nods. "Good idea. I don't think a three year old would understand seven days of mourning. In fact, as a grown man I have a hard time seeing the sense in such an act but we must do everything according to custom, it's what father would have wanted."

Sophie smiles somberly. "Of course, David, we will do what we must, no question." Sarah wriggles out of her father's arms and slides down to play with the makeshift toys. Sophie settles in next to her husband, wrapping her thin arms around him in a loving embrace.

He speaks barely above a whisper. "Somehow I never believed the day would come. When I was eight I remember one of the kids in school asking me if he was my grandfather. That was the day I realized that dad was too old to have a son my age. I suppose that fact always hovered somewhere in the back of my mind but I tried not to pay attention to it. I wanted to believe he would live forever. Childish I know. At least he lived to see Sarah."

Sophie pulls him closer. "At least he lived a long and prosperous life and made an impact on so many people. I know you miss him but I know in my heart that he's happy."

"I'm sure you're right. He's with mom now. It's just going to be hard for a while," He says watching Sarah, his face lined with grief.

"I know. I'm here, my love. Through thick and thin, sick and sin, remember," She replies rocking him gently as if he were a child.

"I don't know what I would do without you." He buries his face in the hollow of her neck.

"You won't ever have to find out," Sophie replies and gives him a soft kiss on the top of his head. "Oh, I almost forgot, something came for you today. I left it on the desk." She reaches for the small paper wrapped parcel and hands it to him.

David examines it but finds no note. He opens it gingerly. Inside is a small golden box with handles on either side, and the words Ano Lucis primitively carved onto the bottom along with a sun, moon and stars.

"Mine." Sarah says and she reaches for the tiny box. David studies it for a moment longer, his brows knitted. "Sure, Sarah. Yours," He replies and shrugs. "I wonder who would have sent this... "

Chapter 99

City of Angels

The dark room is cool and still. The iconic music producer sits back in his chair, legs propped up on a table, master of his domain. "Bravo my man." Abaddon claps loud and slow after Jesse finishes the song. The rest of the studio's occupants sit in amazement. Not a single one having ever witnessed such power, such grace. Abaddon stands and absently fingers the meticulously carved talisman hanging from his neck—Jesus on the cross, rests against his pale chest.

He makes his way into the soundproof booth where Jesse sits, eyes still closed. A pained expression twists his beautiful features. He is clearly shaken, each song, each performance a soul shattering feat. "How about some lunch and an afternoon of R & R. I think we've earned it. Right, gang?" The mixer and assistant, flash broad smiles, well acquainted with Abaddon's version of R&R and looking forward to it in spades. "What do you think, Jesse, my boy?"

Jesse nods. "Yeah, sure, sounds great," He replies and runs a hand through his hair. The dark gold locks fall in waves around his sullen face, his eyes haunted.

Abaddon slaps him on the back. "Come on, man, why you look like somebody just died?" He turns and shouts to Mara. "Your boy's a brooder, that's for damn sure."

Mara smiles uneasily, her attention on Jesse through the glass. "I think he just needs some air." Taking her lead Jesse joins her outside and lights a much-needed cigarette.

"He's really something, huh?" She asks, her expression hard.

"He is, but don't worry, Mar, it's exactly how I thought it would be. I know I should lighten up but I see too many images while I'm in there. My head feels heavy. When the headaches come I just keep singing. I don't know what else to do." He takes a drag and throws her a shy glance. "Am I any good?"

Mara turns to him with a confused look. "Are you kidding? You're like a miracle." She studies his face, the lines much too deep for a man his age and the pale amber eyes tired, their depth unfathomable. A mystery brewing behind them that she desperately hopes to solve. "An absolute miracle."

Chapter 100

Adis Ababba, Ethiopia

"This tea is even stronger than the Turkish coffee," Michael says then takes another sip of the brew from a gold leafed glass cup.

Stuart nods. "Yes, these people need their strength. They do the work of four men everyday." Stuart looks at his watch then down the narrow dirt road. "He's late."

"How will he know us?" Michael asks and takes a bite of an almond cookie.

Stuart laughs. "Look around, we're the only white people here." A sudden bustle of activity gets their attention. They glance up to see a pair of donkeys pulling an old wooden carriage painted in bright colors, its wheels kicking up dust onto the faces of the nearby peddlers. A young man sits behind the reins wearing a smile a movie star would covet. He ties the reigns to a tree then strides toward the two men who watch the cotton clad driver with reverie.

"Hello, I am Obeje. You must be Mr. Stuart?" He says in a thick accent and holds out a sun-scorched hand.

"Yes. We have been anxiously awaiting you, Mr. Obeje."

"No 'mister' necessary. Only Obeje," He replies, the dazzling smile still in place. "Come let us go to someplace private. The walls have ears here," He says with a discreet nod toward two men who sit at a table to their right.

He leads them to the cart and they ride towards the southern mountains. When Obeje is certain they are beyond earshot of the café he shouts. "I am taking you somewhere we can stay for the night. We will dine and discuss the information I have learned, and there is someone there I want you to meet. Then you will head for the city where I believe you will find exactly what you are looking for." He glances at Stuart, a mischievous gleam in his eye.

"Are you saying you have found more information about the Ark?" Stuart shouts over the rattle of the old wood wheels.

"My friend, I have more than information, I have a witness. Someone who has seen and touched the Ark and knows precisely where it was hidden those many years ago," The Ethiopian states, brazen.

"I am intrigued, Obeje," Stuart looks out over the dusty terrain, the anticipation inside him electric, "Where exactly are we headed?"

Obeje laughs. "To the mouth of the volcano my friend," He shouts, finger aimed at a distant mountaintop.

Chapter 101

It all seems like a dream. Each day I wake up and my connection to the earth is stronger. Yesterday we all went swimming in the ocean. Me and the guys took a couple of hours and drove to Malibu. We climbed down to El Matador beach. When I was in the water I could feel its energy, each wave felt like the ocean's music. It sang a sad song of how it had been abused by mankind. The fish followed me, literally circled around me. I could touch them and hold them easily. They were docile in my hands. I don't know what any of it means and I'm afraid to tell anyone.

No one will understand.

Chapter 102

Dallas, Texas

Roy enters the restaurant, uneasy and out of place. He spots Rogerson who sits with a stacked plate of oysters on the half shell at a corner table, a linen tablecloth spread beneath fragrant lilies. He sprinkles one with Tabasco as he spots Roy approaching the table. "There you are, I was starting to wonder if you'd show. Have a seat and try one of these tasty little suckers." He slaps a blue point onto an empty bread plate.

Roy chuckles, "Tempting, but I'll have to pass, cuz. That looks like something I mighta blown out my nose."

Rogerson gives him a stern look and whispers, "Now don't talk like that in a place like this. Geez Louise, I can't take you anywhere."

Roy rolls his eyes. "I apologize, your highness. Now we got bigger fish to fry and that's why I wanted to talk," He stops, pausing for effect, then leans back in his chair and lays his hands behind his head, "Seems you may have a traitor in the O.R.G."

Rogerson drops the empty shell onto the plate. "What in the Sam Hill are you talkin' about?" He whispers. "That group has been around for centuries and passed down through family ... or lucky for me I climbed my way in with money, of course being a Bonesman didn't hurt matters none since half the O.R.G. are in the club, but the point is that group cannot be penetrated." He grabs for his wine glass and takes a generous swig. "Well... spill your cockamamie story already."

"I was watching the girl, she was hangin' out at this fancy hotel in La La land. She was with a group of people, some guy showin' off, flaunting his money, and I noticed someone else. Some guy who was watching her. Now he was good and sly about it and I wouldn't have even known except he bumped into me on the way out to the pool and got my attention. I watched them and sipped a virgin colada while they sat down to ten types of seafood they barely touched. The other guy sat there the whole time too. Watching. Waiting. It got me wonderin.' "

Rogerson wrinkles his forehead. "So that's it?" He sits back with his napkin spread across his belly and scratches behind his ears. "Hmmm. Nothin' concrete but you're right, it's worth checkin' out. Well, just stay on her and we'll see what we see." He tosses back another oyster. "If we have a rat we'll get him and may God help him when we do."

Chapter 103

City of Angels

"Come on, man, this is the life. This is what being a rock star is all about. Eat, drink, be merry." Bathing beauties strike poses as Abaddon and Jesse sit beside the Peninsula Hotel pool enjoying a five-course luncheon. The swank Beverly Hills hotel has become Jesse's third home second only to Abaddon's lavish estate.

The table is lined with decadence; caviar, thinly sliced salmon topped with capers and every other food a person would equate with extravagance and success. The producer is courting his new client and he's certainly not being subtle about it.

Jesse smokes, barely touching the cold lobster salad in front of him and the rest of the band lounge nearby. Mandy's porcelain smile gleams as he waves an arm gesturing to the nearby girls. "And those, my friend, are another perk, one of my personal favorites. I'm telling you, you haven't lived until you've watched two women go down on each other in the back of your limo. Mag-fucking-nificent."

Jesse stubs out his cigarette and squints at Mandy through the Los Angeles sunshine, "It's not my thing. I don't see women like that. I see their souls—and I know what being here costs each one of them." He glances at the row of girls one prettier than the next as they chat and suggestively rub oil on their tanned bodies. "I know what they're here for and it's not what it seems. They want husbands and babies and security. They want to be respected and talked to as equals. They are not whores to be used and tossed aside. No women are. Random sex costs them. A piece of their soul lost with each transaction."

Abaddon rolls his eyes. "Jesus Christ, man, you can be a real fuckinging buzz kill, you know that? Okay, whatever, suit yourself.

But all this talk of transactions is making me want to make a deposit." He winks and makes his way to a busty blonde, lips lacquered in gloss. Wordlessly, he holds his hand out to her and they disappear inside the hotel.

Jesse watches the girls and lights another cigarette. A young one catches his attention. She looks over and waves, flirting shamelessly. He acknowledges her with a half smile. She takes this as a sign to make her move and saunters over in high heals and a skimpy swim suit cover up.

"Hi, I'm Missy," The brunette, not a day over twenty, smiles showing off her deep dimples.

Chapter 104

Langley, Virginia

A naked bulb flickers in the doorway of an unmarked brick building at the far end of an alley. Rogerson grabs the ornate handle and enters. Inside, the club is in full swing. The white-collar crowd out in force. "Mr. Rogerson, so good to see you," The maître d' says as he smiles from behind the podium. "The V.I.P. room, I presume?" He escorts Rogerson through the crowd. Behind velvet curtains sit several men smoking cigars and drinking from various sized crystal glasses, Deputy Director Henry Johansen is one of them.

"Rogerson, you fat bastard. How the heck are ya?" He shouts across the plush room. Rogerson's face flushes.

He crosses to the group as Johansen stands. "Henry, you old dog. It's been too long."

"You're been getting your fair share of BBQ from the looks of it," Henry says and smacks Rogerson on the back playfully. "Join me in my private room." The deputy director leads him to a doorway on the far side of the club.

Inside, the fire is lit and Rogerson takes in the smells of anise seed and lingering cigar smoke. "I always wondered how much you pay to keep this room all to yourself. Must be a pretty penny."

"It's worth it. I like my privacy." Henry shuts the door and joins Rogerson in the brand new club chairs.

"It's a good thing too. Thank God those two idiots are out of the picture. You scared the crap out of me when you told me the story they'd come to you with."

"Makes you wonder who's giving information out so freely."

"That's why it's good to have Bonesman around you can count on," Rogerson says with a wink. "Remember our first time out on Deer Island? I miss those Yale days, don't you?"

"Not really. I was barely getting laid." Henry smiles. "Now let's get down to brass tacks shall we? I've read all his files and Goddamnit, Rogerson, this is a big deal. This isn't just throwing a few bucks at some rag heads. This is something I'm not sure I want to be messing with."

A deep crease mars Rogerson's forehead. "What are you tryin' to say, Hen?"

"I'm saying this is something huge you're messing with here. I don't want to be responsible for that, Rog." He brushes a hand over his head now glistening with sweat.

"Listen here, Hen, my group has been planning for this for years. Trust me, it's for the best. You like havin' this fancy club and your fancy house on Martha's Vineyard don't you?" He locks eyes with the deputy director. "War is big business old buddy, we don't want the public goin' all peace and love on us now do we? War sells guns and oil and all that good stuff. I for one want to keep my business running in the black." Rogerson leans in speaking softly. "Now I need your help on something else. Some artifacts have been found in a cave with inscriptions on lead. Codices, the small metal books they talk about in the Bible. There's one particular book that's said to be sealed. I need to get my hands on it and there's no limit to what I can pay."

"What's inside?"

Rogerson unfurls a devilish grin. "It will blow your mind old friend. Absolutely blow your mind."

Chapter 105

Jerusalem, Israel

The blazing desert sun sets in the distance, casting its orange and red glow on family and mourners—assembled to pay their respects to the wise old man who touched their lives in so many ways. A rosewood casket is harnessed by several pallbearers as a young Rabbi prays. "God full of mercy who dwells on high, grant perfect rest on the wings of your divine presence. In the lofty heights of the holy and pure who shine as the brightness of the heavens to the soul of Rabbi Ashkenazi who has gone to his eternal rest as all his family and friends pray for the elevation of his soul." Elijah throws the first shovel full of dirt onto the casket. This act of mitzvah, the kevurah, is to be replicated by each mourner, the line long. The prayer continues. The mourners wait their turn, heads bowed.

"His resting place shall be in the Garden of Eden. Therefore, the Master of Mercy will care for him under the protection of his wings for all time and bind his soul to the bond of everlasting life. God is his inheritance and he will rest in peace, let us say amen."

"Amen," the mourners repeat. Sophie holds David's body close, her tear stained face alive with mourning, flushed and vibrant. Little Sarah stands grasping her father's hand. She suddenly pulls away and bends to grab a pile of dirt in her small first and throws it onto her grandfather's grave then blows him a kiss, her dirty hand outstretched. David fills with emotion as he watches this innocent act of love.

"How did she know to do that?" He whispers.

"She's like you, my darling. Wise beyond her years," Sophie says and kisses his wet cheek.

In the distance a man watches the ceremony. He does not cry or mourn in any way. He only smokes a long cigarette near a giant oak, its limbs swaying in the breeze.

It's quite beautiful, these rituals they have to celebrate death. Montbard puts the cigarette filter to his lips. *I wonder what they will feel if another so close dies on his quest to find the One. Certainly this David is foolish and inexperienced. He would be easy to take out, hardly an effort for one with experience in such matters.* He takes another long drag from his cigarette and plans his next move.

Chapter 106

City of Angels

"I like this color," Missy says watching Jesse paint her baby toe, "I never had a guy paint my toes before. And I've certainly never had a guy just wanna talk all night. This is the first time since I turned sweet sixteen that I could just be with a man without feeling like it had to lead to ... you know." She giggles and glances at him, coy. "Not that I would mind it leading to more though, just to be crystal clear."

"Noted. I'd rather keep things platonic if it's all the same to you. Anyway, I would feel like I was cheating on her."

"I don't get it." Missy reclines onto the bed and crosses her legs.

"Ah-ah, careful. You just smudged the middle guy," He says blowing on the bright red lacquer.

"Sorry. I mean, how could you love her so much and spend every day with her and never touch her. That just seems weird. And hard."

"It's both I guess, but it's right. I don't want to hurt her," He replies moving on to her other foot.

"You're probably already hurting her," She states, matter of fact.

Jesse stops mid brush stroke and glances up. "You think?"

"Duh. I'm sure she's stone cold batty about you. It's probably torture for her to be around you and not be with you."

Jesse closes the cap on the nail polish and sits back on the bed, head propped on pillows. "I never thought about it like that..."

Missy laughs and shakes her ringlets of curls. "Men. You guys are so dense sometimes."

They sit staring at Missy's half painted left foot until the door suddenly opens. Abaddon stands in the doorway, a smirk on his face. "I thought I'd at least catch a peak of titty or something." Missy shoots him an annoyed look and heads for the bathroom. "Hate to break up the pajama party but everybody's waiting on you, Jess."

Jesse looks at the alarm clock. "Oh, man, I lost track. Is Mara there?" He asks then rinses his mouth with a cup of water from the nightstand.

"Yeah, she's there, and she doesn't look happy."

"That's great."

"She's not your wife pal, she's your manager. And she's gonna have to get used to you having a little fun from time to time with the lady folk."

"Nothing happened. We just talked."

Abaddon shakes his head in disbelief. Missy walks out of the bathroom, her mouth painted with fresh lipstick. "Thanks for entertaining my man here."

She ignores Abaddon and turns to Jesse putting her pale arms around his neck. "Last night was one of the best nights of my life. If you ever change your mind, look me up. And I wouldn't mind you finishing that pedicure either." She gives him a light kiss on the mouth then walks out, shoes dangling from her fingers, and leaves the two men in silence.

"Nice ass," Abaddon mumbles. "Okay, buddy, let's get you out of here. Guess that sweet, succulent fruit wasn't enough to tempt you, but I'm glad you had a good time. And the fuckin' room service bill was murder. Looks like you're catchin' on to this rock star thing after all." He laughs and puts an arm around Jesse's neck, leading him through the door.

Chapter 107

Sweet Water, Texas

"How can you still have nothing?" The sheik asks in disbelief. Only a few members of the O.R.G. have assembled but all eyes are on Rogerson, their expressions grave. "I cannot sleep at night knowing what it could mean for us all if He is not found and stopped."

Rogerson puts up a hand in reply. "Listen here you son of a gun. You think I don't understand the magnitude of what's going on here? I'm having the girl followed every second of every day. We're assembling clues; it takes time. I don't have a Goddamned magic wand, okay?"

The group exchange glances. Madame Kung strokes the small white dog asleep in her lap, her voice soft, barely above a whisper. "Well you'd better find one and a crystal ball too. Because if you do not find an answer soon, you'll be removed from the group."

Rogerson's face drains; he sits pale with mouth agape. "Are you threatening me, madame?"

The elderly Thai woman stands and glares down at him with a hint of a smile. "You bet your lily white ass I am."

Chapter 108

Death Valley, California

Jude holds an open palm to Jesse as the late summer wind whips hot and dry. "Spot me a smoke brother. It's good to be back here, man. Brings back memories." He says and lights up.

"Yeah, this place will always be special to me too. It's where I met Mara." A deep line etches Jesse's forehead. "In fact, she actually saved my life in that very spot." He points to the parking lot; a dark patch marks the area where he bled those many months ago. "Blood leaves a hell of a stain."

"Man, she's a good lookin' girl. Have you tapped that or what?" He says with a lecherous grin.

Jesse's brow wrinkles. "Don't talk about her like that. She's not like us. She's like... an angel. I don't want you talking about her."

Jude puts his hands in the air in mock surrender. "Okay, man, I got it. She's off limits." He takes a drag of his smoke. "Hey how cool is it that Abaddon's 'leaking' one of our recordings to KRTW? He's a marketing genius that guy. We're lucky to have him," He says as a homeless man brushes past his arm. "Hey, watch it." He glares at the man with disdain. "Disgusting."

Bishop Augustus turns towards the men, his face somber. "My apologies," He says, dizzy with hunger. "I am very tired and was not watching where I was going."

Jesse grabs the man's arm to steady him. "Maybe you should sit down." He leads the bishop to a nearby bench. "How long since you had something to eat?"

The bishop shakes his head. "Not since I left Los Angeles two days ago."

"Well, I think it's time you had a bite don't you? Hey, go inside and grab one of the sandwiches and a bag of chips. And a couple of apples and some water too." He shouts to Jude who stubs out his cigarette.

"Okay, O saintly one," He replies rolling his eyes.

Jesse turns his attention back to the man and studies his tattered clothing, the cut and fabric obviously of fine quality. "So what brings you out to the desert?" He asks intrigued.

The bishop shakes his head and smiles. "It may sound crazy but I was led here. Something drew me to this very spot."

"Something drew you to Buddy Levine's? I'm sure it's the great rock and roll, right?" Jesse says with a wry smile.

"Not quite. I am on a mission from God. I just don't know how this place fits ... " He replies as he searches Jesse's face.

Chapter 109

Mojave Desert, California

Dust blows in the dry air as a haggard man pumps gas. His children sit inside the late model station wagon looking out the window, arms crossed and sullen. Not a smile to be found. The quintessential survivors of a broken home.

Inside the truck stop is a small but efficient diner with orange pleather seats that haven't seen new upholstery since the Nixon administration. A waitress, her face generously painted in bright blues and corals, delivers a meatloaf surprise to one of her regulars, a pudgy man in overalls and a faded baseball cap who sits alone at a four top table. A lone coffee cup stands empty nearby with several packets of crumpled Sweet and Low.

"Thanks Nancy, sure looks good." He says and smiles longingly at the waitress. She gives a vacant smile in return and chomps her gum with zest. "Sure thing, Mac." She glides by another table and drops a check as the song on the radio plays out its last notes.

"And next we have a single from a brand new band called The Prophets, give me a holler and let me know what you think," booms the polished voice of the radio announcer. The customers carry on as music fills the room, a mournful tune of electric guitar, citar, and tubla for the drumbeat. The effect is eerie, otherworldly, filling each pore and overwhelming the senses. Jesse's voice pipes through the airwaves and one by one people in the diner stop their chatter to listen until the restaurant is silent except for the sound of his fluid voice. It floats like a haunting melody. Even Nancy stops chomping her gum and stands still behind the counter, mesmerized for a full two minutes until the last cord is struck.

"Once again, that was a sneak peek of The Prophet's new single called "Circle." The patrons slowly pick up their chatter, the spell broken as quickly as it was cast. Nancy resumes her smacking and the cook rings a small bell on the counter to announce the next order.

"That wasn't half bad," the big Hawaiian cook says and pops a maraschino cherry in his mouth.

"I'd say pretty damn good, Bubba, that boy's got a voice like butter," Nancy replies and grabs a stack of pancakes from the counter. She nods to the elderly man in booth number nine. "Still can't figure out how old man Fletcher stays so skinny eatin' pancakes for breakfast lunch and dinner."

Bubba grins. "Maybe it's the sex."

"You're nasty Bubba. You're a nasty nasty man," She says with a smile and glides away.

Bubba resumes flipping pancakes and mumbles under his breath, "The Prophets huh? Not bad at all."

Chapter 110

Mount Zaqualia Monastery, Ethiopia

A young monk reclines against the circular building that houses the monastery, his back propped against the wall he wears the traditional garb, a rust colored cap and white scarf wrapped around his shoulders as the three men walk by. "That is the crater," Obeje says, pointing to a serene lake surrounded by endless trees and shrubs. "It was formed by the volcano back when she was still erupting. Don't worry she has been asleep for many, many years." He states with a smile.

Michael breathes in the crisp mountain air. "It's beautiful."

"It is one of the prettiest sites in our city, "Obeje replies with pride. "But of course I did not bring you to site see. Come, we will meet Dabir and he will tell you things that will astound you. I may have to raise my price, Mr. Stuart."

"I will gladly pay if the information is as good as you say. Let's meet this Dabir."

Obeje leads them towards a path behind the monastery.

"Yes, he will meet us for a luncheon in the garden, I will show you the way."

On the ground lay a thick woolen blanket beneath several tin dishes filled with aromatic spiced foods, covered in mesh tents. A large basket holds layers of thin bread resembling pancakes. "I see you have found the spot," An old man shouts. He waves from the rear door of the pale green building and walks towards them, cane in hand, his white cotton robes billowing in the gentle wind.

"That is Dabir, let us sit. It will take him a few moments, his legs are not so good."

Dabir smiles as he approaches the group and rubs a thin hand across his hairless head. "I have not had visitors from so far away in all my years. I am honored," The old man says with a slight bow.

"The honor is ours, sir," Stuart replies as he stands and helps Dabir settle onto the blanket. "And this is quite a magnificent spot you've chosen.

Dabir squints through his wire-rimmed glasses. "Have you never been to Ethiopia?" Michael and Stuart both shake their heads in reply. "Ah, well, you will be seeing much more of it before your travels are finished." He crosses his legs with great care and points to the dishes. "Please, help yourselves, I have made this with my own hands. They are not as nimble as they used to be but still serve me well."

The men eat, passing the small, assorted dishes and filling their bowls. "This temple was built by Manelik, do you know who he is?" The Monk asks, deftly scooping food onto his fingers, which serve as utensils.

"Surely not The Queen of Sheba's son. This place is much too new."

"No no, by his namesake in 1880. But the real Manelik is intertwined with the Ark that you seek," Dabir reveals, a twinkle behind his glasses. "I had a dear friend, part of the Falasha tribe. We grew up together and he told me many things, things that were to remain a secret. I will share what I know today because I believe the time is right. I only hope you are pure of heart in your quest." He locks eyes with Stuart.

"The purest, sir," Stuart replies, his look sharp and gleaming with fire. "Now please, tell me all you know... "

Chapter 111

Something about that homeless man has stayed with me. I keep feeling like we're connected somehow and I think he did too. We talked for a long time trying to place each other... to find if we had met somewhere. But we hadn't. It was just a feeling, I guess. Not based on anything real. Like slight of hand. Feels everything these days is slight of hand.

Not a dream but not quite real.

As I watched him get on the bus I felt something inside me pull me toward him. Strange. But lately every day has been strange. I smoke until my lungs ache hoping that it will bring me a moment's peace. Just some time where my head isn't swimming with thoughts that race, crashing against each other. Nighttime is my only peace and even then I wake with dreams.

Nightmares.

When will it end?

Chapter 112

New York, New York

Henry Johansen makes his way through a dingy hallway, the smell of rotting trash fills his lungs as he pulls a handkerchief from his pocket and puts it to his lips. *I can't believe I've stooped to this,* he thinks and glances at the address scribbled on the scrap of paper. 610 Cross Street, apartment number 11. He finds the door, stuffs the kerchief into his pocket, and knocks. A young man in a stained white undershirt answers, his face spotted with tomato sauce.

"Hello, you are early. You've caught me having lunch. Please come in. You want to eat something?" he says inviting the deputy director inside the cramped apartment. "Azam, we have a guest, get another plate." He shouts in his thick accent towards the kitchen where a beautiful young woman washes dishes, her dark almond shaped eyes glance up and she nods a quick hello.

"No really. Don't go to any trouble, Mr. Abdelmassih, I'm fine," Henry replies looking around the small yet tidy room.

"Please, call me Hasan. Have a seat," He says with a deep dimpled smile.

Johansen looks at his watch then sits on a small stool near the table that's now set for two. Steam rises from bowls of aromatic foods. "I can't stay long, I have another appointment."

"Okay. But let us talk for a few moments before I give you the relic." The younger man dishes some food onto the clean plate in front of Henry. "You see I want you to understand something. What I'm about to give you is very meaningful. Something that, as a religious man, I hold sacred."

Henry squints, suspicious. "What exactly are you getting at?"

Hasan shakes his head. "Do not misunderstand. This is not about raising the price. The amount that was agreed upon is more than adequate. I merely want to tell you that, as a man who respects religion, I have a great weight on my heart regarding this exchange. Christ is not my God but I respect him the same. Understand?"

"Understood." Johansen nods.

"Please try the food before it gets cold. Azam is an excellent cook." He shouts toward the bedroom, "Azam please, come sit with our guest," then turns his attention back to Johansen. "You see, I would never have considered such a trade but we are expecting a baby." He smiles, his dimples deepening. "In my country I was an engineer, but of course in America I must start again." Azam enters, her belly protrudimg slightly from under her flowing dress. She takes a seat on the floor next to her husband as he continues, "We do not mind. It is worth anything to live in the United States. But once we had a baby arriving, I spread the word that I was looking to make some extra money and now here you are." Henry continues to eat and nods, surprised by the exquisite flavor of the food. "I tell you she is a great cook, no?" Hasan says, proud. "In Amman, she was a nurse." He pats Azam's leg. "I am a lucky man."

Johansen wipes his mouth and glances at his watch. "I really must be going."

"Ah yes, let me get it." He says jumping to his feet leaving Azam and Henry alone. She stares at him, her mesmerizing eyes lined with thick dark lashes, her mouth bold and full.

"Have you enjoyed the food, sir?" She asks, her accent strong.

"Yes. Yes I have. Thank you," Henry says, nervous under her gaze.

"I do not approve of what is happening here. I want you to know that." Henry nods as she continues. "The item is very important, please care for it."

Hasan returns to his seat and begins to unveil a small lead codex no larger than a stack of credit cards. Years of corrosion scar the outside of the small book clamped shut on all four sides by metal threads. A tree is primitively etched onto the front cover. "Here it is," He says and sets it on the table.

"How does it open?" Henry asks.

"It can only be opened once sir. It is written in the Book of Revelations that the sealed codex is only to be opened by one person," Hasan replies, brow furrowed.

"And who would that be?" Henry asks, his face hard.

"The Messiah."

Chapter 113

Lalibela, Ethiopia

"Gondar is there between the mountains," Obeje shouts over the sound of the muffler. "It is a shame we could not bring the carriage this far, it would have been a beautiful site with an open roof," He says with a smile. "I love to travel with the wind in my face. Many in my town think I am foolish for keeping the donkeys but I prefer to travel like my grandfather did. These cars that we as people have become so reliant upon are fragile. If the world stopped making only gasoline they would be, as you say, become obsolete."

Michael laughs. "I don't think there's much chance of gasoline going out of fashion."

Obeje raises his brows. "No? What if the world as we know it stops operating? A great war or collapse of government? My donkeys only need food and water which I can provide myself."

"Do you think there will be a great war?" Michael asks as Stuart listens to the exchange from the back seat of the Volkswagen Beetle.

Obeje shrugs. "I do not know but I am prepared at my home. We have planted a garden and have a spring for water. I have two chickens, one male one female and two cows the same. I can mate them you see. The same with my donkeys."

"It's a regular Noah's Ark," Stuart shouts in reply as they drive towards a series of waterfalls cascading down a cliff side. "My God, that's magnificent."

"It is where the Nile pours into Lake Gondar. I jumped from it as a boy," He says with a laugh.

Stuart raises a brow. "Daredevil, huh?"

"Yes, I love adventure," Obeje says and flashes a smile.

As they climb further up the mountain road the city comes into view in the distance. Just beyond it lay castle ruins reminiscent of knights and damsels in distress trapped in ivory towers. "It looks like Camelot," Stuart shouts squinting. "Who built this place? It reminds me of Europe."

"The Fasilidas. They believed this place to be chosen by God. The castle was built first, then later St. Mary's."

"*The* St. Mary's?" Stuart asks his voice betraying his excitement.

Obeje reveals a mischievous grin. "Yes, sir. The one and only."

Chapter 114

City of Angels

Outside the latest club in the string of venues conquered, Jesse stands staring at the moon, lit cigarette in hand. Mara walks out of the back door and comes to stand beside him, "What's so interesting?"

"The moon," He replies. "You know a lot about stars, how about the moon?"

She glances up and the moonlight casts a glow on her face. "My mother used to tell me that if it disappeared we would all just stop being able to think. That creativity and our personalities are governed by the moon." She props her head against the wall still gazing up. "This is a maiden moon which means the full moon or mother moon will be here in about a week. Did you know that we only see one side of the moon's face? Ever. It never shows us its other side. The dark side."

"There's poetry there," Jesse says as he drops his cigarette to the ground.

"You having a good time with Abaddon?" She asks in a quiet voice.

He shrugs. "It's not bad."

The two stand in silence for a long beat until Jesse moves towards the back entrance. "I'll see you inside." He pulls the metal door shut leaving Mara is silence.

"I miss you, Jess," She whispers, still searching the sky for answers.

Chapter 115

City of Angels

As music thumps through the walls of the club and out into the night, a group of drunken girls pile into a cab, their laughter echoing down the dim alleyway. Jesse stands near the back door, face hidden from view in the darkness, he glances at the girls then takes a drag from his cigarette. An old beggar walks towards him holding out his hand. Jesse takes out a dollar bill and holds it out to him, the paper flaps gently in the breeze.

"I'll take you for a bite to eat if you can wait an hour. My set will be over then," He says as the man steps into the moonlight revealing a face scarred with burns.

"Thank you. Maybe I'll take you up on that," He replies, his painful looking face twisting into a half smile. His eyes glisten with the hint of tears. "You're the first person who's treated me like a human being in months."

"What happened to you?" Jesse asks propped against the wall. He holds out the pack of cigarettes, "Smoke?"

"No thanks, that stuff'll kill you," He replies and the two share a chuckle. "There was a fire. It killed my family and left me disfigured. The insurance company wouldn't pay, some sort of clause because my kid was playing with matches. Suddenly I found myself on the street with the face of a freak and a dead wife and kids." He stops and searches Jesse's face before continuing, "I couldn't get it together, I drank a lot and did things to try and forget, and once I did get it together I couldn't find a job. I mean, who would want to look at this face all day right?"

Jesse drops his cigarette and stares at the stranger's face. He places his hands on the scars.

"Hey, what are you doing?" The man shouts jerking away.

Jesse's body glows in the moonlight. Luminous. "Trust me." He steps forward and touches the man's face once more.

After several minutes Jesse lifts his hands away, his body shakes and sweat soaks his brow. The beggar touches his face, now smooth, and gasps. "Who are you?" He whispers and falls to his knees.

Jesse shakes his head, the ache blinding. "I don't know."

Fifty feet away a man stands in the shadows. Roy watches from the edge of the alleyway, eyes filled with wonder, "Well, I'll be Goddamned."

Chapter 116

Dallas, Texas

"I'm a comin', hold your horses." Charlene yells, her hair dripping wet. She answers the door to her small apartment in nothing but a tattered pink towel. "Roy, what in the world? You scared me half to death with all that banging. Now if you want a little sugar you're gonna have to make an appointment just like everybody else." Roy stands still, his face pale, as if he's seen a ghost. "Hun, you okay?" She asks as she leads him inside by the hand.

He settles onto the couch. "I'm sorry. I didn't know where else to go. I don't really got nobody to talk to,"

"Honey you just tell ol' Charlene what's got you all shaken up, alright? I'm a good listener."

Roy lays his head on the back of the sofa and stares up at the ceiling, "Remember that guy I told you I was supposed to find? Well I think I found him last night," He explains, his voice weak. "See he was there the whole time with this girl I'd been following but I didn't think he was important. Until today."

"What happened Roy?"

Roy turns to her, his eyes wide, childlike. "I think I saw God."

Chapter 117

Journal Entry, May 3rd

I'm obsessing but I can't help but wonder what happens at these parties of Abaddon's. I know there are lots of pretty girls around but I find it hard to believe that Jesse would be sleeping with strangers like that. I mean, he's never even come close to touching me and he's had plenty of opportunity. Maybe he's just not attracted to me—or maybe I'm just fooling myself. He never came home the other night and didn't even bother to call. I guess he's playing the part of rock star now.

I wish I didn't care so much.

Maybe I should force myself to stop caring and just be his manager. I have to do something because this unrequited love crap is eating me alive.

Chapter 118

Sweet Water, Texas

"What the hell have you been doing all this time?" Rogerson yells and slams his fist onto the table of his elegant dining room, shaking the crystal candelabra, causing one of the tapered candles to fall onto its side. His usual smugness and superiority replaced with a hunted look he pleads, "Listen, Roy, I'm desperate, okay? Everything I've worked for my whole life could get wiped out by this, I'm dealing with a Goddamned mutiny!" Rogerson pushes away his untouched breakfast with shaky hands.

Roy shrugs. "I sure wish I could help you, cuz but there's nothing there. It's like tryin' to get blood from a stone," He replies, his own hands unsteady under the table. "I'm not even sure that little lady's got anything to do with it."

Rogerson lets out a nervous laugh, his expression ripe with fear. "Find Him, Roy. I don't care where, I don't care how, I just need you to find Him. Fast."

Roy stands, wordlessly staring at his cousin with a mixture of pity and fear.

"Don't just stand there lookin' at me, get to work!" Rogerson slams both fists on the table then stands and pours himself a brandy from the sideboard. Jibril enters as Roy exits.

"Sir is there something the matter?"

Rogerson replies with a hollow laugh. "What makes you think that?"

"I'm not blind, sir." The butler approaches Rogerson and stands a bit too close, speaking into his ear. "I have known you in so many ways, sir. Please allow me to help you."

Rogerson turns and locks eyes with the other man who is only inches from his face. He gazes at his mouth for a heated moment then collapses into a chair. "Oh, Jibril, it's all gotten so complicated. I'm scared. I need help. I have no one. Please help me," He mumbles, erupting into tears.

The butler puts a hand on Rogerson's shoulder, pulling him into an embrace. "Tell me everything. I'm here for you... "

Chapter 119

Langley, Virginia

Hunched at his desk Henry studies the lead codex, pliers in hand, the grooves of the primitive tree etching catching the light. He inserts the nose of the pliers into one of the thick metal threads then stops suddenly. Hasan's words return to him, "...the sealed codex is only to be opened by one person... the Messiah."

Who am I to think I can look inside these pages? And for what, greed?

Disgusted with himself he throws the tool across the room and it slams into a metal file cabinet. He stares at the small booklet inside his hand, his breath shallow. *I will make sure the person who is meant to open it has that opportunity. I don't know how but someway, somehow I will get this to its rightful owner.*

Chapter 120

Bethany, Israel

Montbard walks through a small village near Jerusalem tucking close to crumbling stonewalls, the bougainvillea thorns scraping his suede jacket. His beard is longer and his skin darkened by the harsh rays of the desert sun as he trails David in the open-air market.

David glides between the stands, eyes tired and swollen, collecting breads and fruits for the last day of Shiva. There is a profound heaviness in his walk and all semblance of joy has been replaced with a somber weight apparent in every move. The stalls are filled with aromatic foods and carcasses of chickens hang from ropes, their blood draining onto the cobblestone street. A butcher wearing a crimson soaked apron waves to him in recognition.

"I'm sorry to hear of your father, David. I was away and just got the news. He was a great man, it is a terrible loss to our community." He sighs as he wraps a beef tongue in white parchment. "I only hope that my children will have a rabbi who they can look up to the way my brothers and I looked up to him. Please, from our family," He says and hands David the package efficiently tied with twine.

David bows his head and accepts the gift. "Thank you, Yehuda. The community has been a source of comfort for us during this difficult time." David's spine stiffens as he suddenly gets the sensation that he's being watched, like someone is clocking his every move. He turns, glancing around the market and squints, just barely catching a glimpse of someone ducking behind a row of watermelons. *Or maybe my eyes are playing tricks*, he thinks.

Yehuda frowns, "What is it?"

David shakes his head and turns back to his business. "Nothing, I'm just letting my imagination run away with me. I also need a whole chicken, and some of your special spices for Sophie," He says as Montbard steps out from behind the cart and makes his way out of the marketplace. He moves briskly in the direction of David's home where Sophie and the baby take their afternoon nap. Alone.

Chapter 121

City of Angels

Abaddon appraises Mara's long slender legs. "Well Ms. Mara how are you doing today? Looking mighty fine I must say. I think this is the first time I've seen you wear a skirt. It suits you." He sits back in his seat, focused. "To what do I owe the pleasure?"

"Look Mandy, let's cut the crap okay. I don't like you. I'm probably never going to like you, and I definitely don't like your influence on Jesse."

Abaddon claps his hands together and laughs. "My influence? That's rich. Our boy is not a boy you know. He's a grown man. A man with needs from what I can see."

Mara cocks her head to the side. "What's that supposed to mean?"

Abaddon shrugs. "I'm just saying our Jesse's a red blooded male and red blooded males have needs beyond holding hands and making goo goo eyes."

"Who makes goo goo eyes?" She asks, her face red. Mandy's only reply is an amused grin. "Whatever. Look, I didn't come here to talk about me I came here to discuss my client. I don't like you keeping him out partying all night, every night of the week."

His sharp eyes focus on hers. "Is this the manager or the woman talking?"

"Don't push me, Abaddon."

He throws his hands in the air in defeat. "Man you're pretty pissed off these days Mar, you're just not yourself." He tilts his chin and looks up at her with a smile. "Look, I've only been taking him out for nice dinners and stuff, completely innocent. I had nothing to do with him and Missy spending the night together." The color drains from Mara's face. She grabs for the side of a chair and settles herself into it. The pleasure in Abaddon's eyes is unmistakable. "Oops. Sorry, guess you didn't know. He even painted the girl's toe nails, for Christ's sake." He watches Mara regain her composure.

"Yes, of course I knew," She lies. "That's what rock stars do right? Screw groupies. I just... well. You know he used to have a bit of a... substance problem. I just don't want him getting caught up in that again."

Abaddon flashes his unnaturally pearly whites. "Oh, don't you worry, Madame Manager. I'll keep him off the stuff. I'll keep him pure as the driven snow."

Chapter 122

Something's changed between Mara and me. She feels darker. Distant. I notice her looking at me with an expression I can't quite place but I know her thoughts are full of hurt. I want to reach out but she scares me.

She's so good. So pure.

Maybe Missy's right. Maybe I'm fucking her up anyway.

Mandy's parties are a good distraction. I mainly end up sitting in the corner smoking too many cigarettes but I don't mind. The band seems to like the lifestyle. James, who I've taken to calling Jimmy Fingers on account of his magic on the keyboard, seems to be the only one that doesn't partake in the pretty girls they line up for us. And me, of course. Though it doesn't make a whole lot of sense, I feel like I'd be betraying Mara if I did. And I'd rather stab myself with a sharp blade than hurt her.

I won't lie. Sometimes I take a drink when Mandy insists. Usually a beer or something light. I've got a handle on it. I won't fall off the wagon.

Too much to lose.

Chapter 123

St. Mary's Cathedral, Gondar, Ethiopia

Stuart studies a recent alfresco painting of Jesus' life depicted on the east wall of the building. The red and golden hued pictures cast an eerie and mystical tone surrounding the dark skinned, black haired man.

"This is where Dabir said the Ark was brought to its final resting place after the original St. Mary's was rebuilt by Emperor Sellasie," Stuart says, eyes darting around the dome-covered room. Light shines through the small row of windows that line the top on the ceiling.

Michael walks along the plush red carpet towards the unadorned pulpit. "This place is much more modern than I expected. I thought the cathedral was ancient?"

"This one was constructed next to the ruins of the second St. Mary's of Zion, built by Emperor Fasallidas, and before that, the first one built in 300 A.D." Stuart studies the structure. "The older church is just next door, let's go inside it."

The two men trek across the tall grass towards a stone building lined with arched windows. A robust man guards the entrance, hands inside his pockets looking bored. "We want to look inside," Stuart says as he discreetly hands a folded bill to the guard.

The man steps aside clearing their path "Go ahead. But if you are expecting to find treasure you have come to the wrong place."

Stuart gives the man a long look then the two head inside the darkened cavernous building, the stone walls cold and uninviting. "If the Ark is in either of these places we'll find it. But something tells me that if it really were here it would be much more heavily guarded. Something's not right here. We need to find out what it is..."

Chapter 124

City of Angels

Jibril winds through the dark and shuttered downtown Los Angeles street following a man in his early fifties with a pretty young girl on his arm, her shocking pink dress leaving little to the imagination. The two laugh as the man puts his hand on her firm and ample bosom, groping without any regard for propriety. "Oh, Mandy, you're so bad." She giggles, her pink stained lips curved into a seductive smile.

"How can I keep my hands off those things? They're like candy. Like sweet perfect cupcakes," He says walking backwards jiggling her breasts in his hands. Abaddon leans into the girl and grabs the back of her head as Jibril ducks into an alleyway. The two lock lips, a long and forceful kiss. "Have you ever wanted to do it outside, against a brick wall?" He asks, pulling her into the recesses of an old abandoned building.

"Come on, Mandy, I thought we were going to hear the band play," She replies, uncomfortable now, standing beneath a solitary flickering bulb.

"Soon, baby, soon." He pulls her in further, his hands already up her short dress.

"I don't want to be late. You promised I could sit in on a set, I wanna show you what I can do."

"Don't worry, you can use that nice set of pipes when we get there but for now I've got something else you can use that pretty little mouth of yours on," He says as he pulls her skirt up around her waist and shoves his hand into her black lace panties, pushing her against the wall. She squirms under his harsh touch.

"I promise, you can have a shot. But first you've gotta take care of daddy."

With a smile she crouches down in front of him and unzips his pants. "You're a very bad man."

Jibril watches from a safe distance, his expression solemn. Abaddon runs his ring-lined fingers through the girl's dirty blonde hair and thrusts himself into her mouth, pinning her head to his pelvis. She gags and struggles under his grip. He thrusts again. And again. The struggle grows fierce, her muffled whimpers echoing through the dirty street. Abaddon stiffens and holds his breath; convulsions shake his body. He releases his grip and the girl slumps forward, sobbing silently. Abaddon reaches for her chin and looks down at her mascara stained face. He wipes the black wetness from beneath her eyes as she bites her lip to keep from crying.

"Mag-fucking-nificent," He says. An embarrassed smile plays at the corners of her mouth, her lower lip trembling. He gazes at her another second longer then slams his fist into her face. Hard.

Her limp body crumples against the wall as the music producer zips his pants and steps out onto the desolate street.

Jibril turns his face to the sky, a moonbeam reflecting in his eyes. "Heavenly father, I fear I have found the fallen one... "

Chapter 125

Bethany, Israel

The screen of David's laptop illuminates his face. He sits in a wingback chair in the living room, the still and quiet house dark around him. He searches pages looking for news of an archaeological finding discovered in the early eighties. Tombs buried deep beneath the earth that could hold a clue to the Messiah's location. *Maybe this is a dead end but father always said we should pay attention to our dreams. Or is this dad speaking to me through my dreams and leading me from the grave? It says here the sarcophagus that was found was etched with the inscription Jesus, son of Joseph. Could it be possible that this really was the tomb of Jesus' family and not a hoax? And if so who were the bodies of the other nine people buried in the tomb with him? Maybe it will reveal more of the lineage of the Messiah and the Tree of Jesse.* He rubs his face and looks out the window, the world outside pitch black. Sophie walks down the short flight of stairs from the bedroom above.

"My dear sweet prince, what are you doing this time of night?" She sits across from him on the sofa and curls her long slender legs under her.

"I'm looking for something," He replies, his voice tired.

"Please, David. Tell me what's going on. Maybe I can help."

"I can't, Sophie, it's better if you don't know. Trust me."

She turns her face up towards the ceiling and lets out a deep sigh. "Well I have a secret of my own." David looks up from the computer, his face glowing from the light of the screen. "I'm pregnant," She whispers.

There is a moment of silence as he studies her face. Then he closes the laptop, gently setting it aside and goes to her on the couch, pulling her close. "You've made me a happy man."

"Are you sure? I know we said we would wait till things got a bit better. Financially I mean. Until some of your work was published."

He kisses her on the forehead and closes his arms tighter around her. "We'll make it work my love. I'll get some work at night. And during the summer months off from tutoring I can work days too. I'll start very soon."

"But your writing... "

"My writing isn't much more than a hobby now, is it? A man can't live on dreams alone." Sophie breathes a sigh of relief and curls into her husband. As they sit in silence David is once again consumed in his thoughts. *And now my child is growing who may not live to see outside its mother's womb. Oh dear God, why have I been entrusted with this burden? I must be missing some clue father left behind ... I only hope for a sign before it's too late.* He thinks and stares out the window where dark shadows hide from the moonlight.

Chapter 126

Sweet Water, Texas

"Do you have it?" Rogerson hisses into the receiver. He reclines on the massive four-poster bed with a cool washcloth on his forehead, absently playing with the tassel on a throw pillow.

"It was a blatant forgery. I'm sorry," Henry says and pours a glass of water. "I went all the way to New York but after I had already paid the man and inspected the item closely, I knew it wasn't real. A forgery. Albeit a very good one."

Rogerson quickly sits up. "Son of a bitch. I was countin' on you Hen."

Johansen takes a drink of the water, his throat rough and dry, "I'll keep working in it Rog. I'll find it for you." He rubs his temple. "What is this book, Rog, what will it do for you?"

Rogerson squints. "Don't you worry about that. You just worry about how much you'll get paid when you find it," He says and slams the phone down on the cradle.

Chapter 127

Dallas, Texas

Roy and Charlene lay looking up at the ceiling sharing a cigarette between them. "That was amazing," She mumbles passing him the lit cigarette.

"The sex?" Roy says with a smile.

"Yessiree, Bob, the sex." She turns and looks across the pillow at his lined and weathered face. A face of the old west. "You make me feel like when I was a little girl, Roy. Dreamin' of marryin an old fashioned cowboy." She turns away suddenly embarrassed. "That was a stupid thing to say."

"No it wasn't." He props himself up and puts the cigarette to her lips. "In fact, that's one of the nicest things anybody's ever said to me."

"You ever been married, Roy?" She whispers, her voice unsure.

"Almost. We'd known each other since we were kids and I loved her to pieces. But she ran off with some trucker she'd met at a gas station two days before we were supposed to get married. Somebody told me she got pregnant real soon after that and that's the last I ever heard of her."

"I've never been married neither. I never met a man that stirred me in that way." The two lock eyes. "Until I met you."

Roy looks back to the ceiling, a goofy smile plastered across his face. "I think I've waited my whole life to hear you say that to me."

"Will you marry me, Roy?" She asks with a nervous laugh. "I'll tow the line for you. I'll be there through thick and thin."

Roy rolls on top of her and plants a slow kiss on her lips. "I think that's about the best idea I ever heard."

Chapter 128

City of Angels

Abaddon sits peeling an apple under a canvas umbrella, the sky alive with piercing sunlight. His hands move skillfully with swift purposeful motions though his eyes stay glued on Jesse's enigmatic face. "What are you thinking about?" He asks with a wicked grin.

"Nothing, really. Just wondering how things will be when the album comes out," He says, taking a drag of his cigarette.

Abaddon laughs. "I can tell you exactly how it's gonna be. You're gonna have the press and every woman in the world crawling all over you. Enjoy anonymity while you can, my friend. In fact, I want to start doing some real press soon. National stuff. Plant the seeds, so to speak. Apple?" He says holding a piece of fruit to Jesse.

"No, thanks."

"Come on, man, you haven't eaten a thing all day, I just picked it fresh off the tree. As they say, an apple a day." He smiles again. Jesse takes the offering and has a bite. "There now, that wasn't too bad was it?"

Jesse gives him an odd look, "You're a strange man, Abaddon."

He laughs. "Don't I know it. Ha. The music business will do that to you, pal." The two sit in silence for a moment. "You know most people would sell their soul to the devil for an opportunity like the one you have Jess."

Jesse chuckles. "It's a good thing I'm not most people."

"Yes. A good thing. Here have another bite; we have a long night ahead of us. The girls will be here soon and the games will begin," Abaddon says with a toothy grin. "I've got some party favors for you, thought you deserved it after a hard week of being rock star." He says and sets a vial of white powder on the table next to Jesse's hand.

Chapter 129

Gondar, Ethiopia

The wind howls as Stuart and Michael make their way through a cramped alleyway, the mortar cracked and the smell of urine strong. They find an arched wooden door and knock three times just as they were instructed by the guard at St. Mary's.

"Who sent you?" The man behind the open door asks and peers at them with his one good eye.

"Hakim sent us. He said you would have information about the Holy of Holies."

The man quickly opens the door. "Hurry. Come inside," He says and glances down the alley to make sure they weren't followed before shutting the door behind them.

They enter the low ceilinged room and stand near the hearth, which burns with the remnants of a fire giving the space uncomfortable warmth.

The man studies them from head to toe. "I am Negasi, what are you here to ask?"

Stuart questions the man, his jaw set firm. "I believe the Ark that's currently guarded at the church is a fake. I want to know what happened to the real one."

Negasi laughs abruptly and turns away. "Surely, you are joking. What can you know of this?"

Stuart moves closer to the dark skinned man, "Mr. Negasi, I must warn you. We can do this the easy way or the hard way. The easy way will make you a very rich man."

Negasi turns and the two hold each other's gaze for several heated moments before he replies.

"Please, have a seat." He says, motioning to the low cot that lines the wall opposite the fireplace. Negasi wipes his face with a rough hand. "Yes, you are correct. The Ark was stolen many months ago."

"Do you know who stole it?"

Negasi shakes his head. "No, sir, I do not. I only know what I saw that night. Something I will never forget. There was a woman, beautiful with long black hair like silk and a wide generous mouth painted red. I was the guard on duty that night and I heard some noise coming from inside the church. I had fallen asleep and was woken to the sounds of drumbeats and a woman's chanting." He takes a deep breath. "As I entered with nothing but my lighter to guide the way I saw the woman sitting in the center of the room, her arms thrown in the air and her body writhing. She was screaming in a language I could not understand and suddenly she looked at me and the flame in my hand extinguished. When I managed to relight it she was gone and that was the first time I noticed that the Ark was missing."

"Do you have any idea who this woman might have been?" Stuart asks, his face twisted in grief.

Negasi looks into the smoldering flames, his face expressionless. "No sir. I have no idea, I only know that she disappeared without a trace... "

Chapter 130

Sweet Water, Texas

"You're keeping something from me." Jibril speaks softly from the edge of the bed while Rogerson lays under the covers in a silk robe staring at the ceiling.

"I don't know what in the Sam Hill you're talkin' about. I ask you for help and all I get is questions. And where the hell has Roy been lately anyway?" Rogerson flicks on the bedside lamp and looks at the clock.

"We're not talking about Roy we're talking about you. You're keeping secrets."

The fat man mumbles under his breath. "That no good, lazy son of a gun. He hasn't been any Goddamned help since he showed up here. Teaches me for hirin' family."

Jibril sighs and walks across the room to the bay window, its seat lined with tasseled pillows. "How can we get close if you won't trust me completely?"

Rogerson runs a hand down his flushed face and lets out a breath, the grey in his hair ghost white in the reflection of the lamp. "Yes. Yes, there's more. But I'm afraid to tell you. Damn it, this is a big fat mess." He stands, tightening the belt of the robe and pacing the length of the glossy wood, his fleshy feet slapping the floor gracelessly.

Jibril moves to him and grabs his arm. "You can trust me." His voice is soothing. The two lock eyes in a long and heated silence until Rogerson sits back down on the bed and reclines, his head touching the plush tapestry fabric that lines the headboard.

"Oh, Jibril, there's so much to tell." He looks up at the handsome face standing above him. "There's a safe behind the painting in the my office. The combination is my birthday

including two numbers for the year. There's a wooden box
and a large envelope under it. Bring them here and I'll tell you
everything."

Chapter 131

I don't touch the stuff but I keep the vials in the back of my nightstand at Abaddon's. Not sure why I don't just throw them away but it seems a shame to waste all that blow. He gives me more every now and then. I guess he has no idea I'm trying to stay clean. I'm sure he considers it a reward for a job well done.

I won't lie. I'm tempted to take a hit to make the voices in my head stop. Maybe it'll numb me from the constant pain I see around me. And then there's Mara. I miss her so much it makes me ache. Bad.

I just can't trust myself around her anymore. That's all she needs, a crazy ex-drug addict slowly going out of his mind and thinking he can talk to spirits.

I wake up at night to their voices. They tell me stories of who I am. I'm sinking deeper into this parallel world everyday.

* * *

Journal Entry May 7th

It's three am and I can't sleep. I had a strange dream about Abaddon. He was eating like a glutton and hissing at me and his body writhed like a snake. I don't know what it means. I wish mamaan was alive, she would understand. I did a protection spell she taught me with a rusted nail that I hammered into the back yard. I must've looked pretty weird hammering away like that in the middle of the night in my nightgown. Maybe I'm just being paranoid but it feels like every move I make is being watched.

Like I'm being hunted.

I wish I could talk to Jesse but he's so distant lately, and he's hardly ever here. I'm not sure I can keep going on like this. Maybe it's better if I just walk away and leave him to his new life.

There seems to be no place for me in it.

Chapter 132

Tel Aviv, Israel

"Monsieur Montbard, I have been trying to reach you for some time." Moreau says as he paces, phone in hand.

"I'm sorry, I have been traveling and haven't checked my messages," Montbard replies, his voice weary.

"It seems, sir, that the man we've been searching for is in California. Los Angeles mainly. I have photographs for you. Where can I send them?"

Montbard sits up abruptly in the club chair of the swank Tel Aviv hotel. "I will travel to Los Angeles at once and give you the address of my hotel when I arrive. Moreau, what about the girl?"

Moreau sighs into the receiver. "It's as I thought sir, she's of vital importance to your cause. You may disagree but after research into her lineage I believe she's the next, Migdal."

Montbard shudders. "Are you sure? If this is true it will be the saving grace of the mission. If she is on our side then I can rest assured that everything will go according to plan. Do you know if they have consummated the relationship?"

"I don't. Would you like me to continue tracking them?"

"No, I will take care of it once I arrive in Los Angeles. I will meet you at the hotel and we can discuss the details further. Excellent work Monsieur Moreau, this information is... priceless."

Moreau hangs up the phone in his stark hotel room and sits on the edge of the bed, head in hand. He slowly makes the sign of the cross, a frightened look etched on his face.

Chapter 133

City of Angels

"All right, boys, I've got some news," Abaddon shouts, rubbing his hands with relish. The band members look up from their collective perches near the pool. Paul floats on an inner tube and Jesse, who's spent the better part of the day looking out onto the canyon, glances up and lights a fresh cigarette.

"Do tell, O wise one," Jude says with a smirk.

Abaddon stands near the pool, smile glowing, his wiry body alive with energy. "The album's being released early. The label heard the tracks and they think they're fucking perfect. They don't want to wait another minute."

"Holy crap!" James shouts and jumps into the pool.

Jude stands at the edge of the pool and yells; "I'm the king of the world!" then leaps in with a splash.

One by one, the guys jump in fully clothed, splashing playfully like boys half their age. Thad shouts to Jesse. "Come on man, don't be such a buzz kill. Get in."

Abaddon smiles. "Yeah, Jess, everybody's doing it." He hops into the deep end shoes and all. The guys laugh and splash until Jesse finally gives in. He turns his back to the water, folds his arms across his chest and falls in.

"Yeah!" The guys shout.

Abaddon yells. "It's about fuckin' time you loosened up, man." He dunks Jesse's head under and holds it there. A few long moments pass and the guys go quiet.

"Hey, man, I think you should let him up," Jude says as they watch Jesse's body writhe underwater, his arms flailing.

"He's fine." Abaddon laughs.

"Seriously, man, what the fuck?" Paul shouts and shoves Abaddon's shoulder. His wicked smile widens for a moment then he releases Jesse who rises to the surface coughing and gasping for breath.

"You okay, man?" James asks and grabs his shoulder, holding him afloat. Jesse continues to cough until he takes in a lung full of air as James drags him toward the shallow end of the pool.

Abaddon steps out of the pool and peels off his soaked t-shirt. "Oh, don't act like a bunch of pussies. He's fine." He throws the shirt on a nearby lounge chair. "Congratulations ladies. Today is the first day of the rest of your lives." He saunters through the open doors of the den, dripping onto the limestone floor.

Chapter 134

Sweet Water Texas

Jibril stands across from Rogerson in the massive dining room, the table set for one. "I've found him."

Rogerson glances up with a mouthful of duck and a gleam in his eye. "Well, I'll be Goddamned," He says after washing down the food with a generous gulp of Riesling.

"I saw him with the girl a few days ago but I didn't want to say anything until I saw more. He has powers. True gifts. I have only a sliver of doubt in my mind that he is the One. I just need to be absolutely sure before you alert your group."

Rogerson rubs his thick hands in delight. "I knew I could count on you, Jibril. This calls for a celebration. Bring out the champagne!" He bellows towards the kitchen and pats the seat next to him. "Now how about you join me for dinner and you tell me all about it, Jibril? The duck is fantastic."

The younger man sits, his expression reticent. "You must trust me and give me the papers from the safe." Jibril stops and locks eyes with Rogerson. "You trust me don't you?" He places an elegant hand on Rogerson's with a brittle smile.

"Of course I trust you, Jibril. Please stay with me. I don't want to be alone anymore. I'm so scared that everything I have worked for is crumbling."

Jibril tightens his grip on Rogerson's hand and looks up to the heavens. "Don't worry, everything you have done will be repaid, just as it is meant to be."

Chapter 135

Journal Entry, May 8th

I found a note under my door. It asked me to meet tomorrow morning at the Red Cathedral just down the mountain not too far from the cabin. It's not a church—it's really just a bunch of pointy red rocks—but people think it looks like one of those grand cathedrals in France or someplace. The note said Jesse's identity would be revealed. It's all pretty cloak and dagger if you ask me but I can't say I'm not insanely curious. Maybe I shouldn't go up there alone but I don't know who to tell. Jesse and I aren't talking much lately and if I tell Buddy or any friends from the club they'll think I'm crazy. Or crazier I should say. They've all noticed the change in me since Jesse arrived into my world. I'll go tomorrow morning and see what happens. I'm not scared... but maybe I should be.

Chapter 136

Talpiot Burough, Jerusalem

David crouches through the cramped dusty passageway below a large symbol carved into a stone hillside, his dark skinned guide nearby. "It's not far, sir."

David struggles for breath, the entrance of the tomb narrow and stifling. He aims a small flashlight with one hand and gropes through the semi darkness with the other. He slides his body through a shaft that leads to a larger opening. The handheld light illuminates the dirt and stone walls to reveal an 8 by 10 foot cave with several small low shafts cut into its sides.

"This is where we found the skulls, sir." The guide points, to the corners of the space. "And these hollows are where the tombs were stored."

David crouches down jutting his flashlight into one of the openings. Nothing inside, no writings or inscriptions. "Were all the tombs taken directly to the museum?"

"As far as I know, sir. It was many years ago. Another worker and I made the discovery and the foreman came in to see what we had found. After discovering the tombs hidden inside the holes in the walls we were not allowed back. I heard rumors that one of the tombs was stolen and the other nine were taken to the curator then sold to a collector."

"Did you touch any of them, the ossuaries? Could you feel the inscriptions?"

The man looks at David plainly and smiles, revealing a gap toothed grin. "Yes, sir. I was the one who found the tomb of Jesus's son."

Chapter 137

Addis Ababa, Ethiopia

The airport is alive with activity as Stuart and Michael sip hot black tea. Overhead, white metal beams rise from the open ceiling lending an air of loftiness to the massive edifice.

"I'll miss this." Michael says then takes another drink.

"Yes, it's sad to part with this place. I was hoping this trip would be our final stop." Stuart replies looking grim.

"What now?"

"Now you go back to Israel and your studies and I make my way to America in hopes of reuniting with my brothers."

"Do you think they'll join you?" Michael asks tentatively.

"Dear God, I can only hope that they do."

Chapter 138

Red Cathedral Cliffs, Death Valley

The wind whips Mara's hair in fluid waves as she looks down from the rust colored rocks. The long steep fall below makes her shudder and she steps back and away from the ledge.

"Don't worry, I'm not here to hurt you." A voice speaks from behind. She whips around, startled. Jibril stands before her, his deep blue eyes are pools of sapphire glowing in the bright sunlight.

"Who are you?" She asks, stepping away from him. "What do you know?"

"Who I am is not important, but what I know about your friend is. You see he's not quite... human, your friend. But you probably already suspected that something was different about him."

Mara furrows her brow. "I don't understand."

"Of course you don't. Here, have a look at this." He says and removes a cylinder from the messenger bag strapped across his chest. He opens the tube and pulls out several pages of old documents that he holds up for her to inspect. "This is proof."

She studies the documents, her eyes scanning the text. "What do these prove? I don't even know what they say."

"Allow me," He replies calmly and begins to read. "The sins are kept secret in the hearts of men. They did not realize that the sins would overwhelm them someday and they did not rescue themselves. But someday there will be a world where wickedness is cut off from the light and disappears like smoke and good and kindness will shine like the sun. The truth will fill every pore of the earth and treacherous lies will forever be locked away. When I come this change will be set in motion..."

"And I will deliver your world from death." Mara says, eyes wide in disbelief. "Where did you get those?"

"They were written between 250 B.C. to 100 A.D." He replies in a soothing tone.

Mara laughs uncomfortably. "You're crazy. Those are the translations. The ones Rajwani did. They're Jesse's words ... "

"They were also the words of someone else long before him." Jibril interrupts. A gust of wind whips the parchments from his hand, blowing them toward the edge of the cliff. Mara desperately grabs for them, but the wind is fierce and the pages flutter beyond her reach, toward rock formations a thousand feet below. Mara turns back to ask the man for help but he has disappeared. Lying on her stomach she reaches for a page of the weathered document. It laps at her fingertips just beyond her grasp. A gust of wind swirls it up and out. She grabs at it, and the sudden motion causes her to slide forward. Her toes desperately searching the ground beneath her for a hold.

Anything to stop her fall.

Images of Jesse flash before her eyes. If she could only touch him one last time. If only ... her foot catches on something solid and she jerks to a stop. Shaking, Mara pulls herself back from the cliff edge and climbs to her feet. Red earth stains her chest and legs. She looks for the foothold that saved her life but finds only flat ground covered in fine red dust.

Something was holding me just now.

I should be dead.

She gazes up at the desert sky, giving silent thanks to who ever or what ever spared her. As she dusts herself off and heads towards the jeep, desert sun burning behind her, a figure flies above, wings outstretched.

Chapter 139

Palm Springs, California

Jesse squints into a long row of lights. Someone clips a small microphone onto his shirt and a woman approaches, clipboard in hand. The flurry of activity in the television studio makes his head ache. "So if you get stuck and don't know what to say just look at the teleprompter over there and we'll put something up. Mandy will be in the booth so he'll help us out." The producer says, her smile crisp and frighteningly alert. "I've known Mandy a long time. I'd do just about anything for him. You have a couple minutes to relax."

Jesse fumbles with a cigarette as Abaddon glides over to him. "You're not thinking about lighting that thing are ya? Cyndy'll kick your ass up and down the block if you even think of smoking in her studio. Speaking of asses did you check hers out? I'd tap that again." A lecherous grin crosses his lips.

"I wasn't planning on lighting it. I was just holding onto it." Jesse says.

"You're gonna be great, just be yourself pal. They'll lap it up like crème." Abaddon winks and makes his way back to the booth on the second level.

A guy in a headset stands in front of the camera and gives a countdown. "Live in 10, 9... " A middle-aged woman with a helmet of ash blonde hair takes the seat next to Jesse and clips on her mike.

"I'm Anne Pomeroy." She says with a firm handshake.

"3,2,1..." says the man with the headset and points to Anne.

"Good morning, Palm Springs, today we have a local artist whose rock and roll album is about to hit record stores every-where. The band is called The Prophets and their lead singer is here to tell us more about their haunting and poetic music." She turns her attention toward Jesse. "Good morning, Jesse. I heard a few of the songs and I have to say, they're quite something. What inspires you to write in such a, if I may, almost sermon like manner?"

He looks at her then looks at the camera, eyes wide.

Cynthia paces inside the booth. "Damn it, he's like a dear in the friggin' headlights. Put the first cue on the prompter." She barks.

"Give him a chance, trust me, he'll do great." Mandy replies, arms folded, feet planted firmly on the ground.

"Jesse?" Anne says. After what seems like an eternity he speaks, his voice shaky.

"I write what I feel. And what I feel is that our world is being led astray. We don't love each other. Our neighbors are strangers we compete with, who's gifts we covet. But it's never too late. All we need to do is change our ways today. If we do, paradise awaits us not only in death but in this life too. In a way we have to lose the life we know now in order to save it."

Anne sits staring at Jesse, her polished demeanor replaced with openness. "That's beautiful. You don't hear a lot of people talk like that these days."

Cynthia gives Jesse the thumbs up from inside the booth. "Well I'll be Goddamned, Mandy. Your boy's a natural."

Abaddon smirks, "I had no doubt."

Chapter 140

Journal Entry, May 10th

I don't know what to make of the man I met at the Red Cathedral. Should I tell Jesse? Probably not. Probably he'll think I've lost it if I tell him what the man said. Plus he's acting different these days. Self absorbed. I'm not sure what to make of it. I don't know what to do, so I guess I'll just do nothing.

* * *

I may be getting better at this rock star thing but I still feel like an imposter. Like I'm no good and one of these days everyone's going to see me for the fraud I really am. I mean, I'm just a guy who writes poetry and puts it to music. I'm nobody, really.

Chapter 141

Antiquity Authority Warehouse, Beit Shamesh, Israel

A large metal door slides open allowing the full moon's light onto a slick concrete floor, its glow bathing rows of shelves in a white blue haze. David enters the vast and high ceilinged warehouse and a slight man with a silver mustache shuffles behind him. "We cannot turn on the lights or the night guard may see it through the windows," the man whispers.

"Don't worry, Mr. Malka, I came well prepared." David says and flicks on a small flashlight the size of a pen.

The two walk by several rows of pottery and other labeled artifacts.

"They're not much further." Malka says, his heavy feet scuffing the hard floor. They reach an area lined with several stone sarcophagi. A thin shaft of the moon's light illuminates one in particular. "Here we are," Malka says proudly. There is an uncomfortable silence as he stands in front of the ossuaries blocking David's path. "Sir, we had an agreement only that I would bring you to the tombs. I believe my part of the bargain is complete." He says holding out his hand.

"Of course." David says absentmindedly and takes several bills from his wallet. "I appreciate your help, Mr. Malka, and please know that your efforts are for a good cause."

"That is the reason I agreed, of course." The man says and stuffs the bills into his pocket. "I like to help where I can."

"If you don't mind waiting, I may have a few questions when I am through." David says. The man glances at his watch theatrically. "I will pay you for your efforts of course.

Mr. Malka smiles, revealing a gleaming gold tooth. "I'd be delighted. Always glad to help." He steps aside, allowing access to the artifacts. David shines a light on the one closest to him, its pitted stone surface partially crumbling. Sliding a hand along the top he feels a rush of excitement.

Imagine if one of these tombs was actually the place Christ's body was laid to rest. What would that mean for Christianity? He thinks to himself. He runs his hand along the back of the large stone until he feels the recesses of an engraving under his fingertips. Heart pounding, David turns the tip of the flashlight towards the inscription. The primitive writing, Aramaic, reveals a name.

"James." David says aloud.

"Yes, but read what it says below it."

"Son of Joseph, brother of Jesus." David replies, his voice trembling with excitement. "How can this be?" He says, turning to face a smug Malka.

"This particular ossuary was not brought to us for more than twenty years after the first nine. In 2002, Oded Golan, an antiquities collector, showed a picture of this tomb to Andre Lemaire, professor of Semetic languages at the Sorbonne. The photograph ignited controversy surrounding Golan's acquisition of the ossuary, which he claimed to have purchased for a mere five hundred dollars. There has also been some controversy about the authenticity of part of the inscription, so they were taken to the Rockefeller Museum for study," He says shrugging his shoulders. "I do not really have an opinion either way but judging by the rest of the tombs it's probable that this one is the genuine article."

David reaches further into the deep shelving, his hands groping the next cold stone slab. Feeling an etched marking he slides his head and body into the small opening between the stones. As he shines the light onto the inscription of the tomb he sees a second name. Miriamine e Mara inscribed in Greek.

They hear approaching footsteps outside. Malka puts a finger to his lips and David quickly flicks the light off. The two men stand silent, not daring to move a muscle. After several tense moments the sound of shoes on pavement fades until it is almost inaudible.

"My goodness, my heart is not strong enough for this type of thing. Please hurry, we must leave soon. I cannot risk being caught." Malka whispers.

David quickly goes to the next tomb, the one illuminated by moonlight. He sees an Aramaic inscription cast in the faint lunar glow that says, Yeshua bar Yosef. David looks at Malka. "It can't be."

"It can and it is, my boy." The old man says with a flash of his golden grin.

Chapter 142

Bethany, Israel

I wish I could share this information with dad. David thinks as he rubs the three days growth on his face. *Imagine, a tomb with the family of Jesus inside. How could they have kept it a secret for so long and who are "they"? The only thing that doesn't make sense is this Miriame e Mara inscription. I don't recall ever seeing such a name connected to Christ in the Bible. There was of course Mary, who could be known as Miriam who did have an ossuary of her own, but who is this Mara and how is she a part of Jesus' lineage? If I can figure that out it may be the missing clue I need to track him.*

Sophie enters, her arms wrapped around her. "Lunch is ready."

"Okay, I will be there in a minute." David says, distracted.

She stands for a silent moment bumping the door with her hip. "We need to pay our grocery tab, David." She says quietly. "I went to the market today and I had to hold my head in shame."

David looks up from his writing. "I will take care of it."

"When, my love, and with what money? This secret mission of yours is costing us plenty. I am trying to be supportive but I'm afraid." She leans against the frame of the doorway and whispers, "I thought you were getting a real job."

"I am Sophie, I'm looking for work. It's not so easy." He says angry. "You can't just snap your fingers and get a good position somewhere."

Sophie looks at him, hands resting on her belly thinking of the child growing inside her and the costs it will undoubtedly bring. "I understand. Please come in before the food gets cold." She says and walks away.

If I could tell her what's happening she would understand. Dear God why do I have to carry this burden alone? He sets his jaw, determined. *I will find the answer soon and then I can focus on taking care of my family and our new baby. There's no other way. Maybe it's time I paid a visit to the museum curator, maybe he knows something.*

Chapter 143

City of Angels

"You know, that's really messed up. He does all these interviews and doesn't invite us to a single one." Jude mumbles as he kicks a lawn chair with his Converse sneaker. "I mean, we're his band, man. Where's his loyalty?"

James shrugs and ashes a joint. "He's the star, dude. He's who they come to see. Not us. We're just the background players. The little worker ants building the village for the big... alpha ant." He laughs, feeling the effects of the pot.

"I'm no fuckin' worker ant. No way, man. I'm an artist and I expect to be treated that way." Jude says then takes a hit. "I bet they want to interview us but star boy wants the limelight all to himself."

Mandy walks towards the pool from the garage, tossing his keys in the air and catching them behind his back. "Cat like reflexes." He says with a smile. "What are you derelicts up to?"

"Nothing much." James replies, his eyes bloodshot.

Jude offers Abaddon the joint. "I've got a question, Mandy."

He glances at the smoke. "No thanks, I've got work to do. What's the question, pal? I'm all ears."

"When those interviews and things come in, do they ask for us too? I mean, I'm starting to feel like chopped liver here." Jude lies back on the striped chaise.

Abaddon's expression betrays nothing. "Of course they ask for you guys. Come on, you're becoming big stars now man. Everybody wants a piece."

"So how come we never get to do any interviews?" James asks, his voice quiet.

Abaddon shrugs. "Well... our golden boy doesn't like to share, if you know what I mean." He pats James on the shoulder. "Hang in there guys, you're doin' a great job. I gotta get on some calls." He walks a few steps then turns back. "You guys are the glue that holds this thing together. At least I can appreciate that." He opens the doors to the den and disappears inside.

Jude spits onto the grass. "I told you, man. He's a publicity whore." He shakes his head, eyes filled with loathing. "Over worked and underappreciated. I won't be treated like this. No way."

Chapter 144

Tel Aviv, Israel

The market bustles with activity. Shoppers push their way through the afternoon crowd as Sophie navigates, her child propped on her hip. *Perhaps I should find someone to take care of Sarah and work more hours until the baby comes,* Sophie thinks while she walks the rows of trinkets at the bazaar. Her little girl points at the colorful items and squeals in delight. *If tomorrow wasn't Sarah's birthday I wouldn't have come,* she thinks. A sudden wave of nausea hits and she holds a hand to her face trying to ward off the pungent smells of food and people.

"Mommy, look!" Sarah shouts pointing to a beautiful doll with copper colored hair and bright green glass eyes. Her clothes are made of pure lace and she carries a handbag to match. "Pretty."

Sophie approaches the stand and lays a hand on the doll. "Thirty shekels." The old man says pointing to it with a crooked finger. "She is high quality, madame." The vendor brings his wrinkled face close to Sarah. "This would be the perfect dolly for you, as pretty as you are sweet child." Sarah turns away and presses her face into her mother's shoulder. Sophie digs into her purse counting money, fifteen shekels, and that would have to buy another two days worth of food as well.

"I'm sorry, sir, I simply do not have enough."

"How much do you have?"

"Ten." She replies in a soft voice.

The man tisks and shakes his head. "I'm sorry, madame, that is simply too low."

"But, mommy, I want her." Sarah cries as tears flood her eyes. "You said I could have a dolly for my birthday."

Sophie moves away from the cart brimming with toys and sits down on a bench with Sarah in her lap. "Sweetheart, Mommy doesn't have the money to get you that doll." She says with a lump in her throat. "There must be another one you like."

"I like that one." The girl replies, sniffling. "Why can't you go to the bank, mommy? Isn't that where they keep the money?"

Sophie suddenly wells up with emotion and looks away, the guilt and shame unbearable. "I cannot my darling. Please, pick something else."

Sarah shakes her head petulantly, defiance etched on her tiny face. Sophie picks up the child and briskly makes her way out of the marketplace, cheeks wet and heart aching. I *will not allow my children to go without,* she thinks to herself. Shaking, she buckles Sarah into the car seat of the Vespa and hops on. *No matter what I have to do, I will give my child what she needs,* she thinks as she speeds away.

Chapter 145

There was a crowd chanting my name this morning outside the balcony at Abaddon's. Not a bad way to wake up, even though my head hurt from too much whiskey and playing the Troubadour last night. I'm getting a taste for the hard stuff again... it dulls the pain a little. Keeps the haze on.

I stood outside and watched them. There were about twenty or so. It made me feel powerful. Electric. I think I could get used to this fame thing after all.

Chapter 146

City of Angels

Montbard glances up from his morning espresso to find Mr. Stuart taking the seat opposite him at the Peninsula Hotel. "Surely we cannot keep meeting this way, Mr. Stuart. Another coincidence?" He says, a frown on his thin face.

Stuart drops the accent and speaks in hushed tones. "I need to talk to you in private, I'll explain everything. We're on the same crusade, we don't have a moment to waste."

Stuart walks toward the elevator with long strides, glancing around the lobby for watchful eyes. Montbard hesitates a moment then follows. "This is cryptic talk, Stuart." Montbard whispers, having caught up to him.

"My name isn't Stuart, it's Berg. I'm a Jew and I don't live in Jamaica or Scotland. I was born and raised in Jerusalem."

The elevator doors close behind them. "What is the meaning of all this?" Montbard demands as he presses the sixth floor button with an unsteady hand.

"I lied to infiltrate the O.R.G. I knew they would never let in a Jew so I took over Randolph Stuart's lineage. His father had belonged to the O.R.G. and passed the membership on but young Randy drank himself into an early grave. The mother resented the secrecy of the 'boys club' as she called it and was more than willing to lend me her son's identity so that I could infiltrate the group." He clears his throat. The elevator doors slide open and the two step out. "It was quite easy really."

"But, why?" Montbard asks, his expression somber.

"Open the door and you'll find out." Berg replies and motions towards room number 603.

"So you have been following me I presume?" Montbard slams the door behind him.

Berg settles onto the sofa in the sitting area of the suite and pours himself some water from a bottle on the coffee table. He takes a drink and studies Montbard. "Are you or are you not Andre Montbard the direct descendant of Saint Bernard Chairvaux born in 1090, nephew of a member of the Knights Templar?"

Montbard's expression shifts suddenly, alarm etched across his handsome face. "Who told you that?"

Berg lowers his voice to barely above a whisper. "No one told me. My father wrote me about you when I was just a boy. Both of our families were the original builders of the temple." Montbard slides into a chair as the man sitting opposite him continues. "And, of course, I presume you know what temple I'm speaking of."

"Yes, I do." Montbard replies, clearly shaken. "The Holy Temple of Solomon." He locks eyes with the man in front of him. "Hello, brother."

Chapter 147

Rockefeller Archeological Museum, Jerusalem

Arms held tight at his side, David walks down a long limestone corridor, his excitement apparent in every step. The arches above the doorways lend an air of drama and mystique to the quiet building. He reaches a door marked "Curator" and taps lightly.

A gentle voice replies, "Come in."

As David enters he sees a man seated at a polished wood desk. He looks to be in his early fifties and wears a beautifully cut Neru suit, his silver hair groomed to perfection.

"David Ashkenzari, I presume?" he asks, a slight lilt in his perfect English.

"Yes. Thank you for seeing me on such short notice."

"It's no problem. I was an acquaintance of your father's years back. He was a great man, I'm sorry for your loss." He tilts his head in a slight bow. "Now what can I do for you today?"

David takes a seat in the plush suede chair opposite the curator and fidgets nervously. "I'm not quite sure sir but I'm hoping you could tell me some details about the ossuaries that were brought here in the 1980's."

The curator smiles. "Of course, there is much speculation surrounding those tombs. What is it you would like to know?"

"Firstly, do you believe them to be authentic?"

The older man lifts an elegant shoulder. "I have no reason to doubt their authenticity."

"Even the one marked 'Yeshua'?"

The curator smiles. "Especially the one marked 'Yeshua.' You see I was a privileged member of the team assigned to test the DNA of the bones inside."

David's body hums with excitement. "And what may I ask did you find?"

The curator smiles. "Nothing terribly conclusive other than the man and woman whose tombs were marked Yeshua and Miriamine were not related by blood."

"Which means?"

"Well surely you know who Miriamine E Mara is don't you?"

"No, sir, I don't." David replies, shaking his head in confusion.

The curator folds his hands one on top of the other and states simply. "She is none other... than Mary Magdalene."

Chapter 148

Journal Entry, May 13th

I wonder if this is love. Is love supposed to make you hurt so much inside that you want to rip the heart out of your chest? That's how I feel when I see him now. I feel like I'm losing him. Everyday, little by little, it seems like he's slipping away but I still feel like I'm connected to him somehow. Connected in a way that nothing can change.

Like he's part of my destiny.

Chapter 149

City of Angels

"So really, Jewish mysticism is not all that different from Christianity or Buddhism or most other religions. Yes, I suppose we have some rituals that could be considered 'pagan' but then again what isn't pagan about communion? The blood and the body of Christ? I mean, really." Berg says as he and Montbard eat at the hotel restaurant, the room sparsely filled with other diners. "Kabbalah has been passed down for generations. Only recently has it come into the spotlight."

"I never realized Kaballists were Masons." Montbard replies in a hushed tone. "Though I do remember my father having friends to the house several times who wore the traditional yarmulke. They would lock themselves in his study for hours and they carried garment bags. I always wondered what was inside them.

"Most likely robes and ritual offerings. The B'nai B'rin has many secret customs that are part of our heritage. But as you know, just because something is kept secret doesn't make it sinister."

Montbard glances at the gold ring on Berg's hand. "The Seal of Solomon. I can't say I remember you wearing this at the meetings."

Berg chuckles. "Yes. I can just imagine the ruckus that would've caused. A member of the O.R.G. wearing a known Semitic symbol."

Montbard sits back and raises his brows, disturbed. "I didn't realize."

"There are certain unwritten rules of that particular brotherhood. Especially with Rogerson running the show. So I played along and took on the identity of the Scottish aristocrat. Easy enough." Berg studies his ring. "The symbols were taken from alchemy, did you know that?" Montbard sits mesmerized by the ring and all it represents. "Fire being the upward triangle and water being the downward triangle. And from those two the symbols are naturally created. The downward triangle if divided along the center creates earth and the same division of the upward one to create air."

"So Solomon's symbol is the perfect balance."

"Exactly." Berg replies, a gleam in his eye. "When Michael and I were in Ethiopia we discovered that the Ark had been stolen. That's when I knew that all three of us needed to work together to reclaim it. To battle whoever would be so bold as to have taken it." The two glance at each another, an unspoken understanding between them. "We must leave tomorrow to find the Ark, Montbard. We are running out of time and we must convince our third member to join forces with us."

Montbard glances up from the gold ring that glitters in the candlelight. "I am ready, my brother."

Chapter 150

Bethany, Israel

Hunched over his desk David studies several open books. *So Mary Magdalene and Jesus had a son according to the inscription on the ossuaries. That son was called Judah. It boggles the mind to think of such connections and that the Bible as we know it could be so far from the truth. Yet everything seems to be pointing to this child. Looking at the scrolls through the persharim theory, one sees that clearly there was a marriage between the two and a child born of that union. How would father have felt about this? Or did he already know?*

David brushes errant strands of hair from his face. *Did not the gospel of Philip say 'There are three who always walked with the Lord: Mary his mother, Mary's sister, and Magdalene, the one who was called his companion. And in the New Testament there is reference to a Mary of Bethany, Bethany used as a synonym for the poor, anointing the feet of Jesus and wiping them clean with her hair—a distinct reference to the Song of Solomon and the wedding rituals in that time. It only makes sense that he would take a wife in the custom of that era.*

David stands, pacing the room in long strides. He thinks to himself, shaken. *Am I merely seeing Jesus for the man that he was, in human form, imperfect and with carnal needs? He was after all, according to Christianity, supposed to be God, taken the life and form of man. Is not and was not finding love and marriage one of man's true delights?*

He stops and thinks of Sophie and the child growing inside her. He opens the door and walks to their bedroom where she lays sleeping, her face carefree. He takes her in and feels a heavy weight on his chest. *She looks so unlike this these days when awake. She has a look of worry and sadness. I have to take care of that as soon as I find these answers. My dear sweet Sophie, please don't give up on me. I'm close. I can feel it.*

Chapter 151

I woke from a dream that shook my core. I dreamt I was in a small pool of water. There was a man holding me. My body lay on his arm as he poured water onto my head. Something about it made me feel like it was a long time ago. I feel strange, like my body is not attached to my soul, like I am looking down on it from above. The leaves on the trees seem to dance for me and when I touch them they grow. I don't know what's happening. I'm scared to tell anyone and Mara doesn't seem to want anything to do with me anymore. Alone. Crazy. Who will understand?

Chapter 152

Jerusalem, Israel

Light pours onto an open leather bound bible as David reads at a sidewalk café, his face intense. Montbard, in dark glasses and hat, sits at another cafe across the street pretending to be absorbed in a copy of the Ha'aretz newspaper and Stuart sits at the table next to David's, watching his every move.

So, Lucifer was the angel of music in charge of the ministry of music before his fall from grace. Interesting. I don't know how it fits with the Tree of Jesse but I do remember father saying that Jesus sang the Psalms. And really Psalms are just poetry put to music aren't they? Is the connection to the sprout of the Tree of Jesse attached to music? Or is the connection that the Devil is still the minister of music as he was before he fell?

Many depictions of the Tree of Jesse show him reclined and dreaming as the roots sprout from him and angels play the harp on a branch nearby. Could it be that the One is telling us the tale of the Messianic age through song?

David wipes his hand across his weary face and takes a drink from the small bottle of Coca-Cola in front of him. *Also Abraham and Moses played horns on either side of the Christ child in the twelfth century illumination of the Jesse Tree. Music seems to surround him in most depictions but what could that have to do with a modern day? And will Lucifer try to tempt the new Messiah into using his powers for selfish gain as was recounted in the scriptures by Mark? So many questions I don't have answers to. How will I ever find him?"*

Berg interrupts David. "Excuse me, sir. Do you happen to know where I can find the house of Rabbi Ashkenzari? I'm here to pay my respects to the family."

David glances at the man confused. "I'm the Rabbi's son. What a strange coincidence."

"I don't believe in coincidences, young man. Only destiny." Berg smiles and holds out his hand. "I'm Isaac Berg. I'm sorry about your father, he was a great man."

"Did you know him well?"

Berg shakes his head in reply. "Actually, I didn't know him at all but I've heard a great many things about him." He lowers his voice to a whisper. "Most interestingly I heard that he may have held the key to the location of the Ark of the Covenant."

David's eyes suddenly go wide and he's momentarily lost for words. Berg leans into him. "David. Trust me. Please go with faith. You must help me, we're on the same quest." The older man's expression softens. "Did your father leave anything behind? Any clue to the information he held?"

David searches Berg's face, unsure of whether to answer. "Yes. Yes he did. In his last weeks alive he insisted on making a testimony. My brother videotaped it but said he didn't finish and that the information was unclear. Father's memory was fading for some time and apparently he couldn't always keep track of things during the taping. I haven't had the heart to watch it."

Berg leans in placing his hand on David's. "I understand the loss of a father. It is profound."

"I thought I was prepared. But it still overwhelmed me."

"We can never truly prepare for the parting of a loved one. But rest assured that your father is in a better place. I worry we will all want to get away from this world we live in."

"I understand the sentiment. I have a child and another on the way and worry for their future."

"I worry for the future of mankind." Berg replies, his expression grave. "I need to watch the videos."

David grimaces. "Why? I don't understand."

Berg whispers, "I am a direct descendant of Solomon and it is my duty to rebuild the temple so that the Messianic age may begin. It sounds mad, I know, but I believe your father may have had detailed information about the Messianic age and the location of the true Ark. It's upon us and we must find the Ark so that the prophecy can be fulfilled." Stuart pauses and locks eyes with David. "Do you believe me?"

David studies the man opposite him for a moment, his jaw set, a thrill rippling through him. "Yes. Yes I do."

Berg stands and drops money onto both of their tables. "Then we must hurry, there's very little time. I have a car waiting."

Chapter 153

Tel Aviv, Israel

An arched wooden door opens a crack after Sophie raps it lightly. The old woman inside peers over bifocals perched on the end of her nose. "Hello. You're a pretty one. Come inside." She opens the door further revealing a dim room with an old fashioned wood burning stove and a multitude of herbs hung to dry on clothes lines.

Sophie looks around, nervous. "I have heard you help women who are... in trouble."

"If by 'in trouble' you mean I help get rid of unwanted babies you are correct." The woman says with a slight bow of her head. Wiry gray curls fall forward onto her face. "But I don't want to dance around the subject. You must know exactly what you are doing and the consequences. It is not my decision to make and I am certainly not here to judge you. Nor am I here to counsel, only to provide a service for a small fee."

"Yes, I have money. I will pay." Sophie pulls a small wad of bills from her purse. The last remnants of her savings, tucked away for a rainy day.

The woman studies Sophie's grief stricken face. "All right my dear, we will get to that soon, but for now why don't you sit and tell me the true reason behind your visit."

"I thought you were not interested in counseling?" Sophie replies with a raised brow.

"I'm not, but I can see when someone is in distress. I'm not made of stone." The woman glances at Sophie's finger. "And I can also see that you're married which makes me wonder why you would be visiting me today."

Sophie slumps down in a nearby chair and places a hand to her forehead. "My husband has not had work in many months and since I have become pregnant he has asked me to quit my job. As it is I work part time and with my three year old it's challenging."

"Have you tried talking to him?"

Sophie nods. "I have. But his father died recently and ever since then he has been very secretive and reclusive."

"Secretive usually means one thing." She says and clucks her tongue. Sophie gives her a bewildered look. "Have you ever thought that maybe your husband has another woman?"

"Another woman?" Sophie gasps and shakes her head. "No no. Impossible. He is not that kind of man, my David."

The old woman shrugs, a smirk on her wrinkled face. "All right, whatever you say. I will mix the herbs and mind my own business, it will only be a moment." She says and heads to an adjoining room filled with glass bottles of varying sizes.

Surely she's mistaken, Sophie thinks. *Of course she is. Crazy old woman.* She shakes the ugly thought from her head but as she catches her reflection in the mirror she sees a frightened woman. A woman whose life may be changed forever.

Chapter 154

Journal Entry, May 17th

I walked by a newsstand yesterday and there was Jesse's face staring back at me larger than life on the cover of *Rolling Stone*. The title said, "The Prophet, Who Is He?" I bought the magazine out of curiosity. It was mainly a fluff piece about Jesse coming onto the scene and how he's caught on so quickly with hardcore fans. Not so much an interview. The writer seemed to think he was using religion and preaching as a gimmick to lure people in. No one seems to really get it. He's the real deal. And even though he's acting like a jerk right now I know deep inside he's still the man that laid on my bed, his amber eyes full of pain, wanting to cure the world. I miss him so much it feels like part of my soul is gone. Like it was cut out and the wound left open to the elements.

I feel like I'm rotting inside.

Chapter 155

Tel Aviv, Israel

The three men enter a dark hotel room. Its windows face a brick wall, choking out the light. "This is quite a city," Montbard says. "It even costs extra to have sunlight in your room."

"Mr. Berg, do you live in Israel?" David asks.

Berg nods his head. "Yes, I live in Jerusalem, it's there that I feel my connection to the soil, my ancestors." He motions to the small loveseat. "David, please, have a seat."

Montbard sits at the edge of the bed; "I am very pleased to see you again David. I'm assuming you remember me?"

David nods his head. "Yes. Without the dark glasses I knew you right away."

"Did you find your clue that day?"

"Yes. Yes I did. It was the Tree of Jesse."

Montbard smiles, delighted. "Of course, that makes perfect sense." He lowers his voice and leans forward. "Did it bring you closer to finding him?"

"How do you know that he has returned? Who are you people?" David asks bewildered.

Berg smiles reassuringly. "We know a great many things David, as do you. I'm hoping if we join forces we can accomplish our mutual destiny." He says as he produces the gold pentagram ring from his breast pocket and holds it under the glow of the lamp.

Chapter 156

Sweet Water, Texas

Rogerson paces the floor of his den, drink in hand, as the telephone rings. "Shut up!" He drains the tumbler and slams the glass on the desk. "Stop calling me, I don't have anything new!" He pulls a pill bottle from the desk drawer and spills the contents onto the desktop. He takes two and swallows them dry as the answering machine clicks on. "Mr. Rogerson this is Ms. Kung's secretary, I am sure you know what this is regarding. The members have been waiting and they will not wait much longer before taking action. Please get in contact with us, we have been very patient."

Rogerson stands and goes to the window, peeking around the drawn curtains. "They're coming to get me. What the hell do I do now? Jibril, where are you?" He mumbles as he makes his way to the safe. Inside lays the ornate wood box and stacks of photographs. He pulls one out from beneath all the others.

"My only hope now is that the Wormwood will come." He says staring at the picture in his trembling hand.

Chapter 157

Tel Aviv, Israel

The street bustles with shoppers. Sophie winds through the Hacarmel market, tears brimming her dark lashes. *How can I even think of such a thing? What is happening to us?* She thinks and pushes her way through the aggressive market goers. As she crosses the road she spots David leaving the Hotel Montefiore, his jacket pulled up to hide his face. But there is no mistaking; she would know his walk anywhere. *What is he doing leaving a hotel in the middle of the day? Who does he know that would be staying in such a fancy place?* She remembers the old woman's words and temper flushes her cheeks. *No. I should not be foolish. David is a good man. He would never betray me.* She reassures herself as she watches the only man she has ever loved shuffle down the busy street and into an alley.

Chapter 158

David strides down a deserted side street headed for the bus stop, his thoughts racing. *Surely if father left behind a journal or any other clues I would know.*

He crosses the market weaving through the shoppers. *Could they be right? Could there be a group that wants to circumvent the Messianic age? And if so are there dark forces at work aiding them or is it merely greed that guides them?*

He picks up his pace, suddenly sure he is on to something. *In the book of Daniel it is said that the Messiah "would be cut off," alluding to his death. But who could do such a thing? Surely it would have to be one with unearthly powers...*

Chapter 159

Vatican City, Rome

Pope Benedict XVI finishes reading the letter aloud to a younger bishop. The flowing sleeves of his green robe drape, revealing his pale fragile arms. "I anxiously await your assistance. Your humble servant, Augustus." The pope removes his spectacles and sets the letter on a large bureau, hand carved in rich mahogany. "Now do you see why I've alerted you, Dimitri?"

The younger man nods and bows his head. "No disrespect sir, but it seems he's gone a bit mad."

"Ah, yes. That's one interpretation. One that I would expect from someone so young." The older man pulls a long cigarette from a sterling silver case etched with two angels playing the harp on opposite ends of a sphere with an octagon above it. "I, my son, have seen too much in my lifetime to dismiss this as mere madness. I also have performed an exorcism or two in my day and it does definitely leave one with a sense of connection to the dark side. A very uncomfortable connection." He inhales deeply, relishing every moment of the Italian cigarette.

"But surely you don't believe that the Messiah has arrived and that the devil is here on earth to kill him?"

"Why not?" The pope replies with a shrug and exhales smoke through his nostrils. "But then again it could all be nonsense and our poor Augustus could be completely out of his mind. Either way, I would like for you to find out. The jet will take you to Los Angeles tonight, please make your arrangements." Finished with the discussion, the pope turns away from Dimitri to glance out of the crimson draped window, lost in thought.

"Yes, of course, Your Holiness. You can count on me."

Chapter 160

Dante's Peak, Death Valley

Near the top of the mountain the desert wind blows wild, ripping at two men as they make their ascent. The one in front carries a walking stick and moves boldly forward while the other hunches several steps behind. "I told you, it's better than sex!" Abaddon shouts to Jesse who struggles the last twenty feet to the view site at the top of the mountain. He takes a breath and fills his lungs. "We're more than a mile high." Jesse collapses onto the dense compacted dirt gasping for breath as Abaddon stands with his hands perched on his waist scanning the terrain. "You know Stan Jones wrote *Rider's in the Sky* while he worked here as a tour guide? That's a wicked good tune."

Jesse lays looking up at the clear blue sky. "I never want to have this much exercise again in my life." The sporadic clouds look like pure white cotton and the air, though thin, has a crisp, clean texture.

Abaddon laughs. He stands at the edge of the peak looking down onto the ocean mirage that consists only of solid halite salt. "You know why it's called Dante's Peak?" He asks, as he circles the perimeter of the Cliffside shaking his walking stick. Jesse lays silent. "It was an homage of sorts to the *Divine Comedy*. You know it?" Jesse lights a cigarette and listens, wordless. "It's a poem really, one man's view of the afterlife in three parts. *The Inferno, Purgatario* and of course *Paradiso*. Paradise. It starts in the year 1300 when Dante was... oh, around your age I guess. He felt he was halfway along life's path and he was, as he says, 'lost in a dark wood' and unable to find the straight way, the 'dirrita via'. Inside he knows he is falling into a deep place, where 'il sol tace'. Where the sun is silent, the underworld." Abaddon turns to look at Jesse, now sitting, lit cigarette in hand. "Am I boring you?"

"Keep going. I'm interested," He replies and watches Abaddon stroke the top of his walking stick shaped in the head of a serpent.

"Well, once Dante escaped the depths of hell he found his way to an island where he claims the mountain of purgatory stands buried under Jerusalem. But I'm thinking maybe good ol' Dante practiced the peace pipe if you know what I mean." He gestures with his thumb and forefinger. "Anyway, the mountain has seven terraces, like the seven deadly sins and interestingly enough the description perfectly matches this place here."

"I think I've lived the inferno already. Maybe I'm in purgatory now..."

"No no, you *were* my man. Like Dante said in *Purgatorio*, 'To tell you who I am were speech in vain, because my name as yet makes no great noise.' But that's all changed now, don't you see? You're a god to them Jesse. And with everyday that passes your power grows. You can have paradise on earth my friend; you can have everything you want and more. Women, money, power, women. Hah! You could probably get away with murder."

Jesse stubs his cigarette into the ground and thinks to himself that maybe for the first time in his life he could feel like he was important, like he was worth something. "So what's paradise like according to Dante?"

"Fuck Dante. "Abaddon says with a smile. "We'll make our own paradise. Dante's version was boring."

Chapter 161

Sweet Water, Texas

Montbard strolls by a fountain near the entrance of Rogerson's palatial estate. He looks up at the ornate pillars and arches indicative of newly acquired wealth and shakes his head. *Who is this Rogerson and how did he ever get into the O.R.G. much less end up running it,* he thinks. He turns once and glances towards his car where Berg sits crouched in the backseat. He scans the building and the grounds for video cameras and, finding none, he presses a button on the phone inside his pocket to signal Berg before ringing the doorbell.

Rogerson answers in a pair of silk pajamas, drink in hand, looking as if he hasn't slept in days. "What the devil are you doing here, Montbard? Did Kung send you?" He peers over Montbard's shoulder and onto the grounds.

"No, not at all. I haven't spoken to her in some time. Don't you remember inviting me anytime I was in 'your neck of the woods' as you called it?" Montbard replies with a jovial smile.

Rogerson, distracted, waves his hand in the air absently. "Okay, whatever. Well, you're here now, come on in." He leaves the door open and pads barefoot down the dark hallway towards the solarium. "We'll sit in here. Pardon the mess. My houseman up and left me." He says with a dry chuckle, a pained expression on his face.

"No problem." Montbard sinks into an over-stuffed gold leaf chair. "Lovely home."

"Thanks. Now if you don't mind I'm not much in the mood for chit chat so..."

"Are you alone then?" The Frenchman glances at the wall of glass opposite him that looks into the backyard.

Rogerson downs the rest of his whiskey. "Very much so."

"Well I decided to come see you in private because I believe an imposter may have infiltrated The Organization. Someone with an agenda much different than yours and mine."

"Well I'll be Goddamned." Rogerson says, his words slightly slurred. "Somebody told me that recently but I didn't pay much attention." A creaking door echoes down the long hallway. "What was that?" The fat man's eyes are wide with alarm.

"Just the wind I'm sure." Montbard replies, his face revealing nothing.

Rogerson shakes his head as if to clear it. "Would you like a drink?" Before Montbard can answer he stands and makes his way to a rolling cart filled with crystal decanters.

Montbard glances at his watch. It's not quite noon. "Ahh, no. Thank you."

"So tell me more of what you know." He says and pours himself a generous helping of whiskey. He takes a long drink and closes his eyes for a moment.

Montbard, discretely searches his pocket for his cell phone. "Well, I believe it is someone who is using us to get information to find the One."

"And?" Rogerson shakes the glass, rattling the cubes, and takes another drink.

Montbard's cell phone chimes. He pulls it from his pocket. "Oh my. It completely slipped my mind, I had arranged for a luncheon in town. My secretary programs all my appointments into this handy little thing." He says holding up his Blackberry.

Rogerson glares in annoyance. "Well you can't drop a bomb like that and just take off."

Montbard stands and backs towards the door. "There really isn't any more to tell. I have a suspicion, that's all, I was hoping you would look into the matter." He says as he makes his way towards the corridor.

Rogerson follows him out and slams the door. *Annoying Frog,* he thinks and downs the rest of the drink. He frowns and makes his way back to the beverage cart, his bare feet slapping the cold marble floor. Suddenly a figure slips out from behind the curtain and places a thin metal wire across Rogerson's fleshy neck.

"What in—" Rogerson gasps.

"Time's up." The figure breathes into his ear, then tightens the cord around the fat man's throat snuffing out all signs of life.

Chapter 162

I'm drinking too much. I try to hide it but I can see Mara's disappointment, it's written all over her beautiful face. The face that haunts my dreams.

There are so many fans now. Nameless. Faceless. People seem to be coming out of the woodwork for interviews. I can't say that I mind seeing my face in magazines. I'm getting used to this game and learning how to play it. Well.

But I don't feel like me anymore. I'm starting to feel like an imposter. Like someone is inside my head.

Chapter 163

Bethany, Israel

Sophie pulls the glass vial filled with herbs from her messenger bag. She studies it and thinks of David, remembering how excited he used to be about their future —all the plans they made the night he proposed. Remembering fireflies darting in the cool breeze as they sat on a thin blanket thrown across the dirt floor of Zedekiah's cave, where David said he came to seek solace.

She has such clear memories of that night, as if it were yesterday. He put a ring on her finger, the light in his eyes so bright. "I will always take care of you, Sophie. I want you to be the mother of our children. I want to build a life with you." He had said, his smile boyish and still a little unsure. They had made so many plans that night. The passion they shared exhilarating. But David's lack of success whittled away at that passion over time and stripped him of the excitement and anticipation he used to wake with everyday. In the beginning just listening to him talk about the old world and his writing made her feel so alive. Hopeful. Now the only thing that seems to bring hope into their home is Sarah and the prospect of the new baby. But even they come with a deep fear. A dread that money will only get tighter and that they will never find their way out from under this rock that seems to be pinning them down. *We have been blessed with a child at the wrong time,* she thinks and rubs her belly, still flat and trim. *David does not need the extra strain. There's obviously something bothering him since his father died, something he is burdened with. I only hope God will see fit to bless us again someday.* She looks at the bottle and shudders.

"Mamma?" Sarah cries from her crib and jerks Sophie back to reality. She tucks the bottle back into her bag. "I'm coming darling, mommy's coming."

Chapter 164

City of Angels

Dimitri pulls open a rusted gate. He steps through and slams it shut behind him with a bang. He studies the primitive sketch again. *The west side of 6th and Main Street,* he thinks to himself. *This should be it.* Shoulders hunched forward he makes his way down the dim alleyway, not a speck of sunshine to be found, until he reaches a dumpster. It's propped away from the wall creating a shoulder width opening behind it. Dimitri crouches, straining to see into the recess.

He hears a groan.

He pushes the metal bin aside, and finds the crumpled body of a man wheezing and gasping for breath. "Bishop Augustus! Dear God what has happened to you?"

Augustus looks up, his eyes blurred, "Who's there?"

"It's Father Dimitri, sir, the pope has sent me to help you." He shakes his head in disbelief. "We had no idea it had come to this. We must take you to hospital immediately, come with me." He demands holding out his hand.

Augustus's body jerks with a violent cough. "I have slept outside for many days." Delirious with hunger he holds out a withered hand. "Do you have anything to eat?"

Dimitri looks down on the pitiful man, eyes filled with concern. "I will get you something immediately. Wait here." He says and walks briskly toward the metal gates. *I remember a market around the corner, he thinks. Maybe there I can get him some sustenance until we reach the hospital. My God, what's happened to the man? He truly has gone mad, it's as I thought all along.* He gets a sudden rush of emotion.

Or maybe... is it possible, he could be right?

Chapter 165

City of Angels

Mara exits Abaddon's house through the back garden, filled with fruit trees and luscious patches of shade. Frustrated from another exchange with the infuriating man she ruminates on the conversation. She walks around the apple tree, brushing its trunk with her fingertips as she replays the conversation in her mind. Jesse stands watching her. They graze shoulders but she barely acknowledges him, lost in thought. "What's your problem?" Jesse asks, the smell of whiskey on his breath.

She stares back at him, suddenly aware that she's not alone. "What's my problem? I don't even know who you are anymore."

"Don't give me soap opera speak, Mar, you've been acting like this for weeks."

"Oh, I didn't think you even knew I existed anymore. And I'm serious about not knowing you. I don't recognize the person you're becoming, Jess. You used to be so good... so feeling. Now there isn't enough space in the room for your ego. What's happening to you?"

He lights a cigarette with a shaky hand. "Well, you said I was special right? Well this is what special acts like."

"You smell like shit."

Jesse laughs, his voice cracking. "Yeah, well this is what special smells like too."

She brushes past him. "I can't even talk to you, you're drunk."

He grabs her arm violently. "Hey, don't walk away from me. You're supposed to be my guardian angel."

Mara searches his face, softening. "What does that mean, Jess?"

"It means... I don't know what it means." He releases her arm. "Go if you want to."

She looks at the fresh red marks on her wrist. "I used to think you were some sort of angel too, that you were somehow different and now... Now I don't know what you are." She says, her voice barely above a whisper. She turns, her body suddenly weak, and walks through Abaddon's garden gate without looking back.

Chapter 166

Abaddon pours scotch into two crystal glasses from an etched decanter. "Screw her, man. Or maybe you shouldn't screw her. You'd be a goner." He smirks. Jesse sits studying the veins on his hands. "Come on, she's just a woman. There are millions of them, billions even."

"You don't get it, she's just... "

""What, special?" Abaddon shakes his head.

"She's like... an angel."

Abaddon rolls his eyes. "I never did go for the angelic type. Bo-ring." He says with a wicked smile. "You're like a god, Jesse, you could have anyone."

Jesse pulls a Marlboro from a crumpled pack. "You're not too bad for the old ego you know that."

Abaddon's voice is cold and flat. "Listen, man, you've got power. You know that and I know that, no reason to kid each other here."

"What do you mean power?" He asks fiddling with the unlit cigarette.

Abaddon sits back in the leather chair and glances around the den. His well-soled shoe taps a rhythm on the floor. "Let's not play games, man. I know. We don't have to talk about it if you don't want to, but just know... that I know."

Jesse releases an uncomfortable laugh. "You're talking in riddles."

"Suit yourself." Mandy takes a generous drink of the imported liquor and settles deeper into his chair, his face still as stone.

Chapter 167

Dallas, Texas

Berg paces the plush carpet of the Ritz. "What I don't understand is if Rogerson didn't have the scrolls then who does and what are they planning on doing with them?"

Montbard shrugs and ashes his cigarette, "I am wondering this myself. Maybe David will find something. And hopefully he will be able to determine the significance of the picture of the star you found inside the safe. I can't see the connection." He glances out the window at the view of downtown Dallas; the lights of the buildings still illuminate the upper floors. "American's work into the night." He says distracted.

Berg glances at him then follows his gaze. "Yes. Capitalism. It takes the place of everything I suppose." They study the tall buildings. "I hope it's worth it." Berg replies then sits at the desk and buries his head in his hands. "I should have taken the stone, it's our only connection to the Ark. And now with Rogerson dead who knows who has it." He glances at the front page of the newspaper article about the oil tycoon's death, a picture of the empty safe below the headline suggesting a robbery gone awry.

"Don't be foolish. He would have known I was involved, and how could we have anticipated that he would be killed? Thank goodness you wore a mask since whoever killed Rogerson was most likely in the house at the same time as the both of us." Montbard puts the cigarette to his lips, "I received a call about an emergency meeting of the O.R.G. in New York tomorrow, we need to be there. I think they want to elect a new leader. I'm sure it will be Madame Kung after her boldness in confronting Rogerson. She is a strong woman, not to be underestimated."

Berg, still deep in thought, responds with a blank stare. "What if the stone has powers as the Rabbi eluded to in the video? What if whoever has the stone uses it before we can stop them?" Berg says, his face twisted in grief.

"I suppose that is what they plan. Why else would they have gone to such lengths to steal it? My head is swimming, could the Rabbi's claim that the Ark's location is coded into the Book of Revelation also be correct? He seemed to know about Axium. And if what he said is true how did Rogerson get his fat fingers on the contents of the Ark in the first place?" Montbard studies his companion's pained and gaunt face, the result of the several days efforts. "I admire your devotion to the cause, I have never seen you this upset in the time we've been acquainted."

"It is my destiny and the destiny of my ancestors before me I must fulfill. My father sat me on his knee when I was ten and told me of the prophecy, about how our elders had built the temple with their bare hands."

"We will fulfill it. Nothing will stop us, even if we have to pay with our lives." Montbard states, then in a low voice barely above a whisper, "I never really had a family, not in the way that you describe. It was more like a business arrangement."

Berg turns to face Montbard, his heart heavy. "I am your family now, till death do us part, brother."

Chapter 168

There was a woman in my dressing room tonight. Abaddon must've let her in. She had long black hair that hung like silk and her lips were the color of ripe cherries. She undressed and touched her body with her pretty, skillful hands. I just stood there as she moved, her hips writhing to the pulse of my music, playing in the background. She said that it made her excited, to hear me and see me at the same time. I thought of Mara afterwards but not during. I could only think of Dante while the woman danced in front of me and smiled with her large porcelain teeth.

I feel like I'm sliding, like something dark is taking a hold but, God forgive me, I like how the people respond to me. How they treat me like I'm somebody. Like I'm important. I don't want to go back to being invisible.

Is there a way to be "somebody" without feeling like you've sold your soul to the Devil?

Chapter 169

City of Angels

Jude blocks Jesse on his way outside the latest venue, an after hours party in full swing in the courtyard behind them. "What the fuck was all that showboating tonight?" Jude asks, flaming with anger. "You change songs mid way and smash up a guitar? What is this, glam rock?"

Jesse shrugs. "I was in the moment." He replies and pulls a fresh cigarette from the pack in his back pocket. "I gave them what they wanted, didn't I? They wanted a show they got one."

"You're your own biggest fan these days aren't you, man?" He says bumping Jesse's shoulder as he brushes past.

"Watch yourself."

Jude turns. "No you watch *yourself*. I'm sick of your shit, man."

Jesse takes a drag from his smoke and replies without turning, "You can be replaced. Remember that. I'm the one they come to see." He steps down and onto the stone patio and is quickly flocked with fans leaving Jude standing in the reflection of an overhead lantern, eyes full of wrath.

"I have an announcement to make, everyone!" Abaddon shouts over the crowd, champagne glass in hand. "Come on, settle down. Listen up." He says as he climbs onto a stone table preparing to hold court, his smile gleaming in the moonlight. "Seems our band here is quite a sensation." Cheers all around. "I just got word that we will be playing Madison Square Garden in two days to replace the headliner. Seems somebody up and died and left an open slot." He snickers, "Their loss our gain." He locks eyes with Jesse and raises his glass. "To the Prophet, may he live long and prosper."

Chapter 170

Bethany, Israel

David reads aloud from the open Bible. "Revelation 8:10-11 And the third angel sounded, and there fell a great star from heaven, burning as if it were a lamp, and it fell upon the rivers, and upon the fountains of waters; And the name of the star is called Wormwood: and many men have died of the waters, because they were made bitter."

The Wormwood prophecy. Of course. It's been interpreted in so many ways but surely it's the most powerful star second only to the Star of Bethlehem, which many believe to be symbolic of Christ. He scratches the three days growth on his face. *But how is Wormwood connected to the Messianic age? And which meaning should I interpret? If taken literally it means that a comet would crash to earth and poison the bodies of water. So no one dies from the impact but only the "bitter waters." And what causes bitterness? Evil I suppose. And what other bible verses are connected to bitterness?* He flips through already knowing his destination.

Of course. Luke 10:18, "And He said unto them, I beheld Satan as lightning, fall from heaven." Often times angels were referred to as stars and Lucifer was an angel and the most bitter star of all. Could it be that that the One is somehow going to be affected by Satan? Will he try to tempt the Messiah in some way? He studies the frayed edge of the holy book and a feeling of profound dread washes over him.

Or is his plot even more sinister... He breathes deep and flips back to the Book of Revelation, to Christ's own words dictated by the Prophet John. *"Revelation 16:4 And the third angel poured out his vial upon the rivers and fountains of water and they became blood."*

David looks up from the page, grief lining his face. *Could this blood he speaks of be the blood of the One? If so does it mean that Lucifer is here on earth to shed his blood and circumvent the Messianic age?*

He picks up the phone quickly and dials. "I think I've found something. I think there's a connection with Lucifer. I believe he has returned to earth," He whispers as Sophie enters the room. "Yes, I'll come as quickly as I can." He hangs up the phone and notices her standing close.

"Who was that?" Sophie asks, her voice revealing an edge he's never heard before.

"No one." He replies and stares at her face, thinking how beautiful she looks. How he wishes he could put all his research away and make love to her, to tell her everything.

"If it was no one, why the whispering, David? Why all the secrets?" He sits mute, his face pale. "I asked you a question!" She screams and sweeps a hand across his desk, knocking his papers and the old leather bound Bible to the floor. Its spine cracks with the harsh landing. "I am sick to death of all these papers!" She shouts and pulls her long hair with her hands, a look of madness spoiling her delicate features.

David stands and tries to comfort her. "Sophie, please calm down... you'll make yourself sick."

"Don't!" She shouts backing away. "Don't touch me!"

"Mommy?" Sarah stands in the doorway rubbing her eyes. Sophie turns to her and the sensitive child bursts into a fit tears. She bends to pick her up and glares at David, her face a flawless picture of hurt and anger.

"Sophie, I can explain everything..."

She holds her chin high, rocking to comfort the child. "Then why don't you. Why don't you tell me where you go and how you are spending our money?"

David turns away, his voice filled with pain. "Not yet. I can't explain just yet. But it's something that is very important." There is a moment of thick silence then Sophie turns to leave, tears streaming down her face. "I have to leave tonight," He says, his words drowned by the slamming door.

He bends to gather the papers from the floor and shudders. *Maybe I shouldn't keep her in the dark anymore. But I don't want to scare her. I've heard a mother's fear can hurt an unborn child. Better she not know the End of Days is looming, it's for her own protection as father said. I'll explain everything when I have the answers. I'm so close. I just pray the star has not arrived already...*

Chapter 171

It's my last night in the desert before I hop a plane. I've never flown before. I wonder if the pressure will make my head hurt worse than usual. There will only be the eight of us and a flight attendant that Abaddon says wears too much makeup. He told us all this over a bottle of 100-year-old scotch and the guys passed a joint around. I didn't touch the stuff and neither did Mandy but it sure smelled good. I got a high just thinking about the crowd at Madison Square. Looks like I've finally arrived. I wish Mara was here.

But I still can't shake this feeling... the feeling that I'm being swallowed whole.

Chapter 172

Death Valley, California

The backroom of Buddy's club is dense with smoke and voices. The band celebrates their last night of relative obscurity huddled together around a picnic table doubling as a dining room where Chinese food containers lay empty. "How do you feel?" Abaddon asks slapping Jesse on the shoulder. His hand clamps down like a vice. "You're gonna be king of the world in less than twenty four hours, my man."

"I think it'll be good to be king," Jesse replies and stubs another cigarette into the overflowing ashtray.

A tall thin man stands in the doorway squinting his eyes. "Hey Jesse, is that you man?" Simon shouts, "Hey guys, Jesse's in here," He says to a group of men packing their instruments.

"Who's that?" Abaddon asks.

Jesse lights up. "My old band."

"Oh what fun. Let the drama begin." Abaddon, amused, watches Simon, Peter and the others make their way towards the table.

Peter holds out his hand. "Hey, good to see you man. It's been a long time." Jesse sits still, making no effort to return the gesture.

"Yeah, it's been a lifetime," Jesse replies and blows a ring of smoke. "This is my band." He motions to the guys who sit watching the uncomfortable exchange.

James passes a freshly lit joint. "You part of the old band?"

"Yeah, we were together a long time."

"Well, lucky for us it didn't work out." Jude cackles and takes a toke.

"So how are you, Jess? Things seem good." Peter asks, searching Jesse's face for some connection.

"Look, man, I'm not really interested in taking a walk down memory lane." Jesse takes a slow drag off his cigarette. "In case you haven't noticed I'm somebody now ... or actually maybe you did notice and that's why you suddenly want to reminisce about old times. Either way, I'm not buying."

Peter studies his old friend's face for a moment before he replies, "Maybe you're not Jesse after all. The guy I knew would never act like such an egocentric piece of shit." He glances at the band before he walks away. "I don't envy any of you. He's turned into a fucking nightmare."

The guys sit mute, not sure how to reply. Jesse stands and pushes his way through the back door heading out into the dark night alone.

Chapter 173

I didn't sleep all night. Peter's words kept running through my head. He's right. I have turned into a nightmare. What happened to me? I used to care and lately I've been pushing those thoughts from my head and only thinking of myself. It's like something dark got inside my head.

My greed and thirst for fame took over.

I have to find my way back...

Chapter 174

City of Angels

Abaddon watches Jesse push open the French doors of the Solarium. "How's the golden boy? Sit, have some breakfast." He motions to the chair beside him.

"I'm not hungry, I came to talk." Jesse paces, taking the room in long strides.

"Okay, talk."

"I don't like myself anymore." He pulls a fresh pack of cigarettes from his back pocket. "Is that the way it's supposed to be? I don't like what this fame has done to me. I mean, I used to care about people."

"Caring is overrated," Mandy says with a smile. "Fame on the other hand is fucking awesome."

"Come on, Mandy, I'm serious."

"So am I," Abaddon replies, carelessly tossing his linen napkin onto the unfinished plate. "You think you've had a taste of it? You ain't seen nothin yet. People will be lined up just to get a glimpse of you. Women will literally throw themselves at your feet for just a chance at a taste. Fame is everything you ever dreamt it would be and more. It's the ultimate power."

"I'm not looking for power. I never was."

"Well, you've got it, Jess. In spades. We'll use that power when the time is right." He says, an enigmatic look on his face.

"Look, I'm just a guy who can sing a little and play the guitar. I'm nothing special and I told you, I'm not interested in power."

Abaddon twists the stem of the single white rose adorning the breakfast table. "What about the leaves, Jess?"

Jesse turns to him, his expression suddenly alert. "What are you talking about?"

"You think just anybody can make the leaves grow just by touching them? Or hold the fish inside their hands?"

Jesse stands frozen. "How do you know about those things you weren't even there..?"

"I know about a lot of things. I knew who you were before you even knew." Mandy snaps the stem in half dropping the pieces onto the fresh linen tablecloth.

"Who am I?" Jesse whispers, eyes locked on Abaddon.

"I already told you that on Dante's Peak, remember?"

"And who are you?" Jesse replies, his voice hollow.

"Well... I'm just a lowly music producer pal. A bottom feeder." He grins. "Now about tonight, I really want to work this Prophet angle, really give the audience a show."

"Didn't you hear me? I said I don't feel good about this. I wanted to reach people in a different way. Not from above them... not as a God. Not as the 'Prophet.'"

"Well, kumbaya, Jess. Fuckin' kumbaya." Abaddon smirks and stands. "I've got things to tend to for tonight. Let me handle everything. You just be on that plane at noon. And don't think too much, you might hurt yourself." He climbs the stairs and leaves Jesse standing alone in the center of the room.

He watches the older man, a deep frown etched on his face. He whispers to himself, "Who are you, Abaddon?"

Chapter 175

Lone Pine, California

The wind howls giving the dark day a foreboding quality. Rows of dense pines are covered with the remnants of a morning shower and the clouds loom low on the vast horizon. Jesse makes his way to the door of the cabin and knocks softly, hands trembling and hair blowing with the violent gusts. Mara stands in the picture window staring, as if she's seen a ghost.

"You look different." She says as she shuts the door behind him. Jesse looks at her for a moment, the silence deafening. He slumps onto the floor, his face buried in his hands, body shaking with tears. She kneels beside him, "Jess, what is it? What's wrong?"

"So many things I never told you. Something has been happening to me ever since the night we met." His face is twisted in anguish. "I can hear things I'm not supposed to hear. I feel too much. Too deep." He glances up at her, his cheeks stained with tears. "I can make things grow and heal people... and other things. Too many other things," He says clutching his head, alive with pain. "I only started drinking again to dull the voices and the thoughts, but they won't stop."

"You're back." Tears brim her soulful eyes as she reaches for him. "I don't know who you are, Jess, but I know that the words you said on my bed those months ago have been said before... thousands of years ago."

He stares at her dazed. "What do you mean?"

"Someone showed them to me." She touches a hand to his face. "A man who knows who you really are. Jess, I know it sounds crazy but think he was an angel. I think he saved my life and I never believed in God before that day. I believe now."

"What are you saying?" He asks her bewildered.

"I don't know, but I know that you were meant to lead people with those words. That you were chosen."

"That's crazy, Mar, I'm just a drunken loser... "

"Don't say that. You're just a man who feels too much, who knows too much."

"God wouldn't choose someone like me. There's nothing pure about me. I've seen dirty things. Done bad to myself and others."

"But now you've seen the light. Isn't that what redemption is about? Isn't that what God is meant to be? The one that loves us and sees our potential even when we can't see it ourselves? The one that sees what's inside of us even when we get caught in the trappings of our lives here on earth? You can understand them Jesse. You can help the ones that have been led astray because you've been there."

Jesse stands still and quiet, wanting to believe but afraid. Mara feels something guiding her, a hand directing what had been destined long ago. "This is your destiny."

"I can't do this. I just want to sleep, I can't go out there in front of all those people tonight."

"You have to, Jess, they need you. They need your message."

He explores her face, noticing tears on her pale cheeks. "Why are you crying?" He asks, his hand brushing the wetness.

"I've missed you Jess, I've missed you so much. I can't lose you again." She feels the longing inside of her, the pain sharp and deep. She stands suddenly and bolts out the door leaving it flapping in the intense gusts of wind. The sky has darkened and the rain ripened clouds loom. She runs toward the pond tearing the clothes from her thin body and sobbing. Guttural cries twist from her throat. She reaches the edge of the water and slows, walking in with the sole intention of taking her last breath.

"Mar, what are you doing?" Jesse yells as he approaches the water's edge, watching her naked body slide deeper into the water.

She glances up, voice filled with sadness. "I told you, I can't lose you again. I can't go through that a second time." Her body shakes uncontrollably.

His reflection ripples in the water as he pulls off his shirt. He swims violently toward her, grabbing her face in his hands. "I'm yours, Mar. Forever." He whispers and touches her lips for the first time, crushing her with the force of his passion. The clouds erupt with a torrent of rain and the sky lights up with jagged bolts of electricity. She pulls at his belt and the last remnants of his clothing float to the surface. Their bodies intertwine. The deep burn inside their souls is finally quenched; the intense longing vanquished under thunderclaps and dense drops of rain. Their hands search, greedy, enveloping one another as their union is complete. As they become one.

A hundred miles away Abaddon sits starring into the storm, his gaze distant, burning with rage. He raises his hands and crashes them together with a clap as lighting strikes the edge of the pond. The lovers take each other body and soul unaware of everything around them and the impending danger that hangs in the air like a ring of smoke.

Chapter 176

Bethany, Israel

Sophie opens the small glass bottle. Tears run down her pretty face. She mixes the herbs in a cup of steaming water just as the old woman told her to. She drinks the dark green liquid and waits... knowing there is no turning back.

Chapter 177

Lone Pine, California

The remnants of the storm trickle down the windowpane. The two lay on damp sheets, bodies curved into each other as Jesse runs his hand through her wet hair and pulls the strands to his lips. "I think I loved you from the moment I saw this mane." She turns to him, her face streaked with tears. "Why are you still crying, Mar? We're together now." She shakes her head. "What is it?"

"I've had dreams Jess. And in them I'm alone. Always alone."

He kisses her forehead lightly. "They're only dreams." He whispers. "You know when I was a kid I used to have this dream over and over that my hands were bloody. It was so real it was like I could feel the blood draining from my palms. But it never happened Mar. It was only a dream. Sometimes we dream our darkest fears... almost willing them to happen to stop the pain of the unknown. The unknown is what we all run from isn't it?"

"I never thought about it that way, but, yeah. Most of the time the future scares me to death."

"That's because we can't control it." He kisses her forehead gently. "The only thing we have is the present."

She takes a deep breath. "We have to go, Jess, they need you."

He pulls her closer to him, tracing her porcelain face with his fingertips. "They can wait." He whispers and brings his lips to hers.

Chapter 178

Bethany, Israel

Sophie washes her face at the sink, trembling from the sheer force of the pain inside her. She drops again at the foot of toilet convulsing with another wave of sickness, grateful that her mother had been able to take Sarah for the day. She can feel her insides churning, the poison taking hold, the child melting inside of her. She clutches her stomach as another surge of pain strikes. She looks up to heaven and prays. *Dear God, what have I done?*

Chapter 179

New York, New York

The cab driver honks out of sheer frustration at the dense evening rush hour. "Sorry, I get a little road rage every now and again. My wife thinks I should see someone about it." The portly man says with a chuckle. "Mind if I turn on the radio?"

David shakes his head, distracted, remembering Sophie's sobs from behind their bedroom door before he left to catch the plane last night. *Please my love; hold on until I can tell you everything.* He rubs a hand over his nearly full beard.

What else am I missing, is there something else in father's words? Some sort of code? I know that there is some connection to music... Suddenly a voice floods the interior of the taxi, an unearthly voice.

Preaching.

Preaching with song.

"Can you turn the radio higher?" David asks the driver. *It's a psalm.* He reclines onto the vinyl seat, his head swimming.

The announcer's voice interrupts once the last cord is struck. "You've just heard the hit single 'Reverie' by the Prophets. They're headlining tonight's free concert in Madison Square Garden just a few minutes from starting. We'll have live coverage of the event."

David's heart races. *Could it be? Could this voice belong to the man who is integral to the world's uncertain fate?* Passages flood his mind. He looks up at the television screens that line Times Square, all focused on the unlit stage at Madison Square Garden.

In the book of Matthew he said, "The coming of the Messiah will be visible to all." He also said, "The coming will be audible and he will send his angels with the sound of great trumpets." Thessalonians 4:16 "For the Messiah himself will descend with the voice of an archangel." David suddenly gets an overwhelming feeling that his father's spirit is there beside him. Guiding him. He suddenly knows without a shadow of a doubt what he must do.

"Change of plans, please take me to Madison Square Garden."

The Cabby's face lights up. "In the mood for a little music?"

"You could say that." David reveals his first smile in days and dials his cell phone. "Yes, Montbard, it's me. I've found him. Meet me at Madison Square Garden as quickly as you can... and bring a gun."

He hangs up the phone and lets out a sigh, running a hand through his hair.

I must get to him... and the woman he travels with.

They are the key to everything.

Chapter 180

City of Angels

High above the Los Angeles pavement the bishop mumbles in deep sleep. A nurse checks his IV bag and glances at the woman lying in the next bed. "Chatty Kathy over here keepin' you up nights?" She asks with a snide grin.

"Boy is he. He blabs all day and night about God and the devil and the great battle between them." The woman says rolling her eyes. "I mean who believes that crap anymore right?" The two share a laugh as the bishop is jolted awake by another nightmare.

He glances at the women then pulls his partition shut. *It was him, he thinks,* remembering the face in the dream. *It was the young man from the Desert, the one who was so kind to me. Could it be that he is the Chosen One? Does he know? Surely he is in grave danger with the serpent here on earth to defeat him.*

He turns his face toward the window and spots a lone star in the night sky. He says a silent prayer. *Please God in heaven, protect him and keep him from harm. Please take me in his place. Save him from the forces of evil that surround him. I give myself unto you.*

Chapter 181

New York, New York

Mara clings to Jesse as the two make their way toward the dressing rooms, backstage at Madison Square Garden. James pulls on a hand painted t-shirt and lets out a sigh of relief. "Hey, man, we were starting to worry."

Jude shoots him a look. "Yeah, nothing like waiting till the last minute."

"I'm sorry. I had to handle something." Jesse kisses Mara's hand and looks into her worried face. "I'll see you guys out there." He says and pulls her into the hall.

"What's going on?" He gently takes her face into his hands.

"I have a bad feeling." She shakes her head. "I told you, I feel things."

He rests his cheek against her face, pressing his body into hers. "I don't know what's coming for me but I feel it too. I only hope we have more time together." He kisses her mouth lightly. "I want to touch every inch of you. I want to take walks with you and tell you everything. I'm so sorry I waited this long but I know now I can be the man you deserve."

Mara trembles and buries her face in his chest. She breathes him in, filling herself with his scent. "I don't want to let you go." She says, her voice broken and distant.

"You can stand backstage and watch. I'll be so close you can practically reach out and touch me."

Suddenly Mara doubles over in pain clutching her stomach.

"Mar?" Jesse crouches down beside her. "What's wrong?"

She shakes her head in reply. "I don't know." Hands on her stomach, she looks to Jesse —a mournful and absolute fear in her eyes.

Chapter 182

Dallas, Texas

Two thousand miles away Charlene sits in front of a television set in her tiny apartment, a bowl of popcorn propped on her lap. "Baby, come on, it's starting!" She bellows. Roy walks in with a bottle of Tabasco. "What the heck are you planning to do with that?" She smirks.

"I'm gonna change your life right now. You will never be the same again after this." He sprinkles the hot sauce over the buttered corn.

"You've already changed my life and rocked my world darlin.'" She grabs his face, kissing him hard.

"Okay don't distract me, we gotta watch our boy here." He grabs the remote and turns up the volume as an image of Jesse flashes onto the back wall of the amphitheater.

* * *

New York City

David watches the screens all around him, lit up with the image of Jesse's face, "Dear God in heaven help me," he says aloud, his heart racing.

"You praying?" The cabbie asks with a curt nod of his head. "I can respect that."

"Is there any way to get there faster?" David asks searching desperately for an opening in the gridlock surrounding the yellow car.

The driver smirks, "Not unless we fly."

David pulls some bills from his pocket. "I'll get out here." He grabs his duffel off the bench seat and steps out into traffic.

"You forgot your change!" The Cabbie shouts but David is long gone, weaving his way through the sea of metal.

I have to get there before it's too late. He runs as fast as his legs will allow, the burn in his muscles growing hotter by the second. Cars honk and the sights and sounds of the city whip by him in a blur.

"Which way to Madison Square?" He shouts to a homeless man pushing a cart full of rattling bottles.

The man gestures over his shoulder with a dirty thumb. "Thata way. Take 6th and right on 32nd. You ain't far."

"Thanks." David shouts and whips past him.

The homeless man watches David sprint like lightning down the street. "That boy's in some sort of hurry." He mumbles, scratching at his beard.

Chapter 183

The glory that surrounds him is unsurpassed by anything that mortal eyes have yet beheld. His voice is soft and subdued yet full of melody. In gentle compassionate tones he presents some of the same gracious heavenly truths which the Savior uttered.

Revelation 1:13

Jesse stands center stage, covered only in a tattered pair of jeans. His pale body is ethereal, bathed in a flood of white light. His voice, clear and true, penetrates the crowd, who stand awe-struck, tears streaming. Ten thousand lighter flames flicker in the massive theatre.

Mara watches from the side of the stage, her heart pounding. *I was meant to love this man my whole life,* she thinks as a gust of wind whips past her and Abaddon approaches yelling into his phone.

"What do you mean he refused to use the wires? That's the grand finale! He's supposed to rise above the crowd. He's supposed to play the part of the Goddamned Prophet!" He hurls the phone to the ground and turns on Mara with a furious smile, his rage burning red. "You had something to do with all this didn't you? The change of heart. The sudden pathetic need to be *among the people.*"

"No, Mandy. He doesn't want it your way." Mara feels herself retreating, her body alive with fear.

"I made him. Do you get that? He was nothing, now he's a star. He's my star." Abaddon snarls, backing her against a wall, his menacing teeth just inches from her face.

From the corner of her eye, Mara sees the crowd swaying, enveloped in Jesse's song. A calming certainty spreads through her and she looks up to meet Abaddon's fiery gaze. "No, he isn't. He belongs to them." She says, her voice steady. Powerful.

Abaddon lifts a hand ready to strike but changes his mind and composes himself, unfurling his signature grin. "Okay Mar. I understand." He says with a low bow. "My work is done here."

He backs away from her then heads out the metal door, a gust of wind trailing behind him.

* * *

David slides through a side door, breathless, and enters the venue. He runs toward the heavenly voice, his face twisted in fear and exuberance.

Across the country Bishop Augustus lays hooked up to several monitors and a breathing apparatus. A doctor stands above him, an open chart in his hands. "I don't understand, he was doing so well. We were going to release him tomorrow." He says to the young priest who sits holding the bishop's hand.

"Sometimes these things happen." Dimitri replies focused on the bishop's face. The doctor exits leaving the two men alone, the intensive care unit silent. Dimitri leans close and whispers into the old man's ear. "I believe you."

Chapter 184

New York City

Jesse stands at the edge of the stage, arms outstretched, face streaked with tears. The sound of his voice penetrates every soul, drowning the thunder and heavy rain outside.

Lightning strikes, it shatters the roof of the building and pours shards of glass and debris onto the crowd below. Scattered screams ring out but the crowd does not move.

Enraptured.

Mesmerized.

Rain pours onto them from the open roof. Gusts of wind extinguish the flames clutched in their hands. The rain and wind strike the crowd like weapons, angrily pushing its way inside the venue.

A shot rings out, echoing through the amphitheater. Everything goes still and silent as the bullet rips through Jesse's outstretched palm. He looks at his bleeding hand, his expression serene.

It's exactly like the dream.

David sees the blood and yells, pushing his way toward the stage. He pulls the metal cross his father left him from his coat pocket, holding it in the air in desperation. Montbard and Berg enter from the other side of the theatre and recognize him in the crowd, his grief stricken face awash with tears.

Another shot.

Jesse holds his wounded hands out to his sides and tilts his head towards the heavens.

Now that I look back on my life I see it was all leading to this. My hands are bleeding but the true pain is inside my heart. Pain for the suffering of my fellow man. Was I able to reach them?

Mara's screams ripple through the auditorium as the third bullet strikes his chest, his body caving to its force. She grabs her stomach in pain and drops to her knees. She turns her face to the sky, finally understanding the meaning of it all. Jesse turns to look at her one last time; the blood draining from his pale body.

I will return. In one form or another. I will return.

His eyes close and he drops to the ground, arms outstretched while thousands of miles away a bishop draws his last breath, a smile across his face.

Outside Madison Square Garden a black limousine pulls away from the curb. Inside Abaddon taps his fingers to "Sympathy for the Devil" on the radio, Mick Jagger's edgy voice floods the leather interior.

Chapter 185

Six Months Later

Only be careful, and watch yourselves closely so that you do not forget the things your eyes have seen or let them slip from your heart as long as you live. Teach them to your children and to their children after them.

Deuteronomy 4:9

A group of three kids skateboard near a record store in a middle class suburban neighborhood. One of them spots a bargain bin filled with hundreds of discs stamped with dollar price tags in bright orange.

"Cool! Check this out." One of the boys shouts, his backwards baseball cap holding his long hair out of clear blue eyes. He digs through the bin, carelessly tossing CDs to the side. Another boy with a matching hat approaches.

"Score! Maybe there's somebody decent in here."

The third boy kicks his skateboard into the air and catches it. "Nah, it's probably all crap our parents would listen to."

"Don't be such a downer man. Check it out, it's Sade. Circa 1984. Totally retro. My Mom would wet herself over this."

"Hey look, it's that guy who was famous for like five minutes. The one that got shot. There's like a million of his CDs in here."

"That's really jacked up how he got killed."

"Didn't Lennon get shot by a crazy fan too?"

"Yeah, I think so."

One of them squints at a group of girls across the street. "Holy crap that's Jenny Meyer, let's cruise by." He says and tosses The Prophet's CD back into the large plastic bin. It lands cover side up, Jesse's luminous face framed by his golden hair facing the sky.

Chapter 186

And there shall come forth a rod out of the root of Jesse, and a flower shall rise up out of his root.

Isaiah 11:1

Mara stands at the long kitchen counter cutting the crust off of several pieces of bread, her enormous belly braced against the edge of the tile. She smiles, slathering peanut butter on one of the slices and glances at David. "Looks like he takes after his papa. I've been craving peanut butter and banana for months."

David and Sophie share a smile as they set the lunch table in their new home. The windows are shut tight against the winter storm that howls at the Judean mountaintops and a raging fire burns in the hearth.

"Have you heard from Montbard or Berg this week?" Mara asks, her voice hesitant while she watches David pour water from the pitcher into the rich amber colored glasses.

"Not this week but don't worry they'll find the Ark. They won't stop until they do."

She touches her swollen belly, her smile bitter sweet, thinking of the child growing inside her and the message he will bring to the world.

EPILOGUE

New York Times December 12th

My fellow brothers and sisters, I have been a scholar for many years. I grew up reading the holy books under the guidance of my father, Rabbi Askenzari. He told me of the Messianic age and I waited all of my life believing that mankind would be ready, that we would all be absolved of our sins and enter the kingdom of heaven. That is not quite what happened when the Messiah came. In fact, many of you may not even know that he came at all.

My words here today will not recite dates or important facts or anything else of scholarly import. In fact, my words may seem unusually passionate for a scholar. But I'm hoping that this passion will unlock your hearts and minds so that you will be ready when he comes. So that we may not be lead to kill our messengers, our prophets, who come to us selflessly. Let us not martyr yet another Mahatma Gandhi, Martin Luther King, Joseph Smith, or John Lennon. Men who spoke profound truths and paid a heavy price.

Have you noticed that history has a way of repeating itself? Anyone, any "cult of personality" who speaks out against our evil doings pays a dear price. And we, my brothers and sisters, are left on this earth to grow more weary and impose more suffering. The Messianic age is not what many of you believe. The kingdom can be here, right in our own backyard.

A common Rabbinic interpretation is that there is a Messiah in every generation. That he can be anywhere at anytime. In fact, there have been many throughout the generations who have been given the title of Messiah, for example, Cyrus The Great, the Persian King, who was also referred to as a prophet. The Talmud, which often uses parables and stories to convey a moral point, tells of a rabbi who found the One at the gates of Rome and asked, "When will you finally come?" He was surprised when he was told, "Today." Overjoyed the man waited all day. The next day he returned to the gates confused and asked, "What happened? You didn't come?" The One replied, "The scripture says, 'Today if you will but harken to his voice (Ps. 95:7).'"

So when we finally open our hearts to the gospel of the Messiah, Mother Earth will be reborn. You see we all want the same thing, Jews, Christians, Hindus, Muslims. We want a God who is good and we want to feel his presence. It does not matter what name we give it. Earth, Fire, Jesus, Mohammad, the Force. It's all one and the same. For example in Hinduism they embrace Jesus as an "avatar" which is an incarnation of God. Muslims believe that Isa, also known as Jesus, will return near the end of days. In almost every religion it is the same, just a slight variation on a theme. Just a different name or idea leading to the same out come. We want love. The only thing that separates us from this love is greed and fear. Fear of something different than what we have been conditioned and taught to believe. So when he comes, have no preconceived notions of what or who he could be. He could be standing next to you on the subway...

Just open your hearts to each other and to the future of our world. We are all brothers and sisters, united we stand, divided we fall.

Your humble servant,
David Ashkenzari

www.ingramcontent.com/pod-product-compliance
Lightning Source LLC
Chambersburg PA
CBHW020537020726
47494CB00006B/1804